# I KILLED SATAN

## THE GREAT WAR OF MAN AND SATAN

NAVEEN MULLANGI

ISBN:979-8-9986711-1-1

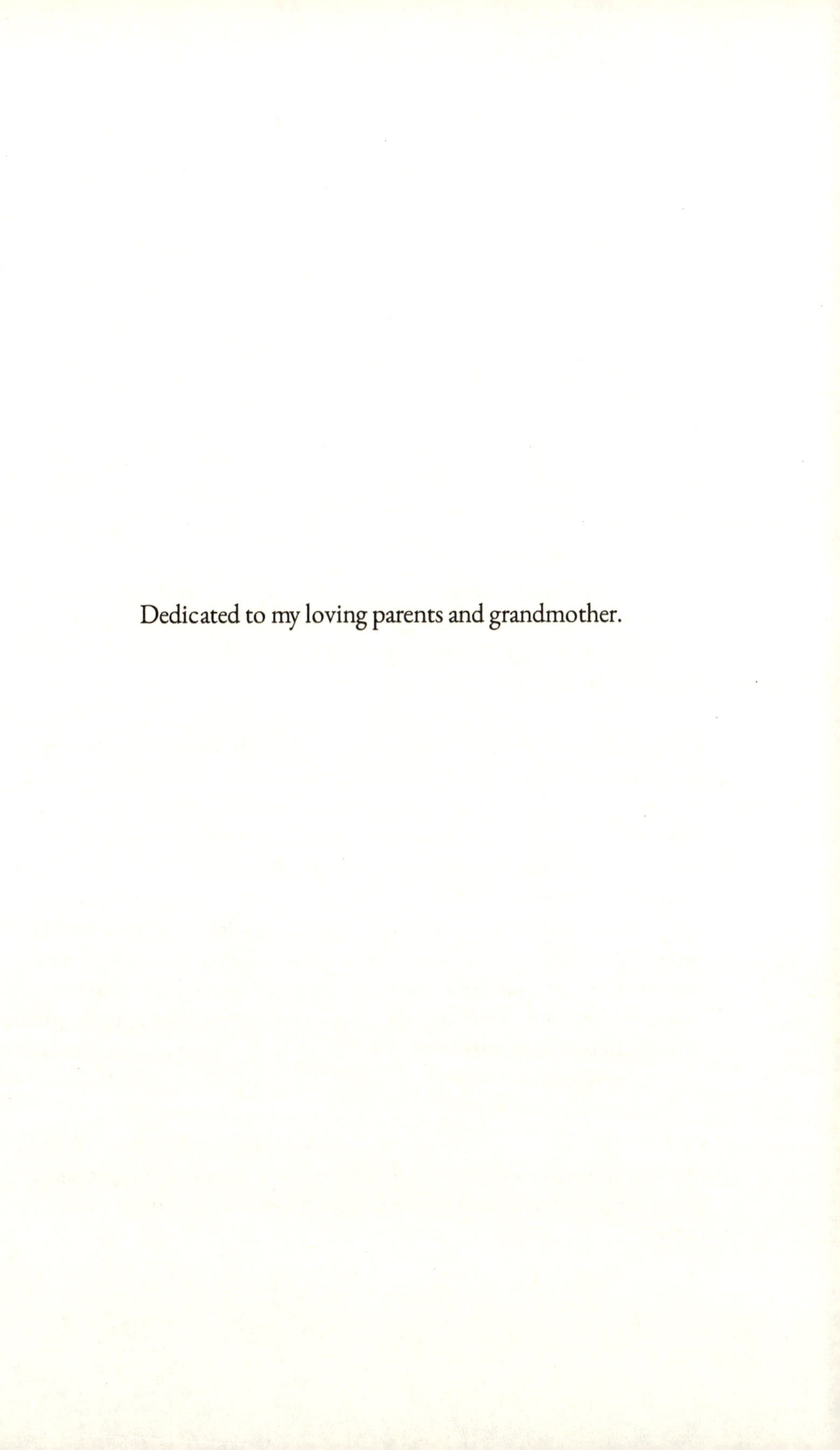

Dedicated to my loving parents and grandmother.

# 1

In Wizbome country, there is a city called Relsar. On the outskirts of Relsar, there is a small village called Beruk. The national highway beside Beruk village is essential for business activities in Trigadha state and Relsar City, its capital.

The majority of people in Wizbome country are Ateestans. Ateestans are people who follow the path of the Ateesta Religion. The people of the Ateesta religion do not worship God Yinta, but God Yinta is the only true solo God of the Ateesta religion. God Yinta teaches people to use common sense, rationality, and morality, and God Yinta asks people to reject any kind of blind belief in any type of supernatural powers or elements. God Yinta teaches rationality and critical thinking, which are more important than expecting some supernatural powers and their blessings to make things better in people's lives. God Yinta teaches Ateestans to work hard to earn great things and be happy rather than believing in any kind of supernatural powers or elements.

God Yinta teaches Ateestans to live in reality and work towards improving reality rather than becoming delusional in the process of believing in supernatural powers to get great things and happiness in life.

* * *

The women in Wizbome country are beautiful. Women are free to choose whom they want to marry and what they want to do in their lives. The men in Wizbome, too, had the same freedom as women. The men in Wizbome are a little afraid to marry. It is because leaving the wife and children after marriage is viewed by society as an incompetent man leaving his family because he can't take care of his family, and it is discouraged. The women are also asked by society to be reasonable with their husbands. A woman is asked not to marry a man if the woman has any second thoughts about a man's financial life. Women are asked to adjust to their husband's financial position, and they should be Okay with it before marriage to avoid problems after marriage.

It is because the Ateestan society thinks it is better not to marry if something feels not alright than to marry and divorce later, which affects the lives of married couples and kids too.

Nathan is a 20-year-old man. He is an Ateestan. Nathan lives in Beruk village with his parents. He is the only child of his parents.

Nathan came out of his home and got into his old car. He is studying Electrical Engineering at Reznova College of Engineering and Sciences in Relsar City, the capital of their state, Trigadha. The college is in the middle of Relsar city. He reached college and parked his car beside many big and luxurious cars.

He walked into college and entered his class. The class is already full. Nathan sat in his chair in the corner at the back of the classroom. Nathan opened a book, and he saw a new girl in the first row. Nathan is looking at her.

Nathan's friend Jiza is in the next chair to Nathan. Jiza is observing Nathan, while Nathan is looking at the new girl in the first row.

"You like her?" asked Jiza.

"No, she is new, right? So.." said Nathan.

"So, checking her out?" said Jiza.

* * *

"Ha ha, leave it. Did you complete the project?" Nathan asked nonchalantly.

"Nope, did you?" asked Jiza.

"Yup!" replied Nathan.

"Oh good! Show me your project, and we have already talked to the new girl. After the class, we planned to go to a restaurant. Come with us," Jiza told Nathan.

"Who else is coming?" asked Nathan.

"That new girl, Keizha, and his gang. It is like a meeting to get to know each other," said Jiza.

"Oh, I will come!" said Nathan.

"Okay, you came to college in your car, right?" asked Jiza.

"Yes, why?" said Nathan.

"We must get some girls into our car!" said Jiza while smiling like an idiot.

"For sure, but my car is super old. I don't think any girl wants to get into my old car, while Keizha is standing there with a big car," Nathan helplessly said.

"Come on, bro, I don't even have a car. You are better than I. You can go anywhere you want with a girl. If you find one!" said Jiza.

Nathan laughed.

The class is completed, and everyone is coming out. In the parking lot, Nathan and Jiza are waiting for the new girl, Keizha, and his gang.

Keizha came first to the parking lot and gave a handshake to Jiza. Keizha also gave a handshake to Nathan. Keizha saw Nathan's car and laughed at it. Nathan felt bad. Then, the Keizha gang came. His gang has a fat guy, a skinny guy, and one mean girl.

Then, the other girls came to the parking lot. Sabrina, the new girl, came to the parking lot with them. She saw Keizha's car and said,

"Nice car!"

Nathan felt disappointed and small.

Keizha said, "Thanks," with a big smile.

Jiza said, "There is a restaurant in the Kaisar area called Lizona Restaurant. We have to go there, and I know the route. The food is awesome there."

Kezha said, "Ok, let's go then!"

Keizha and his gang sat in Keizha's car. Sabrina sat in the front passenger seat of Keizha's car.

The two girls who came with Sabrina sat in the back seat of Nathan's car. Jiza sat in the front passenger seat of Nathan's car.

Nathan introduced himself to the two girls. Prina gave an irritated look at Nathan and didn't respond to him. She looked at the car and hated it. The second girl, named Ira, responded kindly to Nathan and said, "Nice car."

Nathan said, "Thank you so much."

Nathan started driving, and Jiza started giving directions to Nathan. While giving directions to Nathan, Jiza is looking at Prina. Jiza was admiring her beauty.

Nathan asked Jiza, "How will Keizha know this restaurant's location without you?"

Ira said, "There is something called maps on your phone. You can use it instead of your friend."

Nathan laughed and said, "Yup!"

"It's a rich restaurant!" said Prina in a serious and mocking tone.

Nathan said nothing, and no one said anything.

The traffic is heavy that day. And the heat is a little high in the car. Even though the AC is on in the car, it is not helping.

Prina said, "Too hot here!"

Nathan said, "Sorry, this is a very old car, so the AC is not that great."

Prina was in constant irritation.

Ira said, "Lower the glasses."

Prina said, "Yuck! No, the air is polluted. I will get sick!"

Jiza said, "We have to change the air, right?" in a sarcastic tone.

"We have to change the car!" said Prina.

Nathan is silent and driving the car.

They reached the restaurant. After getting out of the car, Nathan apologized to Prina for the inconvenience. Jiza didn't like it and said to Nathan, "Bro, the AC is fine. Ira said nothing. Prina did overaction. Why did you apologize to her? You helped her come here and still apologized. Why?"

Nathan gave a small smile and said nothing. Jiza said, "God, bro!"

They went into the restaurant. Nathan sat at the end of the long table.

Sabrina sat opposite him at the other end of the table. Keizha sat next to her.

Sabrina looked at Nathan and gave a small, friendly smile. Nathan smiled back and nodded his head respectfully.

Jiza sat next to Ira. Jiza found Ira more beautiful than Prina. Food came, and everyone was eating.

Sabrina told everyone at the table, "I'm new to the city. I'm happy to meet you all in the college."

They said "Welcome!" with smiles.

Keizha asked, "Where are you from?"

Sabrina said, "I'm from Ruhtaak. My dad is a government employee. He got transferred here. I heard there are great places here to see."

Ira said, "Yes, Kalsa River is awesome. It is said that Satan hated the Kalsa River because it helped God Yinta when he fought Satan. God Yinta asked Kalsa River not to let Satan worshipers cross it or get in it. The Kalsa River area is called Nazreck in the ancient scriptures of Ateesta. Ateestans believe God Yinta and Satan fought a war on Earth at Nazreck at the beginning of time after the creation of the Earth was done by Mother of the universe, Adis."

Sabrina said, "Oh, that's interesting, awesome!"

Keizha said, "Yeah, there is a big Yinta Temple, too, with Five Pillars of Ateesta descriptions inside. There are also many amusement parks, movie theaters, and other places."

Sabrina said, "Oh, looks like there are many religious places here."

Nathan said, "Ha ha, they are not religious. Anyone can go there and have a good time."

Keizha said, "Yeah, I'm a Krisen, but still, I visit Ateestan temples."

Prina asked Sabrina, "So, you don't know about the Ateesta Religion and God Yinta?"

Sabrina replied, "No, I'm a Krisen like Keizha. Our family is originally from Orut, and we follow the Krise Religion."

Prina said, "Oh! Me, Keizha, Ira, and our gang are mostly Krisen. Jiza and Nathan are Ateestans."

Nathan asked Sabrina, "Tell me more about the Krise religion and culture of Orut."

Sabrina said, "Well, it's not different from usual Krisen practices, but Orut culture specifically commands Krisens to give utmost importance to human emotions, feelings, and it orders unquestionable faith, trust, and devotion towards the one and only true God of Krise Religion, Regor. Regor is the solution to all problems, and he is the creator of the universe. No one can say anything against Regor and do anything that questions the faith and purity of the Krise Religion."

Ira said, "Ateesta is the total opposite of what we follow. I don't mean it negatively. I just saw the difference."

Jiza asked, "What about men, women, marriage, etc., in Krise?"

Sabrina said, "Women mostly do what men say, and Krise is patriarchal. It controls women, but for men, it is different. They can have multiple wives and are free to do anything they want. But what about men and women in Ateesta?"

Nathan said, "No one controls anyone. Women choose their lovers and husbands, or their parents can do it for them, but there is no pressure. Also, monogamy is strict for men and women in marriage. Ateestans are always encouraged to question their beliefs in God Yinta to gain clarity through rationality, understand the world and people around them, and not undermine or hurt others while doing it. We question God Yinta in search of the truth and answers in life. The followers of Ateesta aim to gain rational consciousness at all levels within themselves."

Sabrina asked, "So if you have a problem in life, then do you pray to God, Yinta?"

Nathan said, "No, we don't worship anyone. We ask him within ourselves to give us the strength and intelligence to face and solve the problem."

Sabrina said, "You like science and logic here too much!"

Nathan said, "Ha ha, that is a good way to put it."

Keizha asked Sabrina, "Shall we watch a movie after this?"

Nathan is also waiting for the answer from Sabrina, along with Keizha.

Sabrina said, "Sorry, I have to go home."

Ira said, "We will go tomorrow, then?"

Sabrina said, "Perfect!"

They ate the food and came out of the restaurant.

Keizha said, "Come with me. I will drop you off at your home." To Sabrina.

Sabrina said, "No problem, I live far away from the city in Beruk village. I will take a taxi."

Jiza said, "Hey, Nathan and I live in Beruk. You can come with us."

Sabrina said, "Oh! That's awesome. It seems like a storm is coming," looking up at the sky.

Nathan said, "Don't worry, storms are common here."

Keizha got angry and looked at Nathan, then left.

Prina went with Keizha, and Ira left in a cab.

Sabrina sat in the front passenger seat of Nathan's car, and Jiza sat in the back seat. Beruk is approximately 14 miles from Relsar. They started and, in a few minutes, entered the Beruk highway.

It started raining. Even though Nathan's car is old, it is heavy.

Sabrina can feel the royal road presence of Nathan's car and its weight and stability from inside in the rain.

Sabrina said, "It looks like an ancient car!"

Nathan said, "Yes, my dad bought this for me to go to college."

Sabrina said, "But it feels very heavy and strong."

Jiza said, "Yes, Nathan bought it from his dad."

Sabrina asked Nathan, "You said your dad bought it for you?"

Nathan replied, "Actually, my dad gave this car to me. He bought a new one, and I paid for that new car. I don't have to, but I thought it would be helpful to him. You can't explain all this to everyone, right? So, I'm just saying my dad bought it for me."

Sabrina laughed, saying, "It's great you paid for your father's new car. So I'm not like everyone else, then?"

Nathan said, "No, you are not!"

Sabrina asked, "Why?"

Nathan said, "Because you are my friend now..!"

Sabrina said, "Ahaaa!"

Nathan said, "I mean our friend!"

Sabrina laughed while looking at the road. Jiza looked at Nathan sarcastically and said, "Trying to impress her, haa?"

Nathan said nothing.

Jiza asked Nathan to stop at a highway restaurant beside the Beruk highway. Jiza told Nathan and Sabrina that the ice cream was good in that restaurant.

Nathan stopped the car at the restaurant, and the rain stopped. It is an outdoor restaurant. There are big umbrellas, chairs, and tables under those umbrellas. Nathan parked the car. Jiza went to order the ice creams. And Sabrina and Nathan sat at a table.

Nathan asked Sabrina, "Is it okay that you are here?"

Sabrina answered, "Why? Is it a problem?"

Nathan said," If you have a boyfriend and he gets to know this, it might not be good."

Sabrina laughed and said, "I don't have a boyfriend."

Nathan said, "Oh, then who am I?"

In shock, Sabrina asked, "What do you mean?"

Nathan said, "I am your friend, right?"

Sabrina replied, "Yes!"

Nathan then asked, "And I am a boy, right?"

Sabrina said, "I think so, you look like one!"

Nathan understood Sabrina's sarcasm and said, "I am your friend and a boy. What does it make me to you?"

Sabrina said, "Boyfriend?"

Nathan, with a big smile, said, "Exactly!"

Sabrina got serious, and she got up from her chair. Nathan suddenly got shocked, and his smile turned into tension.

Sabrina said, "Please be within your limits!"

Nathan said, "I'm sorry. It's just a joke."

Sabrina was looking at Nathan angrily, and Nathan didn't know what to say to Sabrina. He thought he had crossed his limits.

Suddenly, Sabrina started laughing big, and Nathan was confused.

Nathan understood Sabrina had pranked him.

Both sat again, and Jiza came with ice creams.

He saw both of them laughing and asked them what happened.

Nathan said, "The thing that should!"

They are eating ice cream. They heard a siren and an announcement telling them to get inside in an hour because the storm would pass the Beruk highway in an hour. They got back into the car with ice cream cups in their hands hurriedly.

Jiza said, "No problem, we are only 4 miles away from Beruk. We can reach Beruk in 30 minutes." To Sabrina. Jiza and Sabrina are eating ice cream in the car while Nathan is driving.

Jiza said, "Eat it, bro," from the back seat.

Nathan said, "Don't you see what I am doing?"

Sabrina looked at Nathan's ice cream cup on the dashboard and thought of something.

After a few minutes, she took Nathan's ice cream cup into her hands, took some ice cream with the spoon, and asked Nathan to eat it.

Jiza was stunned.

Nathan saw it and took that ice cream into his mouth.

There was a big lightning in the sky, and the speed of the wind increased. The environment became more rattled.

Satan's shadow shape is seen in the sky at the back side while the car is moving on the road. As they approached Beruk, the storm calmed down. Nathan dropped Jiza and Sabrina off at their homes, and he went to his home. That night, Nathan is thinking about what happened in the car and smiling. He looked through the window outside, and it started raining again. The weather is lovely. He thought about picking up Sabrina the next day to go to college. Nathan slept that night thinking about Sabrina.

He woke up the following day. After getting ready, Nathan called Jiza and told him he would pick him up today to go to college. Nathan told Jiza not to go with his father, as Jiza's father runs a small business in Relsar City.

Nathan's mother called him to eat breakfast, and his father told him not to do anything stupid in college. Nathan said, "Ok," in a dull tone.

He came out of his home. He is in the car now, going to Jiza's house. He picked up Jiza, and both went to Sabrina's home. They are waiting at the corner of the street for her to come out. She came out, and a cab came to pick her up. She sat in the cab.

The cab started moving. Nathan started following the cab in his car. When the cab entered Beruk highway, Nathan started driving his car parallel to the cab. He looked at Sabrina, and Sabrina saw Nathan and Jiza. Nathan signaled Sabrina to stop the cab. Sabrina asked the cab driver to stop the cab.

She got out of the cab. Nathan walked to her and told her she could come with them and save money. Sabrina told Nathan that she already paid the cab money in prepaid. Nathan said the cab application company would refund the money if the trip was not completed and pay the driver the entire trip amount. So, she can come with them.

Sabrina told the cab driver that she was going with her friends and told him he could go.

The cab is gone. Sabrina sat in the front seat of Nathan's car.

Jiza told, "There is a Wuquin reading session on Saturday. We are coming to Nathan's house. You can join us." To Sabrina.

Sabrina asked Jiza, "What is Wuquin?"

Jiza said, "Wuquin is the Holy Book of the Ateesta Religion. We conduct Wuquin reading sessions regularly."

Sabrina asked Nathan, "Are you going, Nathan?"

Nathan said, "Of course, the reading session is at my home in my garage. I'm conducting the reading session."

Sabrina asked Nathan, "What is in Wuquin? Why is it important that much, besides being a holy book? You are talking about it as if it is something that no one ever knew about or something like that!"

Nathan said, "After the war of Nazreck, God Yinta didn't kill Satan. God Yinta told Satan he wasn't worth getting touched by his sword. He taught the people of the Earth many things to protect themselves from Satan. And those teachings of God Yinta were put in order in book form, which is called Wuquin. In Wuquin, God Yinta propagated rationality, a pragmatic approach to life, while considering and respecting human emotions, feelings, and morals, and using common sense. I'm the founder of the Rational Religion and Science Club. I organize these types of events occasionally."

Sabrina said, "Awesome, Nathan, but I cannot come. Krisens are not allowed to attend any other religious programs and festivals. We only read Krizen, the holy book of the Krise religion. Reading other religious holy books and attending their events amounts to blasphemy in the Krise religion. So, I cannot do it. My dad will kill me if he knows I did something like that."

Jiza asked Sabrina, "Then can other religious people attend your festivals?"

Sabrina answered, "Yes, others can come to our house for our festivals. They can eat and celebrate, but we cannot visit theirs."

Nathan asked Sabrina, "Which God are you praying to?"

Sabrina said, "Regor is the creator of the universe and Earth. The most merciful to his believers and the destroyer of the Krise Religion's nonbelievers."

Jiza said, "Oh, good! I hope your God doesn't know Ateestans exist in this world."

Sabrina became a little angry.

Nathan said, "Cool bro, Everyone has their own beliefs and follows their religion. Just like us."

Jiza said, "Ok, sorry, Sabrina!"

Sabrina laughed.

They reached college. Keizha is in class. The class is filled with students. Keizha saw Sabrina laughing while talking to Nathan and felt jealous.

Sabrina asked Nathan while walking to the classroom. "So, Ateestans don't get angry or jealous?"

Nathan answered, "Of course they do, just like any other person from any religion. After all, we are all human beings. But Ateesta emphasizes not to get lost in human emotions and forget the big picture when dealing with something."

They entered the classroom. Sabrina sat with her female friends. Keizha got up from his chair and sat in a chair next to Sabrina. Nathan and Jiza sat in the last row.

Keizha said "Hi" to Sabrina.

Sabrina responded with, "Hi Keizha, how are you?"

Keizha said, "I'm good. You are looking gorgeous today."

Sabrina said, "Thanks, Keizha!"

Nathan is seeing Keizha talking to Sabrina.

Keizha saw Nathan and gave an evil smile.

A professor came into class and started teaching differential equations.

Class is going on. Keizha is looking at Sabrina's waist, face, and breasts.

Nathan observed it. He got angry. He threw a book at Keizha's face.

Keizha got angry and then understood why Nathan did that. Keizha stayed silent.

Sabrina saw the book hitting Keizha and understood that Nathan threw it.

She also knew Keizha was looking at her but said nothing.

The class finished, and everyone came out.

Keizha, Jiza, Prina, Ira, Nathan are in parking lot.

Keizha said, "Let's go to the movie!"

Sabrina said, "Yeah, what do you say?" to Ira.

Ira said, "Ok, for me. It's my suggestion, yesterday!"

Keizha asked Nathan, "What about you?" arrogantly.

Nathan said, "Sorry, I can't. I have to go home. Got work to do."

In a mean tone, Keizha asked, "To pay EMI for this junk?" pointing to Nathan's car.

Jiza angrily said, "No, to send rockets to space!"

Keizha laughed.

Jiza said, "Literally to send rockets into space. He is working on a small rocket engine prototype."

Keizha stopped laughing and was disappointed.

Keizha said, "Enough of this garbage talk. Let's go!"

Sabrina looked at Nathan and gave him a small, sympathetic smile.

Keizha asked Jiza, "Are you coming?"

Jiza said, "No, I have work too!"

"Ok," said Keizha.

Ira, Prina, and Sabrina, with others, left for a movie theatre in Keizha's car.

Nathan asked Jiza, "What work do you have, bro?"

Jiza said, "My dad asked me to help him at our grocery shop today. A worker is absent today."

Nathan said, "Thanks, bro."

Jiza looked at Nathan and gave him a handshake.

Jiza said, "You are my friend!"

Nathan dropped Jiza at their grocery shop.

After coming out of the car,

Jiza said, "Don't worry, bro. She does not deserve a guy like you."
Nathan smiled and felt good as his friend was supporting him a lot.

Nathan said, "Thank you, bro."

After dropping Jiza, Nathan returned to Beruk. In return, on the highway, while driving, Nathan couldn't stop thinking about the smile Sabrina gave him and the evil smile Keizha gave him when Sabrina got into Keizha's car. He returned to his home and is now sleeping on his bed. He looked sad and lost. Suddenly, he got up and went into his garage. He saw the engine he was working on. He looked at the fuel combustion chambers and took the welding machine. He started welding it.

In the movie theatre, Sabrina sat next to Keizha. Keizha gave her popcorn. She said, "Thanks." Keizha was thinking about touching her hand. And he was looking at it. After several minutes, Keizha touched Sabrina's hand. Sabrina moved her hand after feeling the touch. Keizha touched Sabrina's hand again. Sabrina removed her hand from the armrest. Keizha stopped trying to touch her hand. Suddenly, Keizha felt something. He looked at his palm and saw it becoming red. After several minutes, the palm of his hand turned into leprosy-rotten flesh. Keizha got scared to death after seeing his palm. Sabrina saw Keizha's hand and said nothing. Keizha, in fear, looked around to see who had done it but couldn't find anyone. He looked at his palm again. Now, it was normal. Keizha didn't understand what had happened. He was silent and in fear throughout the movie.

When the movie was over, Keizha dropped Prina, Ira, and others at their homes in Relsar. Prina's house is big. Ira is from a middle-class family. At last, he told Sabrina he would drop her at her home in Beruk. Sabrina said she would go in a cab. And she wanted to see Ira's house, so she stayed in the car.

Keizha tried to convince her, but she didn't agree and got out of Keizha's car. Sabrina said, "Thanks, Keizha, I will go by cab. Please, I don't want to trouble you. Reaching Beruk takes more than 40 minutes. Please go home. I will go by cab."

Keizha disappointingly left. And Sabrina boarded a cab.

Sabrina reached her home. She went into her house and washed her face. While looking at her face in the mirror, she saw the face of Nathan suddenly. She looked back and saw no one. She understood what she did. And she smiled at herself in the mirror. That smile became big and bright in a few seconds.

The next day is Saturday.

She covered her face with a cloth but made it look traditional. She went to Nathan's garage for Wuquin's recitation. There are ten people, including Jiza, in the garage. They are primarily young men and women. Sabrina removed the face cloth.

Nathan saw Sabrina while she was entering the garage. She smiled at Nathan while Nathan was reading a verse from Wuquin. The verse goes, "If you have time, then never take any decision instantly and act on it when you are excited, motivated, depressed, sad, or feeling good. Always take time to think about the outcome and how you can achieve a positive outcome. Consider all possibilities of doing it. Calculate the probability of failure and its success after making a decision. Now that you have approached a problem logically and rationally, you will have clarity on your decision. Analyze whether it is correct or not through your gut feeling and intuition. Now, listen to what your gut feeling and intuition are telling you. Keep your decision and your gut feeling, intuition side by side, and now rationally analyze both of them and make the final decision on whether to act on it or not."

Sabrina sat in a chair and listened to the verse.

She is looking at Nathan. He was talking to people about the verses of the Wuquin and clearing their doubts. Sabrina felt good seeing all this. Sabrina's facial expressions show divine, emotional affection and love for Nathan. She is almost in tears while looking at him. Wuquin - The Holy Book of Ateesta Religion reading session was completed, and everyone was leaving.

Nathan came up to Sabrina, and he gave Wuquin to Sabrina. Sabrina took it. He told her, "Read it when you feel like reading it. Not because I gave it to you."

She said, "Sure!"

Jiza said, "Let's go! My girlfriend is coming!"

Nathan asked Jiza, "You got a girlfriend?"

Jiza said, "Yeah, just like you have a girlfriend. I too!"

Nathan laughed and said, "No, Sabrina is not my girlfriend!"

After hearing it, Sabrina's face turned red. She turned away her face in disappointment.

Jiza saw it and said, "Ok, bro."

Sabrina: "I thought you'd come to the movie theatre, but you didn't yesterday."

Nathan: "Yes, I have work, so I did not come."

Sabrina: " Still, I thought you'd come because I went."

Nathan: "You didn't ask me to come!"

Sabrina: "If I'm going, then can't you come?"

Nathan: "You went with Keizha!"

Sabrina: "No, I traveled to the movie theatre in Keizha's car, but I went with my friends, not Keizha specifically."

Nathan said, "Oh, I don't know that."

A cab came on the road and stopped. Ira came out of the cab. Jiza walked out of the garage. Nathan and Sabrina saw Ira. Ira gave a hug to Jiza.

Sabrina was surprised and asked Ira, "When did this happen?"

Ira smiled and said, "Last night. He said I love you. I said Me too!"

Nathan said, "Wow, it's time for a great celebration."

They got in Nathan's car. Sabrina sat in the front seat. Jiza and Ira sat in the back seat. They went to a takeaway restaurant. Took food parcels, water bottles, and soft drinks. They drove to the beautiful banks of the Kalsa River.

The Kalsa River was peaceful when they arrived. The water in the Kalsa River is flowing calmly. Nathan parked his car on the side of the road. They took the food parcels out of the car. Nathan said, "There are concrete benches and tables at the bank of the river where we can eat food."

They walked a bit into the woods and saw a table.

They sat on benches. Sabrina and Nathan sat on one bench, opposite them, Ira and Jiza sat on another. In the middle, they placed the food on the table. They opened the food parcels and started eating food.

The scenery of mountains and the Kalsa River with a deck on its shore felt marvelous to Nathan. Sabrina is looking at the river and observing it. She felt water touching her feet, and she looked down. She couldn't believe what she was seeing. The water of the Kalsa River is touching her feet slowly.

Nathan saw Sabrina looking down. He asked her, "What happened?"

She said, "Nothing!" and smiled.

Jiza said, "We should go on a trip!"

Ira said, "Yes, great idea."

Sabrina said, "My father doesn't like these types of things."

Nathan said, "My father also doesn't like all these types of things. But you know what? I don't tell him that I'm going on a trip with a beautiful girl, staying in a hotel in the same room with her, and return home. I tell him, It is a college trip! All my friends are going so I have to go. It is a trip to see historical buildings and things like that then he will agree."

Sabrina laughed and told Nathan, "My dad will know immediately if I lie!"

Nathan asked Sabrina, "Is your dad God?"

Sabrina, in a peculiar tone, replied, "Almost!"

Nathan said, "Ha ha, I'm Satan, then we should fight!"

Sabrina asked, "Why will you fight my dad if he is God?"

Nathan said, "Someone who says he is lord or God without showing clear rational and scientific proof is mostly Satan trying to deceive people by doing good deeds publicly. God must tell his believers that even though he is God and has all the powers to change things as he wants, he as God still wants his believers to work hard in life and stand on their own feet rather than he as God encouraging his believers to mindlessly worship him and beg him to get everything in life through a stupid worship process.

At least God must tell and encourage his believers to ask him for great thoughts, initial support while doing new things in life, and help to get the momentum initially in things they want to do. God should not tell his believers to just mindlessly worship him so that his believers get everything they want in life and the afterlife because it is not true. It is a superstition, not a rational belief in God.

See, many believers pray to their Gods for the things they want in life. Those things could be peace, happiness, money, or whatever they want, and they also pray to their Gods to go to Heaven in the afterlife, and not to go to Hell. But why does no one pray to God for a better beforelife, which means for better things happening to them before their birth and the start of their life? Is it illogical? Or their Gods only can change and improve their believers' current life and afterlife, not beforelife or before their birth?"

Sabrina angrily said, "So, you are saying my dad is Satan?"

Nathan defensively said, "No, I'm just telling you a verse from Wuquin, that's it."

Sabrina is still angry.

Nathan started saying," Sorry, Sorry!" Sabrina turned her head left and right, disapproving of Nathan's apologies. He continued apologizing, "Sorry, sorry, sorry!"

Ira and Jiza are looking at them.

While apologizing, Nathan got closer to Sabrina. His face is very close to Sabrina's face. Sabrina angrily lifted her head, and accidentally, Nathan's lips touched Sabrina's lips.

Ira and Jiza saw it and were shocked. They looked at each other and smiled. Sabrina was silent and don't know what to say. Nathan was surprised and he went silent in awe. Sabrina started feeling shy and Nathan started apologizing again for what happened, but his voice was shaking and unclear in amazement.

Sabrina got stiff in shyness and looked at Nathan. Suddenly Sabrina came closer to Nathan and hugged him. Jiza started shouting and whistling. Ira said "Yeah, that's my girl!"

Jiza said, "You did it bro. My bro got a girlfriend now!"

Kalsa River started getting aggressive. Waves are hitting shore strong. Water splashed on the heads of Nathan and Sabrina.

They started kissing on lips.

The Kalsa River flow suddenly appeared to get heavy and looked fierce between the mountains. Water started coming out of the usual river's path. Nathan and Sabrina's feet are submerged in water. Birds are making loud noises. Nearby animals in the mountain forest, deer and cows in the fields, started running away from the river. The wind became aggressive, and dust filled the sky. When Sabrina and Nathan stopped kissing, they saw the weather and were shocked.

Nathan looked at Jiza and Ira.

Ira is Krisen and Jiza is an Ateestan.

In the chaos, with a cool tone, Nathan asked Jiza, "How will you convince her parents, bro?"

Jiza said, "You have to help us, bro. And God Yinta should help us. I will talk to her father after our graduation."

Nathan smiled, saying, "I don't know about God Yinta, but I will help you, bro. I will talk to her parents on your behalf."

"Thank you, brother!" said Ira happily.

The weather kept getting worse with loud hymns from the mountains.

Ira said, "I think we should leave!" Nathan doesn't want to leave that place.

Sabrina looked at the mountains. Her face changed instantly, and she looked serious. She said, "Yes, we should leave now."

Nathan said, "Wow, what happened? We still have food left. The messy weather will go away in a few minutes!"

Sabrina gave a quick glance at Nathan with suspicion. She then changed her expression to smile in a split second.

The water slowly went back into the river, and the weather became calm. Surprisingly, there was no dust in the food. While eating, Sabrina sat opposite Nathan and looked at Nathan's shoulder. She saw the shoulder in particular a few times. While eating food, Sabrina suddenly stood up, came to Nathan's side, and sat beside him. She rested her head on his shoulder. She leaned her body on him.

***

Nathan took a sip from his soft drink. He offered it to Sabrina, and she also sipped his drink. While drinking, Sabrina looked at the mountains and wondered about something for a few seconds, then looked at the face of Nathan and smiled. Nathan looked at her and smiled back. Sabrina then looked at Nathan's face for a few seconds, and she couldn't control the happiness on her face. Her face is full of energy and happiness. She said, "Uhh. Uh.. Not here!" and she stood up and sat on the lap of Nathan perpendicularly. She placed one hand around the neck of Nathan, and with another hand, she took a chicken piece and asked Nathan to take a bite.

He took a bite, and she ate the rest. After that, she hugged him while still sitting on his lap. She hugged him very tightly for more than 2 minutes and started giving him kisses.

She then asked him, "Do you know who I am?"

Nathan said, "My property!"

She said, "No, I'm not your property. I'm the owner of you."

Nathan said, "Then we should fight first, and whoever wins is the owner of the other person."

She said, "Come on! Get up then."

He said, "Not here, in my bedroom!"

She laughed very loudly and said, "I'll kill you!"

He said, "What's the use? You can still see me after that, right?"

After hearing it, Sabrina said, "Uhh?"

Nathan said, "I know you will follow me to death, too. So,"

Sabrina got emotional and hugged him again. She said, "I'll never let that happen.."

Nathan said, "I wish it works like that!"

Ira and Jiza are having sex in nearby bushes. They saw a shape that looked like a man with a scythe. They stopped sex. Jiza took a photo. They got up and walked to Sabrina and Nathan hurriedly. Jiza said, "Hey guys, did you see this a few minutes back in the sky?" while showing them the photo he took. Sabrin and Nathan saw that photo. Sabrina said, "No, what is this?"

Ira said, "We saw it in the sky a few minutes back."

Nathan said, "Clouds form shapes. It's normal. Don't worry!"

Sabrina closed her eyes. She saw a very dark place with lava and volcanoes. A man who is more than 20 feet tall sitting on a throne atop a volcano is very angry. Suddenly, Sabrina opened her eyes. She is sad inside and a little scared.

Jiza said, "Can we go now?"

Nathan said, "Yeah!"

Nathan, Jiza, and Ira started walking toward the car. Nathan placed the leftovers in the car. Sabrina looked at the mountains and saw a bright white light on a mountain.

Everybody in Beruk village knows about the big God Yinta temple on that mountain. She saw the bright light coming from God Yinta's temple.

They went back to Beruk after dropping Ira at her home in Relsar. Nathan dropped Sabrina and Jiza off at their homes and reached his home. He bathed and wore a T-shirt and shorts. He entered his garage and saw his equipment, books, and rocket engine parts. He had a big 2-screen computer with a TV connected to it. He opened a rocket science course, took a notebook, and started watching the course videos and taking notes. He saw 4 hours of course videos for 8 hours straight, then he went to sleep at 2 AM.

He woke up the next day at 10 AM. It's Sunday. His mom is in the kitchen, and Nathan's father is a carpenter. His father's shop is beside the Beruk highway. He asked his mom for coffee. She said, " How many times have I told you not to study after 11 PM? You again slept late last night, and it will affect your health, Nathan!"

Nathan said. "It's okay, Mom. I won't do it again. Sorry, but I'm working on a problem, but I'm not able to find a solution to that problem."

"It's okay, but taking care of your health is more important than anything," said his mom. He kissed her on the forehead, took coffee, and went to his room. He had books on maths, physics, chemistry, biology, and other sciences in his room. He opened his laptop and again started watching the rocket science course videos. Ten minutes into watching, Sabrina called him. He answered the phone. "Hey, baby. How are you?" said Sabrina.

***

"I'm cool, sugar. What are your plans today?" asked Nathan.

"You should plan... I'll follow," said Sabrina.

"Ha ha, come to my home," he said.

"But what about your parents?" she asked.

He said, "We can meet in my garage, and no one can see us."

"Perfect!" she said, and after cutting the call, she screamed in happiness.

She changed her clothes, did makeup, and spent a lot of time in front of the mirror to look good.

She walked to Nathan's home. Nathan was waiting outside and took her straight into the garage quickly. When she entered his garage, she saw images of God Yinta, the God of Ateesta, who had no beginning and end.

"So you don't believe in supernatural things and ghosts, demons, etc.?" asked Sabrina.

"Well, if there is scientific evidence, then I will," replied Nathan.

"But how are you so sure that they don't exist, and you don't believe in them just because there is no evidence scientifically? It might also be because we are not as developed in our technology to find those supernatural things scientifically, right?" asked Sabrina.

"There is a chance of that, but what difference does it make if I believe in supernatural or paranormal things or don't? I believe in the real world. Other than that, those ghosts or supernatural elements increase the list of my fears, and that's it," replied Nathan.

"It's hard to talk to you. Logically," said Sabrina. Nathan laughed.

She asked, "But we still don't know the actual proper beginning of the universe, right? At least about what is there exactly before the Big Bang?"

"Yes," said Nathan.

* * *

"You can come up with all the logic and science ever developed by humanity till now, and you can also come up with science and technology that will be developed by humanity after one hundred thousand years, but there will always be something you don't know, and that is the key to find where and when the universe was started, but you will never know that. At least mathematically. Because in a place where one can be two and two can be one and also twenty, twenty million, or anything for that matter. Then, the mathematics of humans will not stand and fit to explain those unknown elements. Because in those unknown elements of the universe, there is a place where the variables act as variables, and also as constants, and both at the same time or nothing sometimes, Nathan," said Sabrina.

Nathan was thinking about what Sabrina said and replied to her, " There is a chance. And I'm sure God Yinta knows that maths." They both laughed.

Wuquin is on Nathan's bed. Sabrina saw it.

The book cover is so beautiful. It is named 'Wuquin - The Holy Book of Ateesta Religion' on the cover.

Sabrina read the page of the Five Pillars of the Active Mind. And laughed.

"What happened?" asked Nathan.

"Where is God? Where is the story of your God Yinta in this Holy Book of Ateesta religion?" asked Sabrina.

"There is no story of God Yinta!" said Nathan.

"What do you mean by no story of God Yinta?" Asked Sabrina.

He is the only God in your religion, right?" she asked.

"Yes," he replied.

"Then there should be stories of how God Yinta was born, his childhood, life, marriage, powers, and healing stories by people. This book should have all those things." Said Sabrina.

Nathan said, "Ha ha, there is no beginning nor end to God Yinta.

There are no stories of God Yinta because he wasn't born like a human and will not die.

However, we can explore who he is through Wuquin, and no one knows who wrote Wuquin.

It said that Wuquin had been revised thousands of times according to the time people were living in, but core principles mainly remained the same, and

We see Yinta not just as a God, but as the universe itself, because he told us to go out and find how this universe was born and how everything works in this universe, which we know. And also about the universes that we don't know.

So Yinta is a manifestation of the universe in a symbolic God form in the context of the Ateesta religion, but he is not a typical God to whom we should pray.

God Yinta said in Wuquin that you should not pray to him. It is stupid. Instead, sit in silence, close your eyes, and use your mind to get clarity in thoughts about what you want to do in your life.

And he also said to remember, every time you make a meaningful contribution to humanity and other life forms, every time you do anything positive, no matter whether it is a tiny thing or a thing that can change the world for the better, then you should know that you are with God Yinta and God Yinta is with you.

And every time you behave stupidly and do bad things just out of rage or emotions, you drift away from God Yinta.

So be happy and chill with positive vibes, intelligence, rationality, and consciousness.

God Yinta said we must respect someone who tried to do a great thing and failed instead of being an idiot and making them feel bad about their failure.

You already have that book at home, you can read it to learn more about God Yinta. God Yinta is the universe, and the universe is God Yinta.

* * *

If we want the story of God Yinta, then it means that we are asking for the story of the universe, which we must research and discover." Explained Nathan to Sabrina.

"Then how do you know your God is helping you, which means the universe is helping you? " asked Sabrina.

"Through our thoughts! He will tell you what to do through pristine, clear, conscious, intellectual, and rational thoughts, but it is not easy. It takes a lot of time to develop that ability," said Nathan.

"So your God talks to you regularly?" asked Sabrina.

"Yes!" replied Nathan.

"What? How?" asked Sabrina in surprise.

"You will know how when you read Wuquin!" said Nathan.

"I thought you would say you will establish a connection with God Yinta or the universe, but you said it is an ability," said Sabrina.

"Everyone is already in connection with the universe. That is why we are here physically and mentally, but the ability to understand the language of the universe is, in rationality and the five pillars of the Ateesta religion. So you have to learn a lot about the universe technically through intense study to understand who you are as a person. You should also learn about how things are made literally in the universe. That is why Ateestans love science, which is also an integral part of the Ateesta religion. You must also study the five pillars of Ateesta too." Said Nathan.

"In a way, your religion is only for smart, intelligent people who seek the truth in a very technical, scientific, or mathematical way. It's like you are bored with all the oldest religions because they are getting outdated with newly developed technologies. Also, these old religions did not describe how to approach the modern world, which is full of science and technology, apart from some ethics and morals. However, newly developing neurological and psychological science studies are also continuously challenging them. So you guys made your religion for only intelligent and rational people on Earth. And also for human equivalent alien forms outside of Earth, right? Also, I observed you never used the word 'Ethics' while talking about your religion.

You talked about only morals. Is it because you do not believe in ethics, or is it because Ateesta takes care of ethics completely through your Ateestan holy book, Wuquin?

Wuquin told you to behave according to your own morals.

But in Ateesta religion ethics come from Wuquin, not from the society, right? " asked Sabrina.

"In a way, yes, but I can say Ateesta is a religion for people with common sense and the ability to think critically. So, our ethics come from Wuquin, not from any external sources," said Nathan.

"So, one cannot become Ateestan by birth. He/she has to prove himself worthy of becoming an Ateestan?" asked Sabrina.

"Yes, you cannot become an Ateestan by birth just because your parents, father, mother, or family are Ateestan. There is a process to become an Ateestan," he said.

"What is it? I heard about it from Ira, but not in detail," said Sabrina.

"It is simple. You have to read Wuquin and five books on five different topics and give a speech or presentation to fellow Ateestans about what you think about Wuquin and what you learned after reading those five books. That's it.

Half of the presentation time is for Wuquin and half for what you learned from reading the five books. And how it is going to help you practically in your actual day-to-day life. No one can make you an Ateestan, but the presentation you gave. And that presentation should only last for 20 minutes maximum or less than that, but not less than 8 minutes.

The idea is to show that the person who wants to become an Ateestan is capable of thinking critically. With no marks and no one approving or rejecting a person from becoming an Ateestan, it gives that person the freedom to express him/herself freely. It also gives that person the freedom to decide how he/she wants to give the presentation or speech, and it also shows how great that person used the time that was given to him/her.

So, how well your presentation would be is entirely dependent on your interest and passion, and even though people are not giving you any marks, they can see whether you have put your mind to work, that is the whole point.

The two rules here are that you should not talk negatively about anyone who gave a speech or presentation, whether it is good or not. Second, the time limit is based on how many people are participating in the event and how much time it is good to allocate to each person to efficiently complete the presentations of everyone who wants to become Ateestans on that day. If you have many people, you can have less time for each presentation or speech, and if you have only a few people, you can have more than 20 minutes for each presentation or speech.

It depends entirely on the number of people and the time available that day. They can upload their full presentations to digital platforms after giving the initial presentation or speech physically in front of fellow Ateestans. The time given here is based on common sense, not on any fixed rule." Explained Nathan to Sabrina.

"Wow.. This is deep. I will read the book!" said Sabrina.

"Ha ha..okay," said Nathan.

In Hell, Satan sat on the throne and saw Sabrina and Nathan in his mind.

Satan's mind voice is saying, "You don't believe in me, Nathan, but you will soon. I will give you the problems that are very hard to express to others, and you have to struggle within yourself completely. Nobody can understand properly about your problems, pain, and the torture you are going through, even your God Yinta too. You will come running to me for help."

Sabrina and Nathan left the garage in Nathan's car, and in the middle of the highway, the car suddenly gave trouble.

Nathan stopped the car at the side of the road and opened the bonnet, trying to understand what had happened to it. He had seen the engine and everything yesterday during his usual car checkup. Everything was good at that time.

He was trying to figure out what happened and closed his eyes. Visualizing every part of the engine and car, he felt like everything was good in his mind.

He then remembered he hadn't gone to the gas station yesterday, and now there is no petrol in the tank, which is why it stopped.

He realized the fuel sensor was not working properly. Sabrina came out of the car and asked, "What happened? Did you figure out what the problem is?"

He said, "Yup, but we need petrol. I mean, the car needs it."

"We are far from Relsar, and no gas station is nearby. The last gas station I saw was more than 10 miles from here," said Sabrina.

"Open your phone and book a cab.

An outstation cab might be costly, but it will come fast. Book from your account on my phone," said Nathan.

"Okay," she said. She took his phone and booked the cab. The cab arrived, and they got the petrol and then started in Nathan's car again.

Sabrina asked, "Why did you ask me to book the cab from my account? You already have the cab app on your phone and an account in it."

Nathan replied, "You are a girl in the middle of the highway, so the driver will not cancel the ride. He will come to us expecting to see you alone after seeing your photo on the cab app. But he might cancel the ride if I book the ride from my account, and it might take us a little longer to find a cab or find a way to get petrol, so I asked you to book the cab from your account."

Sabrina laughed very hard and said, "You played!"

They went to the temple of God Yinta in the Aarvin mountains. The temple is on a mountain called 'Shen.'

A big, beautiful Yinta temple is on Shen Mountain. At the entrance, there are many sacred quotes. The temple is in an inverted triangle shape with two poles at each side to support the structure, and the base of the triangle at the back, with the sharp side to the front. It is making the structure look like a straight line reaching Earth from the sky sideways.

* * *

Sabrina loved the place. Kalsa River was flowing very calmly at the foot of the mountains. They reached the temple through a bridge that was said to have been constructed by God Yinta himself thousands of years ago. It was constructed of rocks and stands stronger than many bridges built using modern technologies. It was said in Ateestan folklore that God Yinta took 12 years to build it, and thousands of workers worked day and night to build it. Those workers were all engineers, artists, and skilled people. Not a combination of unskilled and skilled people. That is why the bridge is powerful and beautiful even after thousands of years.

Sabrina saw the big entrance of the temple and got excited by the massive structure.

As she walked inside, she saw the images and replicas of important discoveries made by humanity, with the names of the discoverers and other inventions and creations with their scientists' names.

It is said that all the entrances of God Yinta temples face east. This symbolizes the teachings of Wuquin that people should seek the truth and enlightenment through their personal journeys of achieving the goals they have in life, with a great purpose behind achieving those goals.

On the temple walls, there are multiple quotes. One quote she read says, 'You are enlightened when you achieve all the goals you had in your life. Or in the process of achieving them.'

The structure of the Yinta temples is precisely the same everywhere. Wuquin talks about these things in detail.

After reading the quotes inside Yinta Temple, she felt a little uncomfortable and went outside. There is an enormous statue of God Yinta there. The wind touching her face is cool and calm. Nathan came outside with her.

Sabrina observed a pimple on Nathan's face and immediately looked away. She understood something. They started returning to Beruk, and she observed a second pimple on Nathan's cheek.

In Hell, Satan started laughing.

Nathan accidentally touched a pimple while touching his face casually and felt it, but said nothing. Nathan's face is known to be very clean and good-looking in the Beruk village and his college. People used to admire his cleanliness and looks. It is because he worked very hard to show himself clean and healthy to the world with the limited resources he had. They returned to Nathan's home, and both slept on his bed in the garage that night.

The next day at 4 AM, Sabrina woke up and saw Nathan with many pimples on his face. She closed her eyes and heard "His suffering started from today" in the voice of Satan. And she was shocked after hearing it. Nathan woke up after a few minutes, kissed her, and went to wash his face.

He saw the pimples on his face and was shocked and a little stressed, too. He looked at all the pimples individually for a few minutes and returned to Sabrina.

He asked her, "Do you see pimples on my face?"

She said, "Yes!"

Then he started thinking about what he had eaten for the past 15 days, the places he had visited, and the people he had met. His diet is clean, and everything seems normal, but he couldn't figure out what happened and why he suddenly got pimples.

He is feeling stressed more and more after seeing the pimples again and again in the mirror in his room. He knew a lot about human nature and how judgmental society is of people with pimples. He is thinking about all the insults and insecurities he has to face starting today.

Sabrina asked, "Are you okay?"

Nathan replied, "Yes! I will drop you off at home."

Sabrina said, "Ha."

Both went out and are now in the car on the road. Nathan was looking at his face in the mirror occasionally while driving, to look at the pimples in different lighting conditions happening inside the car.

***

Sabrina said, "Concentrate on the road, Nathan!"

Nathan said, "Sorry!"

Sabrina knew he was feeling uncomfortable.

He dropped Sabrina off at her home. And returned to his garage. He sat on the bed in stress and dullness. He went to college but did not take Sabrina and Jiza in his car like usual. They called Nathan on the phone, but Nathan didn't answer their calls. They booked a cab and came to college.

Nathan sat in a chair in the classroom, and everyone was looking at Nathan's face.

Some laughed, some didn't care, and some asked what had happened to his face. Some said his handsomeness had lessened because of pimples, and some said he was looking less attractive now. He listened to everything patiently and said, "It's okay!" to everyone and moved on.

But his mind is not with him, and Sabrina is looking at Nathan, and she knows he is feeling depressed now because of the pimples.

After college, Keizha saw Nathan and mockingly asked him, "What is that great face cream you are using, bro? It is working great. Tell me, I will buy it!"

Nathan replied, "I will tell you, but I don't think you can afford it."

Keizha got angry, but he saw Sabrina in the back of Nathan walking towards him, so he stopped. Sabrina came to Nathan and asked him why he was not talking to her today.

He said, "Nothing like that. I'm thinking, that's it!"

She asked Nathan whether they could go out today. He said, "Not today.."

After a few days, Nathan went to his college and wrote a letter asking for some days off as his health was not good, and he got permission from the college.

He is attending outside events, and his family events in fewer numbers than usual, and no one knows why. Even his close friends and relatives don't know that it is because of pimples. He did not spend much time in the places he went and returned to his home as fast as possible. He didn't meet any new people after he started getting pimples. And it is clear that he is struggling mentally because of pimples. He is not meeting Sabrina as frequently as before. And sometimes, not even talking to her on the phone.

One time, he met a beautiful girl when he went to a book shop to buy some books, and usually, girls talk nicely to him and pay attention to him literally because he is handsome. But this time, he had a different experience. The girl in the bookshop is looking at a book, and Nathan asked her, "Is it good?"

She just looked at him and didn't answer; she walked away. Nathan felt very bad that day.

He is not talking to Jiza or anyone. Even his parents, too, didn't see him for a few days while still living in the same home because now, Nathan is mostly spending his time in his garage. He stopped going to college and switched off his phone.

He is having panic attacks and anxiety while looking at the pimples. He is having tears silently at night. He felt he had lost his handsomeness because of pimples.

In Hell, Satan is laughing and said, "Now you will face more problems until you start believing in me!"

After spending 3 months in isolation, not coming out of his home, he suddenly felt like he wanted to go outside, mainly because he was bored and he had thousands of hours of screen time.

Nathan went outside in his car, and he still had some pimples and scars on his face and felt insecure about them. He went to an outdoor restaurant beside the Beruk highway on the outskirts of Beruk village. He is looking dull and sad. After eating food, he started to his home, and while he was returning, a group of thugs stopped his car by pointing guns and threw him out of the car, and when Nathan tried to resist them, they beat him. While he was lying at the side of the road with injuries, they stole his car and mobile. On the mobile, he had all the contacts and important documents. He had tears in his eyes, and with blood on his face, he slowly stood up. The time was almost 3 AM. He started walking slowly towards Beruk village, with serious injuries to one of his legs. Upon reaching home, he fell on the garage floor and cried.

* * *

He saw a poster of God Yinta under his bed that had come off from the wall because the adhesive had weakened, and after seeing it, he remembered what God Yinta said about problems and emotions in Wuquin.

God Yinta in Wuquin said, "You will be under tremendous pressure and stress while dealing with problems, particularly when it comes to your appearance, health, family, and finances. So you have to always make sense inside of your head. Try to think clearly and find reasons for the causes of problems instead of just feeling sad and taking extreme steps because of your emotions. Use your emotions as fuel to solve your problems. It doesn't matter what emotions you are feeling; use them to your advantage and have control over them. Your solution to the problem you are facing might help other people, too. So remember the five pillars and stop being dumb."

After remembering it, Nathan realized how dangerous the emotions are. Even after practicing the Ateesta religion for years, he struggled a lot to deal with emotions and fell right back into the emotional abyss. He realized how serious the teachings of God Yinta were in Wuquin and how important they were in all situations of life, death, progress, failure, etc, on a deep, ecstatic level.

He got up from the floor and went outside, taking a bucket of fresh water with him. The road is empty as it is the middle of the night. He washed his face and the dirt off his hands and legs. The weather is cool and calm. He went back into the garage and ordered a healthy snack on a food app from the computer, came outside again, and sat on the floor in front of his garage. Nathan is thinking about Charles Darwin and his time on the ship when he was exploring the world. In his mind, he saw how Darwin was getting sick on the ship, the human dynamics Darwin observed on the ship, and his attitude adaptation approaches toward people on the ship to make them behave nicely to him. He remembered Darwin's visits to islands that no human had ever seen before and his discoveries there.

Nathan saw the electric poles on the road and remembered Tesla and the sad life he led. The great inventions Tesla brought into this world and the injustice done to him.

He saw stars in the sky and thought of the circumstances faced by Benjamin Franklin that made him stay unmarried and led to his invention of the lightning rod.

In the meantime, the food delivery person came, and Nathan took the food parcel. The food parcel has a water bottle and a not-so-healthy soft drink with it. He went inside and got plates, a small table, and a comfortable chair. He arranged the food on the table outside where he had sat before and started eating it. Vehicles are passing on the road occasionally.

He smiled and felt so good suddenly. He looked back and saw a hammer in his garage. He ate the food in utmost peace and tranquility. After eating the food, he took his second phone in the garage and went to the nearby police station on his father's bike. He had extra keys to the bike in his garage. He filed a complaint, and he had insurance for the car. He claimed the insurance, and after a few days, he bought another car with the extra cash he had and the amount paid by insurance. The car was decent, and it was red. His previous car was white. He searched for a red color car specifically. After many visits to multiple dealers, he found the car he liked.

He took a license to have a gun and bought a gun.

He went to a big bookstore and bought books on basic biology. And many basic to advanced books on dermatology, neuroscience, and cognitive psychology. He went to his garage and started reading those books. He used online courses and materials to get a grasp on topics and continued his studies using multiple sources to understand concepts at a deeper level. He studied many patient testimonials in dermatology. He did all this to find a solution to his pimple problem.

He studied those subjects for 3 months and finally came to the conclusion that lactose intolerance and heavy metal accumulation in his liver were causing the pimples. He realized he had lost the ability to digest dairy products, and when he consumes dairy products regularly, they stress his digestive system, cause gut illness, and produce pimples as a result. He stopped eating dairy products and got his liver treated while maintaining a healthy diet with proper exfoliation of his skin. Slowly, his skin improved, and the glow is coming back with 10x improvement. His scars are fading away, and it's been months since he saw Sabrina, Jiza, and his other friends. Jiza had not seen him since he got pimples, and when Jiza came to Nathan's home once, Nathan was not home.

Nathan realized he was so entangled in emotions before that he told himself visiting a dermatologist was a waste of time. Nathan realized how dumb human emotions make a person who is under stress.

After healing from the pimples, Nathan had a clearer face again.

Nathan went to Sabrina's home without telling her and knocked on the door.

She answered and was shocked after looking at him. She hugged him in extreme happiness.

They went to an outdoor restaurant in his new car. And while eating food,

Sabrina asked him, "Why didn't you talk to me for all these months? Your pimples healed, and you look more handsome than before.. How? What did you do? Did you visit a doctor?"

Nathan replied, "No, I read what a doctor reads to know about a disease. And to get medication, I visited a doctor, then I just changed my diet. That's it!"

"I thought they would never go away, and you wanted to be alone," Sabrina said.

Nathan said, "Ha ha, why do they never go away? They are the result of something, and if we find and adjust it, they will go away. It is not something that we don't know at all, right?"

"Yes, but I thought some evil supernatural powers gave you those pimples because you said you don't believe in them. And how can we make them go away because they did not come in a natural or human way, right?" Sabrina asked Nathan.

Nathan said, "Ha ha, but even for an evil supernatural power to give me pimples and to make me feel bad just because I don't believe in it,

It has to make changes in this world by making changes in my body, right? It has to make actual physical changes in my body somehow. Otherwise, I won't get those pimples. If we assume those changes are caused absolutely by an evil supernatural power, I can still actually detect what those changes are and stop them or cure them if it is a disease. At least I can try.

No supernatural power can do anything bad or good without changing something physically in the world, and those changes are always detectable scientifically. Otherwise, it violates the laws of physics, and it is impossible for any supernatural powers or humans to violate the laws of physics. It is because even if those supernatural powers exist in a world unknown to us, they must operate hypothetically according to the laws of physics of the world in which they exist.

Even if a good supernatural power heals cancer in a patient, it still has to make changes physically to the patient's body to do it. Did you get it?"

"Yeah!" in amazement, Sabrina responded.

"Even if those supernatural powers make changes to a person mentally or psychologically, they too can be detected. Even if it is a little hard," said Nathan.

Sabrina asked Nathan, "Did you meet God Yinta before?"

"What? No, it is impossible. He is not a person. But yeah, if I'm working towards progress and having fun, I can assume I met God Yinta," Nathan replied.

In Hell, Satan was silent, and Satan understood that now Nathan knows the thin connection Satan had with the world Nathan is in. Also, Satan understood that a power in Nathan is rising, opposing Satan's influence from the known and unknown universes to humanity.

Sabrina said, "I love you!" to Nathan, directly looking at his face. With a smiling face, Nathan looked at her with an expression of wonder as to why she said that suddenly.

Nathan told Sabrina, "Wow.. Love you too, and I just got pimples, and there are people in the world without hands, legs, and with all kinds of diseases and problems. I felt so bad just because of pimples. I can't imagine how those people are taking the pain and moving forward in life. It is sad. I hope no one says mean things to people facing these types of problems because no one knows how it feels until they are in that position, but no one wants to be in that position, but make fun of the people in those sad situations instead of helping them."

"You are something else, man. Not the man I thought you were!" said Sabrina.

At the time, Nathan is with Sabrina at the restaurant,

Nathan got a letter to his home from Kehraan State University in Tushak City in Kehraan state. His mom took it and put it in his room. Tushak is 100 miles from Beruk.

Nathan received an invitation letter for a one-year research program at Kehraan State University. He was invited to join the research team working on finding the pattern of skin, lung diseases, and cancer according to Tushak city pollution levels and air quality. The things he learned from reading biology earlier helped him get a good grasp of the subject, and he applied for the research intern program at the university a few days before. After seeing Nathan's contrasting profile and interest in various subjects, the university decided to give him a chance to bring a different point of view to the team and the work they are doing.

Jiza came to the restaurant and met Nathan and Sabrina, and Ira came with Jiza.

* * *

"Bro.. Where did you go all these months?" Jiza asked.

"To Hell!" replied Nathan.

Sabrina was shocked.

Nathan laughed and said, "Just some low phase, bro. That's it." Sabrina hugged Ira and said, "Happy to see you after a long time, Ira."

"Same here, Sabrina," said Ira.

Satan was angry in Hell. He ordered Koshi to go and kill Nathan.

Koshi took human form from his ugly devil form and came to the restaurant on Earth where Nathan was.

He walked into the restaurant, and the table Nathan and Sabrina were at was in an open place in the restaurant. He saw them. Nathan observed Koshi walking towards them, but Koshi was far away.

Sabrina saw Koshi and looked at Nathan in fear. Koshi came right before Nathan, took his ancient sword, and attacked Nathan. Nathan expected the attack and dodged, missing the sword swing and saving his head.

Everyone at the table went back, screaming in fear. Sabrina stood near the table, but Koshi didn't attack her. Koshi attacked Nathan, specifically, fiercely with the sword, and Nathan was trying hard to escape the sword.

Everything the sword touched was melting and turning into dust. Nathan struggled hard to dodge the sword swings. Jiza, Ira, and the other people at the restaurant are shocked and scared, seeing the table and chairs, the sword touching, turning into dust.

# 2

Nathan is not getting any new thoughts on stopping the attack on him entirely, as he is very concentrated and struggling to dodge the sword.

He saw an iron pole in the restaurant building, and Koshi's sword was approaching him. The sword looked like metal, and the color of the sword was silver. The sword touched the nearby chair, which melted and turned into dust in a split second. Koshi saw Sabrina and increased the intensity of his attack on Nathan.

Nathan saw Koshi seeing Sabrina, and the iron pole was behind Sabrina. Nathan suddenly took advantage of the second Koshi saw Sabrina and went back 2 feet and picked up a plant pot. The plant pot had soil and water in it. He threw the plant pot onto the sword. It turned the plastic pot into dust, but the soil and water remained the same, and the plant was cut into pieces.

He understood two things about the sword then. One, the sword has some chemical properties, and two, whatever chemical properties the sword has, they can make everything the sword touches into dust. But it didn't work with soil, which means the sword cannot turn the Earth into dust.

With this, he understood that rocks, soil, everything that is part of the Earth and its natural process of evolution, will not react with the sword's chemical properties, but everything that is altered in a way by humans chemically will react with the sword, and it will melt and turn into dust if the sword touches it.

Since his body is a living organism and the sword is metal, it can kill him by injuring him, and it will not turn him into dust, but his clothes and other things will get turned into dust. He realized it would be a painful and embarrassing death if he died there in that sword attack.

Jiza and Ira are panicking, seeing the sword with supernatural powers. Koshi is in a very strange attire, and no one knows the style of clothes Koshi was wearing.

Koshi's clothes felt dark and distant, inspiring fear in those who saw Koshi. He hasn't said a single word till now. Nathan ran away from Koshi after throwing the plant pot at him.

There are stone fencing poles that are stationed there for fence construction. Nathan took one light stone and waited for Koshi to come to him.

Koshi walked very fast towards Nathan and vertically swung the sword straight onto his head. Nathan held the fence pole horizontally on his head, and the sword hit it.

The fence pole broke into two pieces and injured the left palm of Nathan. The sword missed its target, and Koshi was shocked to see it. Sabrina was shocked at first and felt happy again. Nathan took one piece of the broken pole stone into his hands again. Jiza and Ira were shocked, and Jiza became confident after seeing it. Ira whistled, and Sabrina smiled in happiness with a big glow on her face.

For the first time, Koshi said, "It's impossible to stop the sword of the Lord of the known and unknown universes. You humans will not stop using your minds even in the most fearful moments of your lives. You will pay the price much costlier than your death for not dying by the sword of the Lord and for committing the unforgivable sin."

Nathan, breathing heavily, said, "The universe cannot be destroyed by what it was made of. It can change its form, or it will not. That's it."

Koshi Laughed and said, " Your God Yinta will pay the price for helping you!" And in anger left the place by flying into the sky.

***

Nathan wondered to himself why he and God Yinta would pay the price. As God Yinta is in his mind, God Yinta is given the idea to defend himself.

God Yinta is the universe, and the universe is God Yinta. How is the universe going to pay the price when the attacker and his sword, too, are themselves part of the universe? Then he realized that the attacker wanted to destroy the universes that were not under his control.

And that there might be many others supporting him, and also the attacker might be from another universe.

Jiza came running towards Nathan and hugged him. He said, "Bro.. You are the hero! You defeated and embarrassed a supernatural power that tried to kill you with a dark magical sword. But who is that, and why did he try to kill you?"

Nathan said, "I don't know, and I don't think the sword and the man are supernatural. That sword might be made of a new metal discovered and not well known. And he might have some good secret technology to fly like that."

"No, Nathan!" said Ira. "No known technology to humanity can make a man fly like that. It is supernatural, and it definitely has a strong reason to try to kill you. It makes no sense even if we see it rationally. It is impossible for a normal human being to be like that."

Nathan said, "Maybe, maybe not. We don't know!"

Sabrina came to Nathan, gave him a lip kiss while everyone stood there looking at Nathan, and said, "You know what the universe is now, and I know what you are now."

She kissed the injured palm of Nathan, and Nathan's blood touched her tongue.

Koshi is the son of Satan. He went back to Hell. Satan knew what had happened.

When Koshi tried to explain himself, Satan stopped him with a wave of his hand.

Koshi became silent.

Satan said, "He must kneel before me. A human cannot challenge the power of Hell. His little stupid display of a skill today can give him more confidence in himself and decrease our influence on him and the world of humanity.

You got defeated today not because you are weak and he is strong, but because he knows the thin line we operate on.

I killed your mother in the mortal world and sent her to Udin because no one should be equal to me, even as a wife.

But still, I couldn't take her out of all the universes unknown to me. It is because if something exists somewhere and if it is unknown to me, then the universe will not let me know anything about it because we don't know that it exists until we know it exists. It is the same for everyone, not just for me.

It is the rule of the universe that what we don't know, we don't know until we know, even for me and even for the universe itself. "

"Father, but you are Satan, and no one can go against you," said Koshi.

"Ha ha, anybody can go against anyone, but the thing is, they have to survive the reverse attack of whom they are going against. That guy did it today," said Satan.

"But father, you are like the universe too. You, too, have no beginning and no end. That human will be dead in the next 80 Earth years. His age is not even equal to a sand particle in the desert in front of your age," said Koshi.

"I'm like the universe, but I'm not the universe itself. I tried to be, but it never happened. Something that has never happened cannot be corrected in any form. I know He will die because he is a human, but his imprint of defying me in the universe will never go away even after the death of his physical body," said Satan

"What should I do now, father?" asked Koshi.

***

"Not you! 'The Ante' will take care of him now, and I will lead the forces if needed," said Satan.

"But father, what if he comes to Farush? God Yinta will come with his forces, too. We are going against God Yinta, because that human is an Ateestan," said Koshi.

"Come what may, we should go against that human if he challenges our power," said Satan.

"Ateestans believe God Yinta is the universe and the universe is God Yinta. How can we go against the universe itself, when we are in it?" asked Koshi.

"The universe doesn't discriminate against anyone. Anyone who is for or against it. But we can. It is not easy to summon God Yinta just by that mere mortal himself. He will die the second he sees me. His subconscious fight is now with me for his free will of mind, and it will end after he sees me," said Satan.

Nathan, Sabrina, Jiza, and Ira are at the Kalsa Riverbank.

Sabrina asked Nathan how he knew what could stop the sword of the dark force that attacked him.

Nathan answered, "It can be a sword or stick or could be anything, but the key thing here is it is made out of something, and that something cannot be all-powerful without rules, limitations, and properties attached to it, since the origin of it is in the universe itself. That universe could be the one in which we are or some other universe unknown to us till now.

In this case, it is a sword, and it is made out of a metal or rock, or something. We don't know what it is, but it is certainly made out of something in some universe, and it came to the universe we are in. We are in this universe, and Earth is in this universe. Of course, we are on Earth.

If I can't stop something, the Earth can sometimes, and if the Earth can't, the Sun can, and if the Sun can't, the Milky Way can, or if the

Milky Way galaxy can't, then the Andromeda galaxy can. You can just go with something that is more powerful than what is attacking us. That is how the universe is constructed and the matter formed."

Sabrina saw Shen Mountain from the bank of the Kalsa River.

Nathan said, "Let's go buy some clothes!"

Sabrina started laughing after hearing it.

Nathan continued, "Why are you laughing? It's been a long time since I bought new clothes."

They started in Nathan's car to buy clothes. Reached a shopping mall in Relsar.

While entering the shopping mall, Nathan told Sabrina he had decided to grow his hair.

She asked him what he meant by growing his hair.

He said, "I'm not going to cut my hair from today till the day I feel I served my purpose in this world."

Sabrina started thinking while still smiling about what Nathan said, and told him it was a great decision.

The long hair on a man symbolizes defiance and opposition to what Satan stands for at the Farush, a place in the Master Universe where no power in the known and unknown universes can take over. It was anciently used for battles between God Yinta and Satan.

Hell is where Satan resides physically.

Heaven is where God Yinta resides physically.

Hell is a place where God Yinta is rejected altogether.

It was said in Ateestan folklore that not just Hell in the Master Universe but any place in the known and unknown universes becomes Hell if God Yinta is rejected there.

In the Master Universe, Hell became Hell because Satan opposed God Yinta, and he saw the power for himself in opposing God Yinta.

'The Ante' is a council of manifestations of negative emotions in the Master Universe, which was boycotted by Happiness of Earth because

Happiness realized it is better to come into the life of a person pursuing a higher purpose or avoiding harm to another's life. Happiness of Earth realized it will be in a better place in the universe when it stops coming into a person's life who is chasing short-term destructive things for long-term Happiness.

After knowing what Happiness had decided, Satan caged the Happiness of Earth in his Hell. Satan only started giving Happiness to people on Earth who are more unnecessarily dumb, emotional, criminal, and losing their rational selves rather than being balanced. Through keeping Happiness in a cage in Hell, Satan started drying out the remaining Happiness in the lives of people who are pursuing a courageous, calm life.

He let other emotions roam freely on Earth in the known universe, confusing the masses who unknowingly are feeling every emotion except Happiness. And for people who are in the process of pursuing Happiness through short-term destructive things, Satan was giving them little amounts of Happiness and making them believe that the path they were on was correct.

By feeling other emotions in higher amounts than normal due to the void left by Happiness, the people of Earth became confused emotionally and logically, losing their common sense and rationality, slowly resulting in depressed lives where failure of others are becoming more interesting and destruction is becoming more curious to them than the respect for creation of great beautiful things, success and long-term Happiness of everyone.

Satan planned to take the remaining Happiness out of Nathan's life and decided to intensively push the rest of the emotions.

Nathan reached home and parked his car. He got a cool drink and food. Sat in front of his garage. It is 1 AM. It was hot, so he placed a portable fan outside to compensate for the heat. He started eating the food in peace. It is silent outside, and birds are chirping. He heard a sound inside his home. He ran inside the home, and he saw his mom on the floor unconscious, and his father was crying and holding her. Nathan carried her out. While carrying his mother in his arms, tears are coming out of his eyes. In his car, he took her to the hospital.

***

The doctor said it was a heart stroke and she needed to be in the hospital for a week. Nathan was sad, and he was at the lowest point of his life at that moment.

After a few hours, He asked the doctor about her condition. The doctor said her condition was stable now, but she needs further observation and tests.

Nathan gave insurance papers to the hospital staff. He stayed in the hospital that night. Jiza came to the hospital in the morning. Nathan's father was sleeping in a chair. Nathan sat in a chair and was thinking about his mom.

Jiza came straight to Nathan and told him his father's carpenter shop was being demolished to the ground by the government for the expansion of the highway.

The nurse returned and told Nathan they had to pay an extra 42,000 cials in cash as the insurance only covered part of his mother's treatment. The total bill was 112444 cials.

Nathan, his dad, and Jiza went to their carpenter shop, and it had already been destroyed. Nathan saw it and got tears in his eyes. Remembering how happy they were when his dad opened the shop. The raw materials and tools were destroyed.

People who had their buildings and properties destroyed are crying and asking government officials why they did not inform them before demolishing them. At least they could have shifted the costly machinery they bought with loan money. Now, everything was destroyed, and they had to repay the loans to the banks too.

The government officer handed a notice paper to Nathan's father. The notice paper had a warning from the government asking not to build the shop again without getting permission from the local municipality. The notice also mentioned a tax fine of 24000 cials to be paid by Nathan's father or go to jail for 5 months.

Nathan took the notice paper while his father was reading it, and he read it. He angrily tore it apart, walked into the debris, and started picking up the tools and materials.

Jiza and Nathan's father followed Nathan.

Nathan's father is a Krisen, and his mom is an Ateestan. Nathan became Ateestan because his mother asked him to become one.

After picking up all the remaining materials and tools from the debris, he took them home. And went straight to God Yinta temple alone on Shen Mountain.

Nathan saw a quote inside the God Yinta temple. It goes, "Common sense and rationality prevail, while blind faith kills and was used to organize dumb people so as not to let them go out of control."

He is looking at the statue of the God Yinta outside the temple.

He sat in front of it. In his mind, he is talking to himself, "A son of a politician smuggled 20 million cials worth of watches from Inkaar Country, and no one arrested him. A businessman got the contract to mine in a 10-mile radius, but he mined more than 100, and nothing happened to him.

A middle-class family like mine had a shop, and the government wanted that place to construct a road for the sake of society, but secretly to increase the value of the land of a politician. We suddenly became villains, lost our land, shop, money, and everything else, and also had to pay fines or go to jail.

The stupid, no, no, the cunning insurance company agent said the policy would cover all the costs of major emergency treatments. But now, suddenly, it won't because of some conditions printed with the font size of 0.2 in the insurance documents, which the agent told me not to be bothered with. We were told by the agent that they are just a formality, and the agent didn't tell us about anything important in the conditions in advance, at least at the time when we signed them, either.

As a person, I thought I'd be good and behave with a sense, but what should I do when the world hits me and asks me, nah, forces me to stay down? Just because I'm a nobody, should I accept this injustice? And they will put a police case on me, threaten me, my family if I speak up!"

He started walking there on the bridge, and the Kalsa River was so high that day that the water was flowing at the edge of the bridge.

"It would take years to get justice if I go through the legal route. There is a great probability that I won't even get it." He said to himself in his mind.

He remembered the threats local municipality officials had made to his father, asking him to surrender the land and shop to them with the support of a politician. His father didn't tell Nathan about it because he didn't want to disturb his mind and distract him from his studies and work.

Satan is looking at Nathan in his mind from Hell.

"I might die, but I must do it because it is right. Like my father, hundreds of people lost everything they had worked for all their lives. I should kill the politician who is behind this, and I have to beat the **** out of the CEO of this insurance company," Nathan told himself in his mind.

Koshi came to meet Satan. "Father, what is he going to do?"

"I don't know!" said Satan.

"But you can know what he is thinking," said Koshi.

"You can't, I can't, no one can!" said Satan.

"Why? He is a mere mortal," Koshi said.

"Ha ha, you wouldn't even know what a dog is thinking, too, but you can always guess," said Satan.

"But father, why? You are Satan, and you must know what anyone is thinking or going to think or going to do, right?" asked Koshi.

"If I can know what someone is thinking, that can be a human or a God or a dog, then it is possible that there is a chance of them knowing what I'm thinking too. If they know what is in my mind, then what can I do? Nothing! They will try to stop me before I even start doing anything, right? I will do the same to anyone. But the universe doesn't work that way, my son. The universe doesn't discriminate against the Intelligence of any species, positively or negatively. Believe me, if you somehow can know what is exactly inside the mind of a man or any life form, then you can become more than a God, and others, no matter who they are, they will become your slaves," said Satan to Koshi.

A very old car coming from Lester City is on the outskirts of Beruk village on the Beruk highway.

It has three men who saw the destruction of public property in Beruk village on TV.

Those three men are Kwin, the short guy; Tes, the skinny guy; and Huro, the raging bull.

These three guys love Wizbome country a lot, and they think the unpatriotic, corrupt politicians are running the country now. They saw the tears of Nathan. And Nathan's father and Jiza, picking the remaining tools and materials from the debris. They felt bad after seeing them.

The three guys thought of meeting Nathan. They also saw the social media profiles of Nathan's father's shop and discovered Nathan's profile too.

They read the articles written by Nathan on rockets, philosophy, his journey of healing pimples, the attack on him, and many other things he wrote about in his blog. They admired him and his philosophical ideas.

They decided to meet him and talk to him. Huro admired Nathan a lot and decided he would follow Nathan philosophically. Huro is curious about how a man with many ideas about life will see and deal with this devastating incident.

In the car, Tes said, "You think he gives f** about us, yeah?"

Huro replied, "Yeah, why will he not?"

Kwin said, "He is already at a loss, so I don't think he will become friends with us!"

Tes said, "Yeah, but he is well-read, unlike us bums.."

Kwin said, "Oh! Come on, what is being well-read done to him? Did it stop his property from getting destroyed? Did it stop his tears? Did it give him as much money as corrupt politicians? What good does it do for him?"

Huro said, "He is just like us but educated!"

"I agree," said Kwin.

Nathan took the Kehraan State University letter he received and went to the university.

He met the professor who offered him the internship. He said he would join after 60 days if possible. The professor agreed.

He came back home at 10 PM that day and parked his car. While going inside the garage, he saw a car parked in an unusual way on the road in front of his home. Three guys inside the car are looking at Nathan. Nathan went inside his home through the door connecting to the garage and took money to pay the hospital bill. When he came out of the garage, the three guys walked toward Nathan.

When they were almost 60 feet away from him, Nathan took his gun out of his pocket and pointed it at them. The three guys were scared. Kwin and Tes ran away in fear. Huro knelt in front of Nathan in fear and lifted his hands in the air. Kwin and Tes are still running on the road.

In a scared voice, Huro begged, "Nathan.. Nathan.. Please don't shoot.. Please don't shoot.. We came here to meet you!"

Nathan asked him loudly, "Who are you? Why do you want to meet me?"

Huro replied, "Because we saw you on TV and felt bad about what happened to you and your family."

Nathan asked him, "Why do you care what happened to me.. Is this a new scam?"

Huro replied, "No, please don't shoot. We are patriots. We love Wizbome, and we think this country is wronged by its politicians, and your family suffered a lot because of it. That is why we came here to meet you."

After hearing that Nathan has lowered the gun, Tes and Kwin are looking at Nathan and Huro from far away. In relief, Huro relaxed on the road, lying.

Tes saw it, in shock, said, "I think he shot Huro," and started crying louder.

In the silence of the night, Huro and Nathan can hear Tes's loud cry, and Kwin's too.

Nathan and Huro heard them. Huro stood up and called Kwin and Tes. Kwin saw Huro calling them. He tried telling Tes, but he was crying loudly and not listening to Kwin. Kwin tried a few times and slapped Tes. Tes stopped crying. Kwin asked him to turn around and see Huro. Huro is standing in the middle of the road. Tes started smiling and shouted in happiness after seeing Huro. Huro waved his hands and signaled them to come.

They both started walking towards Huro and Nathan. Nathan saw them. They came to Nathan and offered handshakes to Nathan. Nathan gave them handshakes.

Huro told Nathan in relief, "I thought I was gonna die, boss!

I'm Huro. He is Kwin, this is Tes. We came here from Lester City after seeing what they did to your shop on the TV. We are patriots. We love Wizbome. We feel you've been wronged by the system. And the worst, the system does not even allow us to express our pain to society."

Nathan said, "Yeah, but how can I trust you?"

Kwin said, "My God, we traveled 120 miles just to see you. We will give you our addresses and all our government IDs. You can check them."

Nathan laughed and said, "Not necessary! What do you all do besides this?"

"Besides begging not to get shot?" asked Huro.

"Yeah!" replied Nathan laughingly.

"Kwin dropped out of school. I own a small bakery," said Huro.

Tes looked at Huro.

Huro said, "Well, my father owns a bakery shop in Lester. I work there. Tes completed High school and wants to become a soldier."

"Great," said Nathan and continued, "I have to go to the hospital now!"

Huro concerningly asked Nathan, "What happened? Are you sick?"

"No, my mom is in the hospital. I have to visit her and pay the bill," said Nathan.

"Fine, then we will also come with you. Why travel alone at night?" said Tes.

"We also want to see your mother," said Kwin.

"Okay! Come," said Nathan, and he took them to the hospital in his car.

Tes, Kwin, and Huro waited, and Nathan paid the bill.

Nathan talked to his father at the hospital. The doctor said she is recovering after surgery.

He went and sat in a chair. The Three - Huro, Kwin, and Tes sat next to Nathan.

"I paid the insurance company a lot of money, but I still paid half of the bill," said Nathan.

"Barbaric insurance companies did that to my father, too, when my father got injured in an accident," said Kwin.

"If you are a politician and have a horse with one eye and like it so much, then you can pass a law that requires every horse in the country to have only one eye," said Huro.

"Yeah, but they killed our horse!" said Nathan.

The Three looked at Nathan in sympathy.

Nathan got to know in the police station from an honest police officer that the people who attacked him when he was returning to his home after eating outside a few months back had the support of the ruling party. Local elected politicians always use those goons to do the dirty work.

And with the support of those politicians, they are committing crimes and dodging the law.

Nathan went outside the hospital, and The Three followed him.

They are in the car with Nathan and came to the Hervin forest on the outskirts of Beruk village. Nathan stopped the car in the forest, went out, and started walking.

The Three are wondering what's happening. They got out of the car, ran towards Nathan, and started walking with him.

"Go to your homes," said Nathan.

"Why suddenly? What happened?" asked Huro.

"Are you really patriots?" asked Nathan.

"We love this country. We are ready to die for it," said Kwin.

"Then don't die, Kill!" said Nathan.

The Three are shocked.

"If you stay with me, you will get in trouble," said Nathan.

"The troubles are not new to us. Tell us what you are going to do," Huro replied.

"I'm going to kill that local municipality head and beat the **** out of the CEO of that insurance company. I will also kill the people who attacked me and stole my car," said Nathan. The Three were speechless and shocked.

"But what do you get after doing it? You will go to jail, and they might kill you if you get caught. You can fight them through court," said Tes.

"In this country, do you believe someone who is like me will get justice fairly through the courts?" asked Nathan.

Tes became silent.

"So you thought about it a lot before we met you?" asked Huro.

"Yes," said Nathan.

"Then we kill him. We will help you," said Huro.

"Yeah, for Wizbome and to fight against injustice done to a normal man," said Kwin.

"Yeah, but we should not get caught," said Tes.

"We have to plan and execute it properly," said Nathan.

"Yeah, boss," said Huro.

They all went to Nathan's garage.

Sabrina called him. But Nathan didn't answer her phone call.

They bought food and water for 10 days and grabbed tools and materials from Nathan's garage. Nathan's family owns a small piece of land near the Hervin Forest. Nathan's father built a cabin on their land. The four went inside that cabin.

They are going to kill the local municipality head, who is corrupt. The local municipality head owns a lot of private lands on the outskirts of Beruk village and wanted to expand the Beruk highway to make the highway go near his lands and increase their market value.

Nathan told The Three that they would make an electric shock delivery device. This device will be the size of a phone, but it will give a shock of 1400 volts for 6 seconds.

They should somehow have put it in the heart area of the municipality head to kill him instantly and flee the scene after that. So they have to do it when he is in a public place, but isolated for a short time. For example, when he goes to the washroom or is left alone for a few seconds by his security team while he is talking on the phone, etc. They have to find a situation like that and kill him using the shock device. Nathan gave them gloves to wear now and also to wear while killing the local municipality head so that they do not get electrocuted by the device they will have in their hands. They have to make six devices in total and have to carry 4 of them in their hands, like phones, and 2 of them as a backup in case any device malfunctions at the last moment.

They made the devices by buying materials in multiple shops in Lester, Tushak, and Relsar to avoid suspicion of any kind.

Nathan made the devices in the cabin near Hervin forest.

Nathan tested them on lights. They blasted immediately. They disposed of the remaining materials by burning them in the forest. They celebrated.

They all ate food at that fire that night.

Nathan got to know about the program for the public opening of a new bridge in the Beruk outskirts on the Kalsa River. The local municipality head will attend the bridge opening ceremony. Nathan decided to kill him there. They also got to know that the bridge was constructed by the construction company of the local municipality head himself. But legally operated by his relatives. They learned that a lot of corruption was committed in the construction process, from bidding on contracts to bridge delivery to the government. The president of the country, who is the head of the country, will also be attending the event. He is a good friend of the local municipality head. So the security will be tight.

Nathan and The Three went to a shopping mall in Tushak city. They bought costly suits, black glasses, shoes, and other accessories.

Nathan told The Three to take the handshakes one by one from the local municipality head after the completion of the event, when he starts walking towards his car to return home.

The municipality head would go to his car after giving handshakes.

Nathan told The Three to wait again near the municipality head's car and his security cars with their car and wait for a moment when the local municipality head will have only a few people around him or alone.

At that moment, one of you should give a handshake again, and the municipality head will look at the face of the person to whom he is giving the handshake. At that second, you have to raise your second hand casually and suddenly put the shock device on his heart and press the button to deliver the shock. The device will deliver 1400 volts of electricity for 6 seconds straight to his heart.

They agreed to the plan and went to the event. The bridge opening ceremony was completed.

The Three killed the local municipality head according to plan when Nathan gave them the signal to give handshakes, and they didn't know Nathan had killed the president.

Nathan told them he would drive the car to escape. As planned, they returned to the car running, and Nathan drove the car away without any problem.

They returned to the cabin, shouted in happiness, and celebrated.

On TV at the Cabin, they are not showing news of the municipal head's death, but showing the death of the president of Wizbome.

After seeing that news, The Three looked at Nathan. He smiled.

Nathan told them what happened.

First, they all agreed to the plan and went to the event. The bridge opening ceremony was completed.

The president and municipality head are returning to their cars with security personnel. The rest of the President's convoy is 1000 meters from the President's main car. The president's main Car came directly onto the bridge and reached the ceremony stage for the ribbon cutting. Due to the smaller space on the bridge and the people there, the total convoy stopped 1000 meters from the stage, and only the president's car reached the bridge with security accompanying him by walking around the car. Fireworks started. The president saw it and thought it was to celebrate the occasion. When the president walked to his car, the local municipality head walked with him.

The president went into the car. The municipality head said, "I will meet you later," to the president, and left. Nathan placed a remotely operated robot near the fireworks. He turned it on, and the robot started firing fireworks rockets at people. And everyone started running to avoid getting hit by fireworks.

Suddenly, hundreds of people started running towards the president's main car, and security got confused and stood on four sides of the president's main car. Nathan wore clothes similar to those of the security agents of the president. In the style of a security agent, Nathan went near the president's car and opened the door. The president didn't see his face, thought he was his bodyguard, and let him sit in the back seat with him. After Nathan sat in the backseat confidently, the other security agents thought he was one of their own.

Nathan said, "Are you okay, president?" and looked at his chest like he was checking for a bullet. That is what the president thought. Nathan took his hand and placed the shock device on the president's heart casually. It delivered a shock to his heart, and he died on the spot. Nathan came out of the car and casually walked away from the president's car. Security personnel thought Nathan was going to clear the people or do something the president had told him. So they didn't stop him.

Riots started in the country and all major cities. He told The Three the plan was to kill the president, but he didn't want to say to them, not because he didn't trust them, but because they might get scared. The local municipality head was the one they had to kill, but knowing about the president's part could have scared them.

Huro asked why he killed the president even after knowing the municipality head would be killed by them. And he could have taken them, too, if he wanted to kill the president.

Nathan told Huro, "If we kill this municipality head, then someone else will come. Then what happens? The reason the system is corrupt is that the person who is running the system is corrupt. If the president is honest, the system will be honest; if not, he should make it honest. That is why he is president. But what is his use to people if he can't and won't make the system honest? To enjoy the power and evade responsibility?"

"Then you should have taken us too," said Kwin.

Nathan said, "What could have happened if I had gotten caught? What could have happened if they had gotten to know my face? What could have happened when that political party's mindless followers got to know what I did there? What would have happened if everyone knew you three were also part of this? I thought if I survive, I survive; if I die, I only die. But this country needs an honest leader, not a corrupted bloodsucker."

"Then how do you know the next president will be good?" asked Tes.

"I don't, I hope! And he/she should. That is why anyone becomes a president, right?" said Nathan.

"Or you could become one!" said Huro.

Nathan laughed, and everyone laughed.

The CCTV cameras couldn't capture a clear visual of the president on the bridge as he was inside the car when he died. Nathan's face is not clear in the footage because of the colored smoke from the fireworks.

Nathan went to the hospital. The doctor said they could take his mother home.

He took her home with his dad. The Three stayed at the cabin.

Sabrina called Nathan, but he didn't answer her again. Jiza and Ira left messages. Sabrina has sent hundreds of messages to Nathan, but he hasn't replied.

After taking his mom home, he talked to her. She said, "I know what happened that night you went out and how you lost your old car. I know you didn't sell it. Someone stole it from you and injured you. I know your struggles all along with everything."

Nathan was shocked that she might know what he did to the president, but she didn't know anything about it; his mom said, "I'm your mother! Meet that girl, she is a nice girl."

Nathan smiled.

" What is her name?" asked his mother.

"Sabrina," said Nathan.

No one in the world knew who killed the president of Wizbome and the Beruk municipality head.

The police are searching for the evidence, but the chaos that day, jammers set by Nathan and with The Three looking very casual in the crowd, convoy sounds, fireworks sounds, and colored smoke made it impossible to find clues. Hundreds of people ran toward the president's main car due to fireworks coming toward them that day, which made it more confusing.

The fireworks are made up of natural colors and not with dangerous chemicals. Those natural color bomb sounds were enhanced by speakers set back on the stage.

The people who ran towards the president's car were his party goons from all over the state. Regular People were not allowed to go near the president.

Nathan went to his college at Relsar and wrote a second letter asking them for more days off. He is friendly with all the professors and faculty, so his department faculty permitted him.

Keizha saw him in the parking lot and said nothing.

Nathan saw Keizha too.

Nathan said, "Hey! How are you?" to Keizha.

In amazement, Keizha said, "Great, thanks for asking."

Nathan left in his car to go to his cabin at Hervin Forest.

After he reached the cabin, The Three and Nathan watched all the footage of their assassination of the president and Beruk municipality head available online.

They read thousands of articles. No one wrote about what the assassins looked like.

But one recent article mentioned that of a security agent who left the president's car seconds after his death. And when the security guards checked inside the president's car, they found the president dead. And the driver didn't know what happened because of the partition in the car. The driver said he heard a struggling voice for a second. The post-mortem report said no injuries to the body anywhere, but the president's heart looked like it had taken a high-voltage shock for a few seconds.

Tes said, "We don't need to worry.. No one will believe the bums like us except you," pointing to Nathan, "would have killed a president and a head of the municipality. So we have to maintain our low confidence levels like before so that we will be invisible again."

"Great observation, but you are not a bum. You are a hero!" said Nathan.

"Thanks for believing in me," said Nathan to Huro.

Huro got emotional and said, "Anything for Wizbome and you, my brother," and hugged him.

Tes and Kwin felt happy.

Nathan said, "I need your help."

"Again? I'm just being nice," Huro said.

* * *

Nathan laughed and said, "I haven't met my girlfriend in months, and she called me a thousand times. I should surprise her when I meet her."

"So what should we do?" asked Kwin.

"Decoration to this cabin and other arrangements," said Nathan.

"I will bake her a cake," said Huro.

"We will do a lighting setup, too," said Kwin.

"Thank you guys, I can't say how much I appreciate this," said Nathan.

"It's ok, brother," said Huro.

"You guys don't have girlfriends?" Nathan asked The Three.

Huro said, "Yup, in Lester."

"Not yet," said Tes.

"She left me for a rich guy," said Kwin.

"Don't worry, you can find one in Beruk," said Nathan.

"I can't deal with an Ateestan woman. I'll be happy with a Krisen woman even if she leaves me," said Kwin sarcastically.

Everyone laughed.

After a few days, Huro saw a video on social media.

It is a video of Nathan's fight with Koshi. Huro showed that video to Nathan.

Huro asked Nathan whom he was fighting with.

Nathan answered that he didn't know. He said he just tried to save himself. Huro told him it was viral on social media. Nathan said he doesn't know about it as he does not use social media much other than posting his work and talking to people.

Nathan called Sabrina.

Sabrina answered the phone call.

She angrily asked, "What the hell is this, Nathan? How can you treat me like this?"

"Where are you?" asked Nathan.

"Why?" said Sabrina.

"Just tell me, where are you?" said Nathan.

"I'm at home," said Sabrina.

It's 6 PM.

Nathan went to Sabrina's home, and she was waiting outside.

Sabrina saw Nathan, and she was angry.

Nathan asked her to come with him.

She said, "No!"

Nathan begged her for an hour to come with him.

Sabrina was finally convinced and sat in his car.

He took her to the cabin.

The Three arranged a beautiful lighting setup and decoration with food and drinks there. Jiza and Ira arrived at the cabin.

Jiza said, "I'm not even going to ask, bro! I don't like you, but you are my brother, so I forgive you," to Nathan.

In a little shame, Nathan said, "Thank you, bro."

Nathan took Sabrina near the cabin, and she saw the beautiful lighting setup and the poster saying 'Happy Birthday, My love!'

Sabrina saw it, got emotional, and hugged Nathan.

He said, "In the Farush, I love you."

Sabrina was shocked. And trying to smile nervously.

Kwin, Tes, and Huro introduced themselves to Sabrina. Jiza and Ira met them, too.

Farush in Ateesta means being in a completely lonely state with the world forgetting them. Nothing in the world is there for them, and they are only living to enjoy life in a way that they do not need to commit suicide.

Nathan said it in the context of Ateesta. Sabrina thought Nathan knew something.

After saying it, Nathan behaved as usual, but Sabrina couldn't understand what was happening with him and why he said it. She is trying to behave normally.

Sabrina cut the cake and put a small piece in Nathan's mouth.

Nathan also put a cake piece in Sabrina's mouth. So did others.

After the cake-cutting, Sabrina and Nathan were walking in the woods.

Jiza and Ira sat with The Three at the cabin.

Jiza asked Huro, "Where are you from?"

Huro got tensed and said, "From Anukin!"

"Anukin? Where is it?" Jiza asked.

"In Inna state," said Huro.

"They speak English there?" asked Jiza again.

Tes said to Kwin, "Divert them from the topic. Otherwise, we are finished!"

Kwin asked Jiza, "Where are you from?"

He said, "From Beruk."

"In Beruk, where?" asked Kwin again.

"In Beruk, where? Beruk is the name of my village.. I'm from there," said Jiza.

"Yeah, we get that. But in Beruk, where you live?" Kwin asked.

"In my house," said Jiza.

"We live in our house, too, but we are here, right? So where do you live in Beruk exactly?" asked Kwin.

"Why do you need to know where I live exactly in Beruk?" asked Jiza.

Huro had a knife in his hand to cut the food. Holding it up, he said, "Just to know," looking into Jiza's eyes, and continued, "You asked for our address. We are asking for yours."

Jiza said, "No, I didn't ask for your exact address. Okay! Leave it."

"Haa.. Okay," said Huro.

***

"What do you do then?" Jiza asked again.

Kwin sighed and said, "What do you do?"

Jiza, in frustration, said, "Okay, leave it..!"

"Yeah, this is good! You want this drink?" asked Huro.

Jiza said, "Yes.." And Huro gave him a glass.

"Where are Nathan and Sabrina?" asked Ira.

"They went for a walk!" said Huro.

"We, too, will go for a walk," said Jiza, standing up.

Ira stopped him and said, "No, I don't want to. Let them do it!"

"Intelligent girl," said Tes.

Jiza was confused and continued to drink.

While walking in the woods, Nathan was on the right-hand side of Sabrina. The trees and bushes are very thick in the place they are walking. They sat under a big Banyan tree, and Nathan put his head on the lap of Sabrina and looked into Sabrina's eyes.

She is smiling and looking into Nathan's eyes. She kissed him on the lips. Nathan gently pushed Sabrina's head towards him again. He started kissing her passionately and made her lie on the floor.

He continued kissing her, and she was not under him completely. He removed his shirt, and Sabrina helped him get it off. She saw his body and felt shy.

She said, "What if someone comes?"

Nathan said, "No one will come! I took the precautions."

Sabrina saw the tent on the other side of the banyan tree, stood up, and went into it. Nathan followed her, and upon entering that big tent, she felt less shy as she was confident no one could see them now.

She asked Nathan, "Did you set this up?"

Nathan said "Yes!" in her ear.

Sabrina smiled. Nathan removed his belt, and Sabrina was getting excited.

Nathan came to Sabrina and removed her T-shirt. Looking at her body, he felt his mind blown.

They slept on the mattress and kissed each other, Nathan touching her body everywhere. He got naked and removed her clothes, too. They are having sex.

Sabrina looked at his face and laughed, seeing him struggle, and she was also experiencing a lot of pain.

Nathan looked at Sabrina and suddenly realized how beautiful she was compared to what he had thought before.

Nathan told her, "You don't know how beautiful you are!"

Upon hearing, Sabrina smiled in happiness, and her happiness had no boundaries. She pulled him towards her and gave him kisses.

Then she realized something and, in a tense, asked him, Is he wearing protection? Nathan laughed and said, "I want a son and a daughter, twins."

Sabrina felt happy and kissed him again. While he was doing it, they were talking.

Sabrina asked, "Will you yeessh!! marry me.. uhh.. then?"

To which Nathan replied, "Why would I have sex with you.. pfff.. without protection.. Don't move your hip!! Then? Yeahh.. I will hit you whenever I want from now on!! Not with hands.. Yuss.. With my hip..!"

Sabrina laughed loudly.

He continued, "I love you, and.. I want you to be with me.. until the end.. of times!"

Sabrina realized he loved her a lot.

She said, "For.. Aaah.. sure!"

He was finished after an hour and settled beside her. Sabrina turned to his side on the mattress, put her leg on the lower part of his body, wrapped her hand around his chest, and kissed his chest.

Sabrina said, "I'm going to my grandmother's village tomorrow."

Nathan asked her, "Oh.. When will you return?"

She said, "After 10 days!"

Nathan asked her, "Where is your grandmother's village? I'll drop you and return."

Sabrina said, "No, no, I'm going with my father."

Nathan said, "Oh, ok!"

They slept that night there. The trees and birds heard claps of hips all night.

The next morning, Sabrina woke up and got dressed. And went out.

Nathan was still sleeping. After half an hour, Nathan woke up and saw that Sabrina was not in the tent, so he went out. Sabrina was nowhere to be found.

He got a message from Sabrina saying she went early because her father had called her. And she will meet him after 10 days.

Nathan read it and walked to the cabin. Nathan asked The Three sitting around the fire whether they saw Sabrina. They said no! He felt strange.

As he was outside, he saw the news on TV. It's about the death of the CEO of The Wann Insurance Company in a private plane crash.

He didn't tell the details of the insurance company to The Three. The Insurance company CEO's plane crash happened in Trishone country, which is the money capital of the world.

Nathan went to his home.

Nathan got to know from his father that the new government announced a relief package to the victims of the illegal demolitions done by the previous government. And a new president is going to take the oath in a few days and has promised to end all types of corruption in government.

He also learned that an unknown signal disruption that came from space made a small change to the Wann Insurance Company CEO's private plane's software binary code bit, from 0 to 1. It resulted in the crash of the plane. Three people who are executives of the company died in the crash along with the pilot.

He felt bad as others, too, died in the accident, along with the CEO, whom he planned to beat but not to kill, to teach him a lesson.

***

Nathan went to his mother.

She is getting well, he told her, "Happy to see you again, maa.. I asked Sabrina to come here with me, but she said she would come here after 10 days. She is going to her grandma's house with her father."

Nathan then returned to the Cabin.

Tes said "Hey Nathan, come here!"

Nathan went near him.

Tes asked, "Can you take us to God Yinta temple? I heard it is beautiful."

Nathan said, "Sure!"

Later that day, Nathan took The Three to the God Yinta temple. They loved it.

Huro said he wants to learn more about God Yinta and his teachings.

He got interested in Ateestan theology of how God is in a person's mind and gives that person pure, great, positive, and progressive thoughts even when they don't appeal to that person emotionally but are good for that person based on rational sanity.

And he liked the way Ateestan theology explained how the bad thoughts come from the Satanic irrationality of the mind, even though they appear very good and attractive for that minute inside, but you know consciously, they are not good for you.

Nathan gave Huro a Wuquin from the Wuquin book stacks placed there for the visitors of the God Yinta temple.

Nathan told The Three to take his car and go to the cabin.

Huro asked, "Why?"

Nathan replied that he would meet them at night at the cabin.

He walked into the forest of the Aarvin mountains. He sat under a banyan tree and closed his eyes. He is thinking about the intuition he was getting that something or someone from far away in the universe is calling him.

He is thinking, Is it true or not, or Is he getting an illness or a psychological change in the mind or a chemical change in the brain, or what is happening to him?

The forest is thick. There are just trees around him with birds making sounds, and the wind is heavy.

He was thinking very hard while meditating to get clarity.

He realized nothing was wrong with him.

Huro followed Nathan secretly. And saw a bright light coming out of the forehead while Nathan was thinking, Huro was shocked. And continued to see Nathan.

The light vanished, and Huro was convinced Nathan was not a normal human being.

Nathan heard a voice in his head saying to him, "The war at Farush is coming. Prepare your forces. Otherwise, the universe that you are in will fall. At Farush, ask for the help of God Yinta. He will give his forces to you."

Nathan suddenly opened his eyes and saw a sun ray touching the middle part of his forehead. Nathan saw an odd-shaped black leaf of another banyan tree which is in front of him. Only one leaf is there, like that.

He stood up and started walking peacefully in the forest. He is not scared of anything there. He is just walking deep inside the forest. The animals of the forest are secretly looking at Nathan.

He is talking to himself, but no human is near him to hear what he is saying to himself, "How? How can I defeat him without any power or army forces with me? It's impossible. At Farush, I will perish!"

He heard a bell sound from the temple. And continued, "It's a God Yinta temple. I will ask him here. And also before going to Farush."

Nathan didn't know,

Huro heard it and went back to Tes and Kwin.

Huro said nothing about what he saw and heard but told them, "Whatever Nathan says, we do it!"

Tes asked Huro, "Wow, what happened to you?"

Huro said, "I'm telling you two now! Whatever Nathan asks us, we do it."

Jokingly, Kwin said, "Ha ha, why? Is he God or a Prophet? You got to know it?"

Huro replied angrily, "Hey, stop joking. Do you believe me? Do you both trust me?"

They said yes. "Then please do as I say," said Huro.

"Ok, ok, we will do what he says," said Kwin and Tes, agreeing to Huro.

In the forest, Nathan was walking and told himself, "I might live or die, but I will fight till I die at Farush. He should perish to protect the universe."

He walked into the temple and looked at God Yinta inside the temple. Then came out and sat on a bench. Nathan saw Huro standing far from him. And The Three are looking at Nathan. Nathan signaled them to come.

The Three came to him, and Nathan asked Huro, "I told you to take the car and go to the cabin, right?"

Huro replied, "Yeah, but we liked it here, so we thought of spending some time here." Nathan laughed and said, "Cool!"

They are returning to the cabin, and on the road, Nathan saw his old car with people who attacked him in it.

Nathan was in the front passenger seat, and Huro was driving the car.

Nathan asked The Three, "I want to beat the hell out of those guys. Can you do it with me?"

Kwin said, "Yeah, who are they?"

Nathan said nothing.

* * *

Nathan told Huro to turn the car and follow the old car he showed.

They did, and his old stolen car was stopped at a gas station. Nathan took the gun out and hid it under his shirt.

Tes, Kwin, and Huro had knives in their hands.

The stolen car windows were open.

Nathan stopped The Three and asked them to come back.

They did and asked him why. He said, Let's follow them. After a mile, there are no buildings and CCTV cameras.

They got into the car and waited for the stolen car to move again. The stolen car, after filling the tank with petrol, started moving on the highway, and they followed the old stolen car for a mile, maintaining a distance from it without getting noticed by the thugs in it.

Nathan was driving the car, and on the highway, there were only a few vehicles at the moment. Nathan suddenly accelerated his car, approached the old stolen car, and hit it from the back. The stolen car went straight into a tree.

And Nathan did not stop his car and fled the spot. The Three thought the people in the stolen car must've been seriously injured or could've died too, but they didn't check.

Nathan said, "Justice is important even if it seems extreme sometimes!"

They went to the cabin and parked the car a little more inside the forest than usual.

Nathan said he would be back and walked into the forest.

Sabrina is in a dark place and looking at the sun. She lifted her hands and made a 60-degree and an opposite 60-degree triangle sign without the base with her hands, and changed the sign into an inverted triangle shape.

Then, on Earth, where Nathan was walking, a Satanic creature called 'Ayoon' appeared in front of him. It was named 'Hureraa' in Hell.

Ayoon is an ugly-looking, blood-sucking creature. Nathan couldn't believe what he was seeing. He blinked multiple times to check if what he was seeing was reality or imagination.

* * *

Ayoon came fiercely running towards Nathan. It has six legs and two heads with a tail. It is pitch black in color with vertical red lines on its body. It has a height of 20 feet and a length of 24 feet with a breadth of 16 feet.

It came running towards Nathan. Ayoon attacked Nathan with its claws. Nathan couldn't escape and just leaned back.

The claws caused injury to his chest. He is bleeding. He asked God Yinta for help inside. He fell down after the injury and saw a wooden stick. That wooden stick looked so clean and strong that it felt like someone had placed it there.

The creature went up flying and waited on top of a tree. For Nathan to get up again.

It wants to attack him again and kill him. But the creature was suspicious that if it approached Nathan again immediately now, Nathan might've hid something underneath him, and it suspected that Nathan might use it to kill the creature.

Nathan lay there for a few minutes to recover. And suddenly, he got up and took that wooden stick. Ayoon saw it and came to Nathan, flying very fast.

Nathan is holding the stick, and upon Ayoon reaching him, he hit the head of the creature so hard that it fell on the ground. In pain, Ayoon looked at Nathan.

It made a terrible screeching sound in pain that any human being could get scared after hearing it.

It is looking at Nathan angrily as it spreads its wings on the ground.

Nathan closed his eyes. Ayoon got confused after seeing Nathan closing his eyes.

Nathan opened his eyes and looked at the sky. He smiled at the sky and looked at Ayoon, fiercely lifting his wooden stick, but suddenly lowered the stick and started walking away from Ayoon.

Ayoon is a slave to courage and bravery. It can be tamed by someone who overpowers it and has the power to kill it. Satan tamed Ayoon at the beginning of the times of all known and unknown universes.

Then Ayoon came flying towards Nathan. Nathan looked back at it, waiting for it to come near him. But he suddenly started running towards it, which startled Ayoon a bit and made Ayoon nervous. At the right moment, Nathan hit its leg with the stick so hard that Ayoon fell to the ground in pain. He placed the stick on its neck, and Ayoon looked at Nathan in pain. Nathan then removed the stick from its neck and petted it. He then, with his right-hand fist, slowly thumped at the place of Ayoon's heart, and he petted it on the right side of its head.

He then took the stick into his right hand from his left and sat on Ayoon. It stood up on its legs with Nathan sitting on it and made a screeching sound.

It is 3 in the morning.

And Ayoon started flying with Nathan sitting on it. Tes, Kwin, and Huro saw what happened from far away.

Kwin said, "This is why you said we have to do what he says and not question him, right?"

Huro replied, "Yes!"

"Fair enough," said Tes.

"Fair enough? He is literally a Prophet," said Huro.

Kwin and Tes stayed silent, and after a few seconds,

Tes said, "We should not joke about him!"

Kwin said, "It's a good idea!"

Huro laughed.

Nathan sat on Ayoon, who is flying high now. And suddenly, Ayoon started shaking. They crossed a transparent layer. The layer they crossed is called the 'Brunuck Line of the Master Universe.' Nathan realized Earth was not under him now, and he saw three places afloat in front of him in the endless universe.

One is Hell, the other one is Heaven, and the other one is Farush.

As he looked up and down at them. He felt like he was seeing many dimensions at a time, with Heaven and Hell in front of him.

When he looked at Farush, it made him think of positive, negative, and neutral, as well as everything in between and outside.

He knew nothing of those places he was seeing underneath him and up. He only recognized Heaven, Hell, and Farush with his intuition and appearance of them in his meditation at God Yinta Temple on Earth.

He knew he was not in space, which comes after leaving Earth in a rocket or spaceship. And he did not see any man-made satellites roaming around Earth.

He knew from what he felt that he was in an entirely different dimension. The dimension that comes after Earth and the solar system Earth is in.

He is not struggling to breathe because he is not breathing at all, and he is all right and feeling normal.

Ayoon screeched and landed in a place called 'Nothing' in front of Hell.

He can see Heaven far away from Hell in front of him.

And he can see Farush too from 'Nothing' place.

The three-dimensional world of Earth and the sub-universe the Earth is in is governed by the laws that are made here in this dimension of the Master Universe.

The universe that he is in is the Master Universe, and the universe Earth was in is its dependent universe called the sub-universe.

Nathan got down from Ayoon, and there was nothing in the 'Nothing' place. Only the surface of the 'Nothing' was shining by itself without any light projecting on it.

He saw no end and no beginning of the 'Nothing' place. Nathan understood that along with three dimensions, there is 4th dimension, too, and the fourth dimension is time, and here at the 'Nothing' place in the Master Universe, time is nothing.

Jiza suddenly woke up from sleep at night in his home. He drank some water and looked at his phone.

He got a notification from a news app about a mysterious creature flying above Beruk, and two human legs were seen on the creature.

The same news is on TV too about a mysterious creature flying above Beruk, and two legs of a person are seen on it from Earth. The creature and the person on it suddenly disappeared in mid-air.

The face of the man is behind the creature's body, and the man's two legs are only visible in videos.

There are all kinds of memes and jokes about it on social media. The Three knew who it was, but they had never spoken up about that incident anywhere.

Nathan called Ayoon "Ayoo" with affection at the 'Nothing' place.

It screeched. And Nathan laughed.

At the 'Nothing' place, Nathan remembered the words of God Yinta in Wuquin: ' What we don't know, we don't know, and when we know, we know. Make sure what we know is the truth, and not any other thing.'

Nathan knew something now.

Nathan saw someone coming towards the side of the 'Nothing' place.

Nathan saw a big Satanic chariot with fire and Koshi sitting in it, and two Satanic bulls were burning. The chariot came near Nathan.

Koshi's chariot landed on 'Nothing', and Nathan had the stick in his hand.

He tightened the grip on the stick. Koshi saw it and laughed.

Koshi said, "No, you cannot fight here. Only in the grounds of Farush. There,"

He pointed to the side of Farush.

"What happens if we fight?" asked Nathan.

"Nothing, nobody wins," said Koshi and continued, "You are the first one I will kill at the Farush before my father comes to Farush."

Nathan said nothing.

Koshi left in his chariot. Nathan looked at Ayoo. It is angry and looking at Koshi's chariot. Nathan petted it. Ayoo calmed down.

He heard a voice in his head saying, "Go to your mother and talk to her one last time. Go to your father and talk to him one last time."

***

He felt strange about the voice because it felt like God Yinta was talking to him.

He sat on the Ayoo and signaled it to fly. Ayoo stood up and took off.

It was flying very fast and suddenly started shaking. He then saw Beruk under him. He was still on Ayoo.

Both of them are transparent. Nobody can see them.

When the time of holy war is fixed by Farush, then it takes the responsibility of maintaining the secrecy of universes into its hands, so as not to violate the laws of entropy.

So Farush made Nathan and Ayoo's energy transparent on Earth. It will be like that till Nathan goes back to his normal life, it is not to create an energy imbalance footprint in the Earth - Subuniverse.

Ayoo landed in the Hervin forest near the cabin. Nathan left the stick there.

The Three are outside the cabin around the fire. But they didn't see Nathan or Ayoo, as they were transparent in the sky.

Nathan told Ayoo to stay in the forest, started walking towards the cabin, and came into the normal state where he was visible to everyone.

A deer saw the transformation of Nathan in the forest. Ayoo was not visible to anyone except Nathan.

When Nathan reached the cabin, The Three were sleeping, and Nathan woke up Huro. Huro was shocked after looking at Nathan.

Nathan told him to come with him. Huro said, "Sure,"

He was driving Nathan's car on the Beruk highway. Nathan sat in the front seat of the car, and he was thinking about something. It is 12 in the morning.

What he was thinking was what he had done before he went to the Master Universe for the first time; he was thinking about that time, when he went to Kehraan State University.

Actually, he never attended Kehraan University's internship because he had never intended to.

He just applied as a joke to that university, but he got the internship opportunity, and he didn't want to disrespect the university and professors who gave him the invitation to join the research team, so he met them.

He just wanted to see the people who believed in his capabilities, and he also knew that on the Tushak city outskirts, there are dark mountains called the Sviven Mountains, where humans are prohibited from climbing because of the many mysterious deaths and bad incidents occurring in the mountains.

So, the government authorities closed the mountains for climbing, trekking, and other activities.

No one goes near them in Tushak city because the Krisens believe a demon has been residing there since the beginning of time and will not leave anyone alive who steps into its territory.

Ateestans in Tushak city believe something is happening there, but not certainly because of a demon. But because of Krisens's belief, the government closed the mountains for all activities. Tushak city has a majority population of Krisens.

The day Nathan visited Kehraan State University and spoke to professors, he then secretly went to the Sviven mountain range, and he climbed the Tunique mountain, which is considered to be the residence of the demon Ireena, the Vikroth servant of Satan, according to the Krise religion.

The day Nathan went to the Sviven Mountains was cloudy, and it started raining slowly. He stopped the vehicle at the start of the Sviven mountain range and trekked to the Tunique mountain.

He trekked on 16 mountains of the Sviven mountain range through day and night to reach Tunique mountain.

On Tunique Mountain, in the middle, on top of the mountain, he saw a weird dark Trapzoid rounded shape, which was solid. It is in the air in a fixed position.

It started raining heavily after he saw it, and he suddenly started getting blood from his nose after seeing that mysterious solid material.

Nathan understood what was happening.

Ireena's energy was very strong, and she was playing with him. He closed his eyes, and the time was 3 AM. Nathan was lifted into the air and thrown to the ground.

After getting hit to the ground,

Nathan said, looking at the sky, "In the darkest days, you are in my mind, and in the brightest days, you are in my mind, guiding me and my heart in sync with you."

He opened his eyes, and he was standing on the ground.

He walked up to the dark-solid object and spat on it.

He heard loud sounds of wind in his ears, and something was trying to stop him, but it couldn't touch him.

The wind has become very strong now, and it is raining heavily. The lightning is horrible in loud thunderstorms.

He kicked the solid object with his right leg, and it moved.

He kicked it again.

It moved some more, and he started pushing it towards the edge of the cliff.

And he finally pushed it from the edge.

Finally, the demon who was trying to stop Nathan went down the cliff with the dark object, and the dark object smashed into rocks and broke into pieces.

He destroyed an object that allowed a demon to stay on Earth by doing energy transacting from Hell. That dark object is called Nishiki.

Nathan broke Nishiki, which is a dark, solid object made of unknown material.

Upon being broken into pieces, those pieces burned and disappeared. Along with Nishiki, Ireena went back to Hell, crying loudly and angrily.

Nathan saw the Sviven mountains in his dreams, months back! When he got pimples.

Nathan went home, and The Three - Huro, Kwin, and Tes met Nathan for the first time that night in front of his home after he destroyed the Nishiki that day.

After returning from the Master Universe on Ayoo for the first time, Nathan returned to his home with Huro. Nathan told his parents about a new change in his life.

Nathan's mom and dad felt happy after seeing Nathan. They thought he was returning from Kehraan State University in Tushak city.

Nathan told his mom that he rejected the internship at Kehraan State University and that he was going to Trishone Country because he had gotten a job there.

Nathan didn't get a job in Trishone country or anywhere. Nathan lied to his parents.

And this might be the last time they ever see him.

Nathan's parents felt sad as he had to leave home and go to Trishone country. Nathan told his parents he would return in a year.

His mom cried. Nathan tried to console her. His dad gave him money, and Nathan gave his dad a hug.

Nathan called Jiza. Jiza came to his home. He said the same to Jiza.

Jiza felt happy, and while leaving, Jiza told Nathan, "I will always support you, bro, don't you forget it. No matter where you are, even in your war!"

Nathan was surprised after hearing it, and Jiza left.

Huro was shocked after hearing it. But he didn't question Nathan or Jiza about it.

Satan was angry. Koshi came to Satan while Satan sat on Hell's throne.

Satan said, "Give him the illness which his physical body cannot recover from so that he cannot reach Farush for the war."

Koshi said, "But father.."

"Enough!" said Satan.

Koshi left.

Nathan came out of his house and was in the car, now returning to the cabin.

He suddenly vomited, and blood came from his eyes.

Huro got confused, and in the tension, he took him to the hospital.

In the hospital, after running tests, they learned that Nathan has a condition that was unknown to him till now. It is making his body produce too many red blood cells, and the blood is becoming dominated by red blood cells and very thick.

Doctors said they have to take 1 liter of his blood out, remove excess red blood cells every two weeks, and send the blood without red blood cells into his body again to balance the red blood cells, white blood cells, and other things in the blood and body.

There is no cure for it.

The doctors gave him 1 year maximum to live.

Huro cried after listening to the doctor say it to Nathan.

"I'm sorry!" said the doctor and left.

In a few hours, Nathan's life turned upside down.

He decided not to tell his parents about this and still proceeded with what he told them.

They returned to the cabin. Nathan told Huro to tell his parents that he died in an accident in Trishone country, and his body was not found.

Huro cried while telling Tes and Kwin about it.

Nathan searched for the Ayoo in the forest, but it was nowhere to be found.

Sabrina called him. He told her to come to the cabin. She did, and outside of the cabin, around the fire, he told her about his illness. Sabrina started crying and went unconscious.

She woke up after Nathan rubbed her palms and feet.

She was crying.

Nathan consoled her, and she hugged him and sat there crying for hours.

Huro, Tes, and Kwin are sad, with tears in their eyes, seeing Sabrina and Nathan.

Nathan asked Sabrina, "Baby, do you remember the cab and its driver? We went to buy petrol together?"

Sabrina stopped crying a little and said, "Haa."

"I killed him!" said Nathan to Sabrina.

The Three got shocked, and Sabrina too. She stopped crying.

Nathan continued, "He came to my home, following me."

Sabrina and The Three looked at Nathan, and he continued, "I took him to Ireena!"

Nathan remembered what he did when he went into the Sviven mountains, even though he was emotionally unstable and facing the inevitable.

The cab driver followed Nathan for many days like a spy after he dropped Nathan and Sabrina at their car the day they booked his cab to get petrol.

Nathan knew that the cab driver was following him regularly, but Nathan did nothing that would raise suspicion in the cab driver.

On the day Nathan went to Kehraan State University, the cab driver followed Nathan all the way, from Nathan's garage to Kehraan State University in Tushak and to the Sviven Mountain range.

The cab driver thought Sabrina was waiting for Nathan in the Sviven Mountains, and he would kill Nathan and take over Sabrina.

Nathan actually had no plans to attend that internship. He just wants to meet the people at Kehraan State University.

Nathan had a gun in his car at the time he visited Kehraan State University, too.

After visiting Kehraan State University, Nathan realized the cab driver was still following him, and Nathan wanted to isolate him to kill him. Nathan intentionally went into the Dark Sviven Mountains and onto the popular haunted Tunique Mountain.

Nathan had a gun with him, and the cab driver followed him into the Sviven mountains.

Nathan saw the same 'cross lines within a circle' symbol tattoo on the left hand of the cab driver when Sabrina and Nathan were in his cab, and it is the same symbol the gang who attacked Nathan has on their hands.

Nathan understood the cab driver was from the same gang that attacked him and stole his car.

And they are also committing other violent crimes of murder and rape.

Nathan realized the cab driver's gang who attacked him earlier might have known that he had filed a case against them in the police station and how Nathan, The Three with Nathan's new car hit his old stolen car with thugs who attacked him in it and that could have resulted in serious injuries or death of those thugs but Nathan and The Three didn't stop and checked.

As revenge for what Nathan did, the cab driver wanted to kill Nathan and take Sabrina because he was also in the stolen car that day when Nathan hit it. The two thug friends of the cab driver died in the incident, and others were seriously injured.

The cab driver knew who Nathan was and what he did because he was also part of the gang that attacked Nathan. But they covered their face with masks on the day they attacked Nathan, but Nathan saw the tattoo on their hands.

No matter how many times the cab driver tried to follow Sabrina, he lost her and never figured out where she went after some time when he started following her.

The cab driver orchestrated the attack on Nathan, thinking Sabrina was with Nathan in the car. But she was not with Nathan that night when Nathan was returning to his home after eating outside. So they beat Nathan and took his car.

The cab driver, when he came to pick up Sabrina and Nathan in the middle of the highway, behaved normally. Nathan wantedly booked the cab through Sabrina's account to get petrol.

Nathan, by planning, took the cab driver to Tunique Mountain, knowing that the cab driver was following him. On the Tunique mountain, Nathan hid suddenly, confusing the cab driver, and Nathan shot him with his gun.

When the cab driver fell to the ground, Nathan came near to him, and the cab driver begged him to forgive, but Nathan shot him in the head, killing the cab driver instantly.

Then he pushed his body down the cliff of the mountain. When his head hit a rock, it was broken into many pieces, and his body was smashed between rocks.

Nathan destroyed Nishiki after this. Nathan gave the cab driver as a human sacrifice to Ireena to make her calm and allowing Ireena to take the cab driver's soul as a slave. So that Ireena will not return to Earth ever again and will not trouble anyone who comes into the Sviven Mountain range.

Back at the cabin, Sabrina hid her facial expressions and asked Nathan, "What do you mean by saying you killed the cab driver ?"

Nathan said, "Haha.. I'm joking!"

Sabrina punched him playfully and cried by putting her face on his chest.

The Three are in tears. After that, Nathan visited the hospital regularly and got treatment and blood checkups.

He was getting blood in his cough and in his vomits, which became normal to him. Tes, Kwin, and Huro never complained about anything.

Huro is always sad and dull seeing his boss suffering.

As days turned into months, Nathan occasionally talked to his parents on the phone.

Nathan remembered his garage, his books on rockets, and the rocket engine he was working on. He cried.

Sabrina slowly decreased the frequency of visiting Nathan. She started ignoring Nathan's calls.

She came to the cabin one day, and Nathan felt happy seeing her.

She asked Nathan in a little harsh tone, "How are you?"

He replied, "Doing good."

She gave a fake smile and continued, "I'm sorry, I cannot come here again!"

Upon hearing this, Nathan was shocked.

She continued, "My dad is going to his hometown, and I'm going with him. So I can't come here from now on."

Nathan said, "You can come here and visit me occasionally then, or I will come and meet you."

Sabrina replied harshly, "Sorry, I'm afraid that is not possible. My dad doesn't like all that, and I'm very sorry. This is the end."

Nathan asked her, "Are you breaking up with me?"

She said, "Yes."

Nathan was devastated and full of sadness.

Sabrina said, "I'm sorry, but I have to go. I have some urgent work!"

And she left.

Nathan sat there. It is at 3 PM. He heard the screeching of Ayoo from the forest.

Huro was carrying the wood to cook food. Nathan started walking towards the forest, and Huro saw him. Huro asked Nathan where he was going.

Nathan told Tes and, Kwin, Huro to follow him.

Nathan saw Ayoo waiting for him in the forest. He asked Ayoo to show herself to The Three, too. It did. The Three were amazed and scared after seeing Ayoo closely. Nathan got on the Ayoo and asked The Three to come with him. They got on the Ayoo and sat on it.

Ayoo screeched fiercely and started flying, and in a few seconds, they were in the sky but in transparent energy status enabled by Farush. They observed the shaking of Ayoo, and in seconds, they were in the Master-Independent Universe.

The Three saw Heaven, Hell, and Farush, along with other universes above and below them. Ayoo landed on 'Nothing' place. And they got down from Ayoo.

# 3

Nathan heard a voice in his mind: "Your mortal life is mine from this moment."

He asked Huro, Tes, and Kwin to stay at the 'Nothing' place and told them, "You three are servants of God Yinta now. Please assist me in the future when I'm fighting in the war," to which they agreed by bowing to Nathan.

Nathan got on Ayoo and then started flying towards Farush.

He is going to Farush, which is a very dry and bright place.

When he went there, he felt different. Ayoo landed on Farush. And dust of dry, hard regolith is touching him with a glow. He saw a big waterfall on the right side of Farush, and He saw a massive fire on the other side burning like the sun.

He couldn't even estimate the size of the sacred fire and sacred waterfall. They are that big.

He touched the Farush ground with his hands and felt the power of Farush and the law of balanced entropy of positive and negative forces.

Nathan saw a big fire chariot burning in an uneven way, coming towards him from far away, and for some reason, he thought it was Koshi.

When the fire chariot came near to him and landed on Farush, he saw Sabrina on it.

* * *

Nathan was shocked.

Her clothes are strange and scary. She is pregnant with full months of Master Universe.

Sabrina said, "I know you will come here. Otherwise, you'd be dead by now in your sub-dependent universe. Your God Yinta made you come here, but you will lose."

Nathan said nothing.

Sabrina continued, "At Farush, God Yinta will perish."

Nathan said, "How are you?"

Sabrina stopped talking and looked into Nathan's eyes and her stomach.

Sabrina said, "Your son is making me uncomfortable with his powerful kicks."

Nathan tried to come near Sabrina, but she showed her hand as a warning not to come any further.

He stopped. And looked at his son. His son kicked in her stomach, and Sabrina felt it.

She said, "You might come here, but you will never win. My father will kill you!"

Nathan asked her, "Who is your father?"

Sabrina gave an evil laugh and said, "The Lord of all the known and unknown universes, Satan. I'm his only daughter, and Koshi is my brother."

"The one who attacked me in my universe and met me once at 'Nothing'?" asked Nathan.

"Yes, he is my brother!" said Sabrina and continued, "You don't know anything about my brother. You will die the moment he starts to fight against you."

* * *

Nathan replied, "I already did, and that is why I came here."

Sabrina, in anger, got into the chariot and left. But in the chariot, she was sad.

She went to Hell, and she is in her place in Hell. But she didn't have any pregnancy stomach in Hell.

Satan came to her and asked her, "What happened to God Yinta and his prime disciple?"

Sabrina said in a shaking voice, "Prime Ateestan visited Farush."

Satan said "hmm" in anger.

And Sabrina, in fear, continued, "God Yinta gave his word to Prime Ateestan that he will send his forces to fight by his side."

"I will make him and his forces run away from Farush, never to return," said Satan. And he sat on his throne.

On Earth, Police and investigation teams reached Nathan's house.

They searched the whole house and garage. Nathan's mom and dad were given notice papers of shoot-at-sight orders on Nathan. They are in tears and scared.

The investigation teams reached Nathan's cabin in the forest, too. They searched everything and found nothing except medical reports of Nathan. They took them to the hospital. The doctor said that the patient was not coming for a few weeks, and he thought the patient was dead, according to his reports.

The police searched for Nathan for 2 months and found he never went to Trishone country as he told his family. And stayed at the cabin only. He mostly died, and his friends could have buried him, or he might have gone to an isolated place to die in peace there. They searched for Sabrina and The Three but found no information about them.

The house that Sabrina stayed in, Beruk village, did not have anyone living inside of it for many years after a whole family got murdered in that house.

Nathan never went inside Sabrina's house.

***

After a while, the new government of Wizbome removed all the cases against Nathan and revoked the shoot-at-sight orders and recognized him as a hero. They built a memorial for him.

Every day, thousands of people visit his memorial and thank him for getting rid of the dictatorship of democracy that the country was in before.

They found Nathan's involvement in the assassination of the corrupt president through drone footage of a civilian uploaded to the internet.

They didn't see Nathan's face in the video, but they recognized that an extra security person was there in the security team than the allocated personnel to the president that day, and followed each security agent individually through available footage.

Security agents recognized themselves in the footage and attended the investigation, except one, and that is how they found out about Nathan when he left the president's car after killing him.

Nathan's mom and dad got to know about the news, and they held his funeral without his body, according to Ateestan practices.

Jiza and Ira cried at Nathan's funeral.

Keizha and Prina attended the funeral with other college students. Keizha felt bad for being mean to him. They looked around but didn't find Sabrina.

Nathan at Farush was thinking about Sabrina and his son.

Sabrina delivered the baby in Hell. Satan didn't see the baby. Satan knew about the baby, but he thought of using the baby in war as a tool if possible.

The baby's skin is glowing and has the most divine and devilish look on its face at the same time.

Nathan landed at 'Nothing' place where The Three were waiting for Nathan. And they realized they were not breathing but were alive.

At first, they got scared and then excited.

***

Nathan told Huro he had to come with him to a sacred forest called Yira, a place under Heaven.

The Sacred Yira forest is where the first mortal male, Neehaan, and the first mortal female, Seeha, in all of the known universes took their first breath.

Nathan told Tes and Kwin to go to Farush. They asked how they could go there.

Nathan said Ayoo's friends would come to 'Nothing' place, and they could go with them. They agreed.

They waited for Ayoo's friends. They came. Ayoo's friends are three beautiful White, Red, and Green Sacred Eagles. They came to the 'Nothing' place and landed there.

On the Red and Green Eagles, Tes and Kwin sat and started to go to Farush.

Huro sat on the White Eagle, and Nathan sat on Ayoo.

Huro and Nathan started flying to the Yira sacred forest.

While going to the Yira sacred forest, they crossed Hell. The doors of Hell are closed, and it is Dark and Red from the outside, with burning volcanoes around it.

And they went near to Heaven. From the outside, Heaven is a beautiful white complex with golden poles and designs on it.

The doors were open when they saw it, and inside, they saw a man in the middle of the hall walking. He had long hair, and he was skinny and tall.

His clothes are old, and he has a divine body language. He turned to the entrance side and smiled, but Nathan and Huro couldn't see his face. By the time he turned his head, they crossed Heaven.

They crossed Heaven. The white eagle and Ayoo are going very fast. They entered a time loop under Heaven. They traveled through the time loop and came out on the other side of the loop.

They couldn't see Heaven or anything after coming out of the time loop.

They entered the Yira Sacred Forest, which had unusually big trees and animals. They were like on Earth, but their sizes are at least 10000 times bigger than that of Earth.

Nathan and Huro landed at Sacred Yira forest. Ayoo screeched very loudly after landing.

Nathan saw a massive Roush tree in front of him. The forest is thick there.

There was a snake under the tree, and it wrapped itself around the tree. And Nathan was scared to go near the tree.

Huro is standing behind Nathan. Nathan started walking towards the Roush tree by gathering his courage.

The snake started moving and going into the forest. By the time Nathan went near the tree, the snake had gone into the forest and turned back and looked at Nathan.

He saw the snake but didn't stop, still with the fear in him as he approached the tree. The tree by itself extended one of its branches with Sacred Roush fruits.

Nathan saw the miracle and felt wonderful and happy. The branch came down and stayed there. Nathan took one Roush fruit. And took a bite of Roush fruit.

He felt strange. He went unconscious. When Nathan came out of dizziness, he walked like he was drugged for a few minutes there.

Huro saw it, but he didn't come near Nathan. He was scared seeing the snake. Then the snake came near Nathan and got Nathan on it.

Snake started going into the forest, taking Nathan with it. Huro stood there in fear and did not follow Nathan.

Nathan realized he was on a snake while it was moving very fast in the Yira sacred forest.

He saw the scary forest elephants and lions while on that snake. The snake traveled through the thick forest, and it swam in the river flowing through the forest with Nathan on it.

The water was crystal clear and glowing in a golden color.

When Nathan looked into the sky, he saw nothing. It is pure white and has no sun in the sky.

The snake entered a big, thick bush, and he saw the snake's nest inside a cave. It entered the cave and went inside its nest.

Inside the nest, there is a sacred stone in the middle. The stone is cylindrical with curved ends on top and bottom. He observed five dots on the stone—one in the middle and four on four sides.

He went near the stone. It was very big, and the snake was looking at him. He touched the stone. The dots started glowing. Light came out of those dots, and from the middle dot, a drop of the Seehaal came out in white, rounded, shielded light and touched Nathan's forehead.

Seehaal is what Mother Adis gave to God Yinta when God Yinta told Mother Adis about the Great War of Nazreck on Earth. It is the antidote to Beeliaal's Empty dark liquid given to Satan to take over Earth and the Master Universe through the power of emptiness and depression.

The Seehaal light potion drop went inside his head. He fell on his knees, shaking, and bright sacred light came out from his eyes in front of the stone, and the snake hissed very loudly. When the light blinded the sacred snake for a few seconds, the nest was filled with the brightest white light from Nathan's eyes.

Nathan stopped shaking. The light stopped coming out of his eyes. He slowly got up. The snake revealed its two heads on the left and right sides. Nathan's clothes were changed.

He got a dark cape and into his sacred white clothes. A Trident came out from inside the stone with sacred red light.

Nathan was given the Trident by the sacred stone.

The Trident was glowing with fire when it reached him. He took it. The snake came in front of him, and its size increased.

In the nest, Nathan was growing in height and size. He grew to 18 ft in height.

In Hell, Sabrina took her real form. She has also grown in height to 14 feet.

He walked out of the nest with glowing eyes and a trident. The wind in the forest is bending the great, massive, sacred trees.

The dust blinded the pure sky. He stood in front of the cave.

It started raining heavily with massive thunderstorms. The snake came out, and it covered Nathan's head with its skull. Nathan looked at the sky, and the rain stopped.

Slowly, the sacred snake came in front of him. Nathan sat on. It started moving and took him back to the sacred Roush tree.

Huro saw Nathan. He felt like he was seeing God. He bowed to Nathan, placed his hand on his heart, and said the Krisen prayer used to praise God Regor.

Huro prayed, "In the day and the night or both at a time or when it is outside of day and night, in life and death or not both or outside of life and death, in everything and nothing or not both. Krisaan Regor, I'm you. I worship you. I completely submit myself to you. Protect me and my world."

Nathan got down from the snake. Ayoo saw Nathan's glowing eyes and new form.

It screeched loudly in pride, and it elevated itself from the ground and looked at Nathan. Ayoo screeched again.

Ayoo transformed into a beautiful creature from its ugly-looking form.

The snake decreased its size and turned into light, went into the trident, and increased the trident's power.

Nathan walked up to Huro and looked at him. Huro was trying to talk, but he was stuttering.

"My dear friend, I know!" said Nathan.

Then Nathan sat on Ayoo. He looked at the sacred Roush tree, and his glow in the eyes calmed down.

He started flying back to Farush on Ayoo. But Satan knew if Nathan made it to Farush, the war would come.

So to buy more time. When Nathan was on Ayoo traveling in the sacred time loop to come back to Farush, he sent Koshi to attack Nathan.

Ayoo and Nathan are in the sacred time loop and traveling at higher speeds to return to Farush.

Koshi came in front of them in the time loop and started attacking

Nathan.

Koshi was on his Satanic chariot and attacked with an Inertal arrow on Nathan.

In all the chaos, Ayoo was screeching loudly.

Ayoo activated its outer energy shell. It stopped the arrow of Koshi.

Koshi then attacked Ayoo with another arrow called Sviten.

Sviten was given to Koshi by Satan.

It is said to make any sacred place Satanic by destroying the sacredness of the place.

One of the most powerful weapons. It hit Nathan's trident.

When Nathan swung his trident to stop the Sviten arrow.

The energy released was so high that the sacred time loop collapsed instantly, and both Koshi with his chariot and Nathan with Ayoo fell in a place called Saden, the place where the pisaach demon villages of Satan are located.

In Saden, Heezle, the loyal servant of Satan, is the chief of demons. Saden has all types of demons.

Saden has all the worst dark magic powers, spells, and forces in it.

The demons that create chaos in the lives of humans come from Saden sub-villages, the villages of demons.

It is a dark place with demons everywhere. It appears to someone according to how they imagine it is.

The demons that reside there can play with the mind of any mortal.

It is said in ancient Krisen and Ateestan folklore that if Saden, the villages of demons, exists somewhere in any universe, then even the most sacred and divine powers of that universe should be very careful in facing those demons.

At the beginning of time, Satan hid those Saden villages from the Master Universe energy of Adis so that the common progressive energy of the universe would not reach those Saden demon villages.

***

Ayoo and Nathan came down from the time loop and hit the ground of Saden.

Koshi came down, and while he was about to hit the Saden ground, the demons grabbed him and his chariot from hitting the ground.

Nathan and Ayoo got up, and Ayoo is behind Nathan. Nathan and Koshi were standing on Saden's ground opposite each other.

The demons are looking at Nathan; they are in the ugliest and darkest forms, which are visible to Nathan clearly.

Any mortal will die in fear after looking at those demons. They are angry and want to suck the sacred blood out of Nathan.

Ayoo looked at Koshi's chariot. And the bulls of Koshi's Satanic chariot looked at Ayoo. Koshi came running towards Nathan with his sword.

Koshi elevated into the Sapace fast from the ground and attacked Nathan with his sword.

Nathan, with his trident, hit the Koshi's sword.

The energy was released, and it caused a massive explosion there and made a big hole in the ground.

Nathan, Koshi, Ayoo, Koshi's Chariot, and demons are in this hole now.

Demons are hitting the trident of Nathan. They are trying to take it away from him. They hissed in the ears of Nathan to give up and surrender.

Nathan didn't flinch. The demons are laughing at Nathan for fighting against the son of Satan.

Koshi attacked Nathan again. Nathan defended himself with the trident, and both were swinging their weapons at each other. While fighting, the demons are trying to take away the trident of Nathan and trying to make his legs slip while fighting.

Nathan, while fighting with Koshi, suddenly grabbed Koshi's sword with his trident and drove it into the ground.

When it happened, the cry of demons was so loud that Nathan kicked Koshi on his head, and Nathan was lifted into Sapace and fell far away.

Nathan looked at the demons and took some of those demons,

which were very powerful and ugly, into his fist. He compressed those demons within themselves, placed those demons on the ground, and crushed them under his right leg. After seeing this, the demons around Nathan got scared and ran away.

Koshi stood up, and in anger, he changed his form into a massive ugly insect with eight legs and two wings, which is his true form.

In his insect form, Koshi came to Nathan flying. And attacked him with his legs and teeth. Koshi was attacking Nathan relentlessly, and Nathan was trying to stab Koshi, who was in his insect form, but Koshi was not letting it happen.

With his teeth, Koshi grabbed the trident and threw it away. Demons came near Nathan again, laughing.

Nathan stood there while demons circled him, and Koshi flew high and came down to attack Nathan with his full power and a glow of redness.

Nathan had his two fists ready, and Koshi tried to stab at the heart of Nathan.

Nathan grabbed the legs of Koshi and, while swinging him in circles, said, "In the name of God Yinta, I kill you and reject you for the peace of eternity in Heaven and Earth."

And he tore Koshi's legs and grabbed his head.

In Koshi's insect ears, Nathan said, "You shall not be in the creation of the merciful. You shall not be dead in the creation of the Mother Adis. You will be suspended in infinity where you never came into existence," and tore Koshi's insect body into pieces. The pieces of Koshi's insect body burned there and turned into smoke.

The demons cried loudly. And Nathan walked to the trident and picked it up, and gave it a kiss.

The chariot of Koshi burned along with him in the sacred fire. Nathan freed the bulls from the sacred fire. Ayoo came to Nathan, and he sat on it. Satan got to know the news of his son's death in eternity through demons in Hell. He is angry. Sabrina heard the news of her brother's eternal death through demons. She said nothing and felt sad.

Satan knew what had happened. He went to Sabrina. Sabrina was with her son. Satan looked at Sabrina, Nathan's son, and Satan saw God Yinta's divineness in the baby.

He took the baby into his hands. Sabrina was looking at Satan in fear.

Satan cast the baby into Udin, the place of origin of dark magic. Sabrina tried to stop Satan, but with a head turn of Satan towards Sabrina, she said nothing, and after Satan left, she cried like any mother would.

Udin was the place where Satan took birth in the Master Universe. No sacred energy reaches there.

It was hidden from the rest of the Master Universe and the energy of Mother Adis.

The eight sahani servants of Satan stay there.

Those eight sahani servants have only one purpose in the universe, which is to destroy the creations of Mother Adis. But God Yinta took an oath at the Great War of Nazreck that he would kill the eight sahani servants of Satan the moment they leave Udin, after they go back to Udin, after the Great War of Nazreck.

Satan told 7 of his sahani servants to go to Udin after the War of Nazreck, and Satan told Heezle to go to Saden for his works against the creation of Mother Adis and its protector, God Yinta.

He told Heezle never to return to Udin. Satan told the seven sahani servants at Udin never to let the son of Nathan and Sabrina see the light. And never let him be happy.

Sabrina knew what would happen to her son.

After killing Koshi, Nathan went back to the Sacred Yira Forest to find Huro. He was sitting under the sacred Roush tree. Nathan pushed Huro back into the Yira forest from the time loop when Huro tried to save Nathan.

Huro felt very happy after seeing Nathan. On Ayoo, Nathan, and on the sacred eagle, Huro came back to Farush. There, Tes and Kwin were talking about the sacred waterfall the Farush had on one side. They saw Nathan coming.

Farush treats everyone as an equal. All the extra supernatural powers given to anyone and powers they got after the birth are neutralized at Farush, except the powers from the nature of their birth.

Farush was used to fight the universal wars of God and Satan since the beginning of the creation of universes by Mother Adis. The last war between God Yinta and Satan was on Earth. The war happened with permission from Mother Adis. And Mind of Farush independently supervised the rules of war even though war is not happening on the Farush in the Master Universe.

Even God Yinta and Satan have to fight in the war only by using all the supernatural powers they got by birth.

When Nathan fights on the Farush war field in the Master Universe, he, too, has to fight with his mortal energy and powers only.

All the supernatural powers will be taken away from Nathan by Farush.

The armies of Satan and God Yinta, too, were deprived of their supernatural powers while fighting in The Great War of Nazrack, and they had to fight only with their natural energy and powers. It was the rule set by Mother Adis so that the wars happen in a way that is more natural than fighting eternally forever using supernatural powers, where there is a chance that there will be no clear winner.

Farush can also set rules according to the cause of the war and who is fighting in it. God Yinta and Satan, too, cannot go against Farush because it is a system that Farush follows that no one can alter other than Mother Adis.

Nathan and Huro landed at Farush.

Kwin and Tes got excited after seeing Nathan.

Nathan got down from Ayoo and asked Kwin, "Did you drink the water from that waterfall?".

Kwin replied, "No!"

Nathan said to The Three, "Drink the water from that sacred waterfall. You shall live forever!"

The Three couldn't believe it and were shocked.

Nathan continued, "But after drinking, you have to be in the water for 24 Farush days continuously; otherwise, your body couldn't handle the energy of the sacred water."

The Three nodded in agreement.

Then Nathan said, "Now go, use this opportunity!"

The Three happily got on their eagles and started flying towards the sacred waterfall.

* * *

After The Three left for the sacred waterfall at the edge of Farush, Nathan was alone at Farush.

A Satanic chariot is coming towards Farush.

Nathan saw it and understood it was Sabrina.

Sabrina's chariot landed at Farush, and she came out.

She saw Nathan and felt happy. She smiled in happiness after seeing Nathan's height and appearance, which was polished after being given Seehaal by Mother Adis in the sacred Yira forest.

Nathan is at 18ft height and Sabrina is at 14 ft. They look like giants in comparison with The Three. Sabrina's chariot, too, was increased in size.

Sabrina came near to Nathan. Nathan realized she delivered the baby.

And asked her, "Where is my son?"

She suddenly changed her facial expression to sad.

Nathan saw it and asked again, "Where is our son Sabrina?"

Sabrina started getting tears in her eyes.

Nathan was shocked. He placed his hands on her shoulders and asked her, "What happened? Why are you crying?"

Sabrina started crying loudly.

The dust on the Farush is flying high, and there is some change in the Farush's environment. It is because of the energy fluctuations happening.

Sabrina said, "My dad sent our son to Udin, never to return."

After hearing that Nathan was frozen, he knew what a horrible place Udin was.

In the Dreta years, Satan sent Giur to Udin.

Since then, Giur has been staying in Udin. Because no sacred energy and power reaches Udin.

Udin is at the bottom layers of the Master Universe, and Satan rules it absolutely. Nathan had tears in his eyes, and Sabrina saw it. He was getting angry. His face and body language were changing.

The trident is glowing, and his eyes have turned red.

Sabrina, in tension, said, "No, Nathan, no. We should not go to

Hell. It is impossible to defeat my dad there. He will kill you."

Nathan said, "I will burn the Hell under my feet today!"

Sabrina said, "No, Nathan. If something happens to you, then our son will be in Udin forever." After hearing it, he calmed down a little.

"First, we should go to Udin. And save our baby," said Sabrina.

He was convinced by her argument.

"How can we go to Udin?" asked Nathan.

Sabrina answered, "I know how to go to Udin. It takes 62 Farush days to go to Udin, and there are many worlds we have to cross on the path to Udin. The initial worlds we see are good, but as we go near Udin, we see the worst, rotten worlds with injustice, crime, disease, and filth. Quantum travel is not allowed to Udin.

A world we see on the path to Udin in the Master Universe is a planet according to your human science, but here, those planets we see on the path to Udin exist in different universes, and those planets from different universes are pulled together and placed there in quantum leap through the law of convergence of independent energy by Mother Adis. Because life is only on these planets in those universes they are in, as Mother Adis intended before the beginning of time, and according to what she decided, the creation of all known and unknown universes to us was done by Mother Adis. So, we call a planet a world here."

Nathan looked at Ayoo and went to sit on it.

Sabrina said, "Come with me!"

Nathan told Ayoo to follow them.

Ayoo nodded her head.

Sabrina sat in her chariot, and Nathan sat next to her.

The bulls started running on the ground of the Farush, and the chariot moved forward.

Then, it elevated itself and started moving into the space of the Master Universe.

They started going in a direction that had no end in the Master Universe.

Ayoo was following the chariot.

They are going far away from Farush into the deep darkness of infiniteness.

They traveled 10 Farush days in absolute darkness in infiniteness without any light except the glow of their chariot.

Nathan said while they were traveling in infiniteness, "Thanks for telling me about the sacred Yira forest."

Sabrina said, "I know you are the chosen one. The day I saw you."

Nathan laughed.

Sabrina said, "Anything for our baby." Sabrina put her head on Nathan's shoulder on the 10th day, and he took the reins of the chariot.

He is controlling the chariot now. After Nathan took control of the red-glowing Satanic chariot, it turned into a red-blue mixed-shade glowing chariot.

Sabrina saw the first world. And Nathan saw it.

The first world is floating in the infinite darkness, suspended here by Mother Adis in a quantum leap with a sun. It is orbiting its Sun.

Sabrina said, "This is the Pure Pane World. No crime, no injustice, no hate, no negativity, and only happiness is in this world. People only talk if the words coming out of their mouths are positive or they don't. They are followers of truth, peace, and nothing else. The planet is shining as bright as its Sun."

In the Master Universe, Mother Adis placed all the planets from all known universes she created with any type of life in those planets, she placed them together here with their suns and also immediate natural satellites for the final sacred audit at the time of the Dohona destruction event. Dohona destruction will happen on all planets with any type of life form on/in them once every 52,444 Farush years.

As they moved forward, Sabrina said, "We will visit all eight planet worlds with our son on our return journey together."

As they moved, they saw a little disturbance in the space they were traveling in, and Nathan observed a very little noise. They traveled six Farush days in that disturbance. And Nathan saw another world orbiting its Sun and a small natural satellite object orbiting that planet.

Sabrina said, "This world is called Sub Pure Pane World."

This is the second world.

In this world, people debate moral issues and what is good and what is wrong. They don't know the truth, but they try to find it by considering two sides of everything, positive and negative.

Nathan heard vague noises coming out of Sub Pure Pane World.

As Nathan and Sabrina moved forward in infiniteness, they saw dust in space and felt more disturbance in the time and space.

After traveling for another six Farush days, they saw another world; It had two natural satellite objects orbiting it and the Sun. This is the third world.

As they were beside this world, Sabrina said to Nathan, "This is Pure Panen World. Here on this planet, people talk about sex, money, and wealth, morals, but they try to earn them righteously.

My dad once tried to enter this world directly and sent his demon soldiers into this world, but Mother Adis has her representatives there, and they fought with my father's demon soldiers and stopped them from entering this world. This happened 80000 Farush years before. People know that incident in this world but my father said soon he will conquer this world. The people in this world are very smart and mostly good."

As their chariot moved more into the darkness, there was nothing after that third world. They traveled for another eight Farush days, and they started seeing more dust and small rocks called asteroids in human science, floating in space.

There, they saw the First Sideenis World. The First Sideenis planet had three natural satellite objects orbiting it, and the First Sideenis planet was orbiting its Sun.

Sabrina said, "In this world, they talk about everything. Good, bad, sex, and morals, and they commit sins against their God by being dishonest and lying to others. But those people who lie cannot enter Heaven in the Master Universe, and those sinners and liars come to my father in Hell. Those people are given the status of soldiers of Satan in their afterlife for lying to their fellow human beings. They fight for my father to avoid eternal pain and punishments in Hell."

Nathan looked at it and felt a different feeling about that planet.

Their chariot of courage is moving forward into infiniteness, and Nathan saw more dust and big rocks floating in space.

They saw Satanic stars from far away. Those stars are trying to mimic Mother Adis's creation of the universe.

The chariot is traveling deep into the unknown infiniteness. After eight Farush days, they reached The AndroSat World, also known as The Second Sideenis World.

Sabrina said, "In this world, people lie. They talk about every good and bad thing. Also, they commit adultery and have extramarital affairs with other people's wives and husbands. The people who commit those acts of sin are loved by my father. He likes them."

Nathan said nothing. Four natural satellite objects were orbiting the Second Sideenis planet, and there is also a Sun that the Second Sideenis Planet orbits.

Their chariot moved forward, they saw the stars glowing strongly, and they saw dust and floating rocks forming an orbiting system.

There are millions of asteroids around them. Their chariot is moving forward between the spaces of those asteroids.

As they traveled another eight Farush days like that, they saw The Idine World, also called The Third Sideenis World.

Sabrina said, "In this world, people lie, and commit adultery, talk about everything, and also Jealousy is high, and they try to sabotage those who are working hard and truthfully. People love the destruction of anyone who disagrees with them on anything rather than being rational and sensible with common sense. The influence of my father is significantly high in this world." The third Sideenis world had a sun which it orbits and five natural satellite objects orbiting the planet.

The chariot of courage moved forward. Nathan and Sabrana saw volatile, big floating rocks with dust moving in space in different patterns.

There were millions of them, and they saw brighter stars far away from where they were. After traveling for eight Farush days, they saw The Fourth Sideenis world called The Maris. The Maris has a sun which it orbits and six natural satellite objects orbiting Maris.

Sabrina said, "This world is a relative of Hell. They do everything here. The worst and the best. The bad and the good. But my father's wishes are honored here with the murder, rape, and killings of their fellow human beings because of dirty lust and money.

They kill themselves in the process of attaining material wealth. And my father receives prayers daily from this world. And he actually quickly grants the wishes of people who pray to him."

As their chariot moved further, they were traveling deeper into infinite darkness, and it was all chaos there with big floating rocks, fake stars mimicking the Mother Adis's creation of the universe, and the laughs of demons and screams of people.

After traveling 32 Farush days in that chaos to the side of the edge of the ever-expanding Master Universe, they saw The Fifth Sideenis world.

It is also called The Earth.

Sabrina said, "My father has a great influence on this world. He loves this world a lot as they leave their Gods for material gains, and they worship my father with utmost sincerity. They do all the best and worst in this world, but my father always wins. They lie, kill, massacre, perform immoral sex, and commit adultery. They lose their identities for attention, and they kill themselves in the chaos of mindless stupidity. Most people in this world are addicted to habits that destroy them, and my father loves those people and creates those habits for people of this world. My dad gives them great wealth and health, but they don't know my dad has no one as his favorite. He takes their lives whenever he wants. My father's demon soldiers are plenty here, and they possess people and love to give the souls of those people to my father. The people here are more loyal to my father than to their Gods. They actually go to any extent to get the worldly pleasures my father wants them to have. They commit the most favorite sin of my father, which is watching other people having sex, instead of having sex with another person directly and morally in their real life."

Nathan asked Sabrina, "Don't your father know that you are with me?"

Sabrina answered, "Yes, so what? I like you, and no one can stop me from being with you."

Nathan smiled in happiness.

Sabrina continued, "I know you will die for me and also die again to protect me. So what difference does it make if my father knows I'm with you or not? And I love our son more than my father."

Nathan kissed Sabrina on the forehead.

Nathan said, "God is in your mind. And God gives you good, great, rational, and highly matured intellectual, pragmatic thoughts that will not give you instant kick and satisfaction but a long, fulfilled, happy life. Satan wants to grab that space in your mind through his Satanic bad thoughts. Satan wants to give you instant satisfaction and happiness by destroying your future and making you more cruel, dumb, and aggressive in the process. Don't give Satan that space in your mind. Give all the space of the mind to God rather than to Satan."

After hearing it, Sabrina said, "You really are my husband. No, no! You became my husband because of this nature of yours. I know!"

As they were traveling into infiniteness, suddenly stars and rocks, dust, everything disappeared. After traveling for another 10 Farush days, they entered Sapace and saw the big floating territory in Sapace. It is as big as planet Earth.

They saw eight castles in Udin. The first castle is at the entrance of the Udin, and the Udin is in a shape that it is impossible to land the chariot anywhere except in front of the First castle's entrance.

Sabrina and Nathan don't know where their son is in Udin.

So they landed in front of the first castle. The eight castles are on eight dark mountains; the tallest mountain is first, and the smallest is 8th in descending order.

So they go down into Udin as they move through the castles.

Udin is a dark place damned by Mother Adis and used by Satan for his pleasure, guarded by his seven servants who oversee the destruction of people's lives and make them worship Satan in the Sideenis Worlds.

Satan was born at Udin, but after Satan opposed Mother Adis, she cursed Satan and his beloved things in the entire existence.

Satan likes Udin a lot because it is his birthplace, but as part of the curse of Mother Adis, Udin, which is bright and full of life, has become lifeless and worthless.

Satan loved his mother a lot, but he felt he was ill-treated in comparison with his brother, God Yinta. So he opposed the creations of Mother Adis and has been working against God Yinta ever since in a pact with the Emperor of Emptiness, Beeliaal.

No sacred energy has reached Udin since the beginning of time after the curse of Mother Adis on Satan, but now Nathan has come to Udin.

Each castle is on the top of each mountain. After the 8th mountain, there is a big hole in the ground that leads to Seperna, The Deep Hollow of Dimona. It is where Giur was imprisoned, in a place called Suuyaan Nowhere. To reach Suuyaan Nowhere, one has to travel for 484426 Farush years inside The Deep Hollow of Dimona. Giur was imprisoned for helping God Yinta by betraying Satan in the Dreta times.

Dreta times are the years before the creation of Mother Adis began.

Ira and Jiza are at the bank of the Kalsa River, and they were having sex without clothes.

Ira is on top of Jiza. Jiza was lying on the ground.

Ira is moving her hip, up and down. They are making loud moans.

Jiza said, "Faster, Faster!"

Ira said, "It will come off!"

Jiza laughed and said, "No, it will not. Do it faster.."

Ira increased her hip movement speed. Both were in ecstasy.

Suddenly, Ira changed her facial expression. And looked into the sky. She is still giving hip moments, and she is moaning.

Suddenly, Ira started slapping Jiza. Jiza thought of it as part of the act. But she slapped him again so hard that his cheeks turned red with finger marks on his face.

He shouted in pain, and she was still giving him hip movements, but much, much faster now. And she slapped him very hard again.

This time, he got blood from his cheeks. And she again increased the hip movements to much faster speeds.

He shouted loudly in pain and tried to get up, but she pushed him down and kept giving hip movements.

Jiza wanted to get up now and shouted, "Stop, Stop! I'm already finished."

But Ira ignored him and increased her hip movement speed again.

Jiza pushed Ira very hard and got up. He was bleeding, and blood was on his legs.

He has wiped his tears. He went near the water and washed the blood off which is on his body.

Jiza looked back at Ira. Her eyes turned black. Jiza got scared after looking at her.

He wore his clothes and went near her.

She was lying flat on the ground without clothes with her eyes closed.

Jiza went near her slowly and called her, "Ira.. Iraa.. What happened?" but she did not respond.

She was silent and not moving. He went near her and touched her shoulder. She opened her eyes suddenly and looked at Jiza.

Ira, in pain and confusion, said, "Jiza, what happened?"

Jiza took her into his hands and got her into clothes.

In his car, He took her to her home. He rang the bell of her house.

Ira's mom came out and saw them. Suddenly, Ira started making weird noises.

Jiza got scared looking at Ira. Ira's mom, too, looked at Ira, wondering why she was making those weird, strange, scary noises.

Ira started behaving abnormally. She is hitting her face with her hands and hitting her head against the walls around her.

Jiza is trying to hold her steady, but she is pushing him. Ira's mom got scared and started crying.

Ira is tearing her own clothes.

Jiza forcefully got hold of Ira and took her into her home.

Ira started throwing things at her mom at home.

Jiza asked Ira's mom to bring a rope. She brought it to him. Jiza took Ira to the bedroom and asked her mom to hold Ira's feet down. He quickly wrapped the rope around her hands and legs and tied her to the bed.

In Saden village, demons are crying because Heezle left Saden to possess Ira. Heezle is one of the eight Udin servants of Satan.

Jiza, in his dream, once saw the Master Universe. And God Yinta revealed to him what he should do to help Nathan in the war. Heezle tried to scare Jiza and woke him up from his sleep that night.

Heezle knows Jiza loves Ira, and in order to create chaos in his life, he can create problems for Ira.

Then, Jiza will become weak mentally and kneel in front of Satan to get him and Ira out of those problems and betray Nathan.

Jiza and Ira's mother tied Ira to bed.

Ira's father died when Ira's mother was pregnant with Ira.

Ira started acting weird and shouting loudly. Jiza cried in fear and asked Ira to stop shouting. But mentally, Ira is not in this world. Heezle made Ira's soul a slave to him, and he took the place of her soul.

Heezle has sent Ira's soul to Saden, and demons of Saden with Satanic soul chains tied Ira's soul to a wall of Saden's Demon castle in the room of Ikkayath, Soul Slaver.

Ira went unconscious on Earth.

Nathan and Sabrina are on the chariot at Udin's first castle entrance.

They heard their son crying. Their chariot landed on Udin at the first castle's entrance.

Nathan felt emotional hearing his son cry for the first time, and Sabrina had tears in her eyes.

Nathan and Sabrina are also hearing hissing voices in their ears. But they couldn't find where the cry of their baby was coming from. Nathan understood it was a trick being played by the demons of Satan.

Nathan and Sabrina got off the chariot.

Nathan looked at the first castle. He is walking up to the entrance of the castle. Then Nathan saw Ishrane, the demonic depression servant of Satan.

He came in front of Nathan.

Ishrane said, "Give up! It is impossible to cross me and go to Seperna."

Nathan said nothing.

Ishrane said, "No one lived their life normally after I met them in any way or form. It will be like that for you, too, Nathan."

Nathan said nothing.

Ishrane said, "I'm too powerful and greater than you. Why waste time just to give up after some time and go back? You will suffer more when you want to fight against me than when you opt to submit to me. Go, make another baby, and leave your son to us."

After hearing it, Nathan stopped walking. His trident started glowing. His eyes started turning red.

Sabrina was angry, too, after hearing it.

Nathan's cape started waving itself. He again started walking towards the entrance. Ishrane came in the middle.

Nathan said nothing.

Nathan kept walking. He reached the entrance of The First Castle, Depresna. He heard his son's cry again.

Ishrane came running towards Nathan to attack Nathan with his sword.

Nathan lifted his body above Udin's ground very high. Nathan moved so fast towards Ishrane that the path he was flying in Udin's atmosphere started burning out of nothing.

Nathan's trident started leaking fire storms. Nathan came down to Udin's ground and hit Ishrane's sword with his trident.

The Depresna mountain was destroyed, and the sword of Ishrane broke into a million pieces and turned into dust after getting hit with the trident of Nathan.

Then Nathan's trident hit Ishrane. Ishrane's body was torn, with demons coming out from Ishrane's body, crying loudly, and his body turned into dust.

Nathan was furious, and his rage was increasing.

He is running forward in that rage.

Sabrina felt proud and started following Nathan.

They are now on the second mountain top. Udin has this massive mountain range to symbolically challenge the creations of Mother Adis. This mountain range was created by Satan himself out of his love for Udin, after he got cursed by Mother Adis.

Nathan didn't stop at the second castle, Arron.

Arin, the second servant of Satan, came and said, "You are nothing in front of me. With the power I possess, I can kill you in a second."

Nathan charged forward and looked back at Sabrina, and he said, "I am you!".

He ignored what Arin was saying. Arin attacked Nathan fiercely, but nothing happened to Nathan, and Sabrina didn't even look at Arin. Arin again attacked Nathan with more power.

Nathan looked at Arin, took his trident into his left hand, and said, "I am your master!"

and grabbed Arin's throat and started walking towards Arron castle's entrance. Sabrina was searching for their baby.

Arin is attacking Nathan while his throat is in the grip of Nathan's hand.

Nathan crushed Arin's throat, lifted him up, and threw him to the ground so hard that Arin's body exploded and destroyed the demons, the mountain, and Arron Castle, too.

Nathan continued walking. Sabrina and Nathan are also searching for their son while they are going through the castles.

Nathan and Sabrina are on the third mountain now.

The castle on the third mountain is called Jealona Castle. Jeas stays at the entrance, protecting the castle.

Satan got to know what happened at Udin through his demons and told all the remaining servants in Udin to go against Nathan at once.

Jeas from Jealona Castle, Hatio from Hateso Castle on The Fourth Mountain, Lusy from Lusio Castle on The Fifth Mountain, Greedio from Greeda Castle on The Sixth Mountain, Malice from Malisio Castle on The Seventh Mountain came in front of Nathan.

Heezle from Humiliana Castle on The Eight Mountain, and also he is one of the eight sahani servants of Satan, was not on Udin.

Because Heezle possessed Ira on Earth.

The five servants came together against Nathan.

They took the forms of the five Anti elements of Udin as ordered by Satan.

They are anti-elements to the elements of nature created by Mother Adis.

The first anti-element is Satan's sand called Satsand. Satsand makes the sacred sand created by Mother Adis for all the known and unknown universes, and the Earth and other planets go lifeless, and Satsand pollutes the sacred sand created by Mother Adis and makes it impossible to raise crops that are needed to sustain life on those planets. It kills the essence and sacredness of the soil of worlds and makes the worlds' life forms go hungry and plagues them with death.

The second anti-element is Satan's water. Satan's water is called Sater, which makes the sacred water created by Mother Adis lifeless and useless to be consumed by all life forms. Sater kills life by taking orders from Satan.

The Satan fire destroys civilizations, life forms by taking orders from Satan, and it has always been used in wars by Satan to capture the forces of God. The very nature of Satan fire called Safire is opposition to the light of God, and it tries to pollute the sacred fire created by Mother Adis with its malicious nature.

The Satan air called Sair always pollutes the sacred air of the universe and makes it lifeless.

The Satan space time called Sapace. Sapace always opposes the space-time of God, and it offers immortality to mortals to turn them against God and in favor of Satan.

Jeas took Anti Sacred Sand - Satsand, Hatio took Anti Sacred Water - Sater, Lusy took Anti Sacred Fire - Safire, Greedio took Anti Sacred Air - Sair, Malice took Anti Sacred Space - Sapace. The 5 servants of Satan took five anti-universe elements forms.

Satan figured out that even though Nathan is immortal now after eating the sacred Roush fruit, his mind is still from the mortal world, and his thinking cannot go beyond the scope, permutations, and combinations, possibilities, and probabilities of the five elements of nature of his world.

So no matter what Nathan thinks and does in the Master Universe, even with the divine power he attained in the Yira sacred forest, his mind and thinking patterns will not allow him to think beyond the scope and possibilities of the five elements of nature of his world because that is what he knows his entire life and every decision, move and every single thing inside and out of his mind and body is within the scope of the five elements of his world, Earth.

Even in the Master Universe, his view of the Master Universe and everything he sees in it is constructed by interpreting his existing knowledge of the five elements of his world, Earth, rather than seeing the Master Universe as it is.

Satan knew Nathan was seeing the Master Universe through his knowledge of his world and interpreting the Master Universe in his own way according to the five elements of nature of his world, Earth. That view of Nathan is very limited in understanding the Master

Universe, and Nathan should work a lot in his mind to see the true and real Master Universe that Satan was seeing.

Sabrina, too, has been seeing the real view of the Master Universe all along, but she didn't expect her father to take this step to defeat Nathan at Udin through the weakness he had in seeing the Master Universe and using the rules of the universe in the Master Universe.

Nathan doesn't know those rules of the Master Universe, and even if Sabrina tries to explain them to Nathan, he wouldn't understand, as he does not even see the real view of the Master Universe, but a very limited one till now.

To see the real view of the Master Universe, his mind has to suffer, and he has to take that pain and suffering to learn the rules of the Master Universe to interpret them in broadway, which opens him to the vastness of the Master Universe completely and makes him realize how he can use the energy of the Master Universe to his advantage.

The five servants surrounded Nathan and took the forms of the five anti-elements of nature of Nathan's world.

Greedio Sair came running towards Nathan and hit him with the power of Satan's air through the Verona, a trident that releases Satan's air at unimaginable speeds and poisons the mind.

Greedio attacked Nathan with Verona. Nathan defended himself with his trident. Verona released the poisonous Sair on the face of Nathan. Nathan breathed the Sair.

Sabrina saw it and got scared. Nathan, in his mortal instincts, breathed the poisonous Sair released by Verona. Nathan's strength was gradually getting reduced, and Greedio attacked him with Verona continuously.

Nathan is struggling to defend himself, and Jeas saw this. Jeas came and attacked Nathan with the hammer of Satsand.

Nathan took the Satsand hammer hit on his shoulder.

Hatio with Sater, Lusy with Safire, Malice with Sapace, through their swords started attacking Nathan.

Sabrina stepped forward to fight with them, but Nathan saw it and said "No" to her. She stopped.

They are inflicting all kinds of pain and emotions in him using his memories.

They are trying to confuse him through emotions while still drawing swords at him. Nathan is fighting with five Anti-Natural Universe, Anti-Mother Adis's elements of Satan through the natural Earth's elemental energy, knowledge, and divine power within him.

Every hit made with the Verona trident and swords of anti-elements on Nathan was getting power matched by Nathan's trident. They are not causing any damage to Nathan or his trident.

Safire attached itself to one hand of Nathan and continuously burned his hand.

Sater grabbed Nathan's left leg, and Satsand took his right leg from the ground. Satsand was trying to take Nathan inside Udin's ground. As a result, it is holding him attached to the ground, making him unable to move.

Sair is trying to poison Nathan's mind. Sapace turned everything totally dark in Nathan's mind with a touch of malevolent forces and demons, making Nathan confused about his surroundings.

They got hold of Nathan, and Sater covered Nathan's trident in it.

Suddenly, Ayoo came flying with Sabrina on it. And flying around Nathan, Ayoo screeched loudly.

Nathan heard the cry of his son again, and he couldn't do anything as he knew nothing more than what he learned in his previous world, Earth.

Ayoo screeched again. Nathan, struggling with anti-elements to make himself free, looked up at Ayoo and saw Sabrina in tears. Nathan is trying hard to free himself from those anti-elements. But it is not working. The strength of the anti-elements matched Nathan's.

Nathan heard a voice in his mind, "No one can do anything to you unless you accept what they want to do to you; it doesn't matter whether it is good or not. Even if they do something forcefully to you, you act as if you accepted it, but inside, you don't. Wait for the right time and strike, but strike so hard that no one can escape."

Nathan stopped trying to untangle himself from anti-elements. After hearing this in his mind, he stopped his efforts to free himself.

The anti-elements got him into their control completely. Half of his right leg is inside Udin's ground now, and Satan is laughing in Hell.

Nathan closed his eyes. And looked at Sapace while his eyes were still closed.

# 4

Nathan again heard a voice in his mind: " Free your mind from weakness. Free yourself from your self-imposed limitations. Endure the pain and face it. Only while taking the pain, you fight it and can kill it, not while avoiding it. I, God Yinta now giving you the freedom of thought and freedom to live. And to live, you survive now, and to survive, I give you the truth. The truth is, what is true is the truth. And sometimes the truth changes, and sometimes it doesn't. So seek the truth and know your self-imposed limitations. Then you will not be a slave to anything, even to the death of your mortal body."

Nathan opened his eyes and looked at the anti-elements struggling to keep hold of him. He smiled. He took his leg out of Udin's ground.

He looked at Safire, it is burning his hand, and he said, "It's too cold, right? How is my hand? Is it warm?"

He started walking forward. The five elements are trying hard, hitting him, and attacking him to put him down.

Nathan is taking the pain and walking forward. Nathan, for the first time in the Master Universe, started bleeding through his nose. A drop of blood came out from his nose, and the blood touched the ground of Udin.

Nathan knew where the blood of men touches the ground while fighting against evil. There, the truth will prevail, and justice will return. Udin is the birthplace of Satan and was cursed by Mother

Adis. But now Udin was sacredly polluted by the blood of the last prophet of Ateesta, thought Satan.

Mother Adis is the source of energy for the Master Universe and all the other known and unknown masters and sub-universes.

Mother Adis stays in a dimension unknown to anyone, even to God Yinta and Satan.

Mother Adis favored the positive forces of God Yinta in the universe at the beginning of time. That is how most of the known and unknown universes are comprised of five natural elements of nature: air, sand, water, space, and fire in different forms according to their location.

Mother Adis saw what Nathan was going through, and God Yinta was the son of Adis, making God Yinta's followers dear to Mother Adis. No tiny change of energy happens in all the known and unknown universes without Mother Adis knowing it, even though she doesn't want to control it and lets the energy flow independently of her.

But Mother Adis is the energy of positive, negative, and neutral, and everything in between and outside.

Everything happens in her, through her, and with her; the energy itself is her. But she treats everyone equally, and that is why she didn't meddle in her sons, God Yinta, and Satan's war of Nazreck on Earth, as she loves them equally. But Mother Adis only favored God Yinta because he was defending the sacredness of the universes created and will be created by Mother Adis.

Mother Adis saw Nathan. Did nothing. Nathan doesn't know that Mother Adis saw him.

Nathan walked forward in pain, unbearable to any man and never known to mankind, while the anti-elements tried to tear him apart mentally and physically.

Ayoo landed in front of Nathan. The blood from his nose stopped after one drop. Udin's demons came flying to Nathan after they were told by Satan to stop Nathan's blood from touching Udin's ground, but the blood drop of Nathan went into Udin's ground.

The demons are giving more strength to anti-elements.

No demon and no anti-element touched Sabrina as they knew she was the daughter of Satan. They also know that made Nathan, son-in-law to Satan.

Nathan stopped and suddenly fell on his knees on Udin's ground. Demons laughed. The anti-elements Jeas Satsand, Hatio Sater, Lusy Safire, Greedio Sair, Malice Sapace covered Nathan's body and took control of Nathan completely, physically and mentally.

Sabrina had tears in her eyes, and Ayoo screeched in sadness, not being able to see his master giving up.

Nathan was taken inside Udin into the ground, and he was dragged into the ground of Udin into a massive hole made by the anti-elements.

Nathan accepted his fate through the anti-elements and demons.

But suddenly, inside Udin's hole, he was being dragged into eternal darkness like Giur in Dreta years. Nathan now knew the plan of Satan.

Nathan tore the anti-elements energy shield on his body through his trident and, with his left hand, grabbed the shield formed by the anti-elements and made it into a ball.

With one kick of his right leg down, he came out flying from the massive hole, and, in his hand, he had the anti-elements as an energy ball.

He stood above the ground with bright glowing eyes, and Sabrina saw him and shouted in happiness.

Ayoo screeched in happiness. Nathan threw the anti-elements energy ball with Satan's servants in it into Sapace with an energy thread from the ball attached to his hand.

The ball went near Earth, hitting asteroids and fake Satanic stars mimicking creations of Mother Adis, and came back. While it was coming back, Nathan removed the energy thread of the ball from his hand and took his trident into both of his hands. When the anti-elements energy ball reached him, he hit it with the trident. The energy released by the hit was devastating, and that energy destroyed all of the remaining Udin mountains and castles on the Udin mountains.

The anti-elements energy ball, after getting hit by Nathan's trident, went towards the Unknown, the Origin of Mother Adis. The Angels in Heaven believe Mother Adis's physical castle starts after 88468246 Farush years in the direction the anti-elements energy ball with Satan's servants in it went from Udin.

Udin had only demons now.

These powerful demons who had known Satan since the beginning of times were terrified now of Nathan.

As Nathan started walking, the demons started running away, but the sacred snake of Nathan's trident grabbed every demon and made them stand in front of Nathan.

Nathan said, "Kneel or go to Mother Adis!"

The demons knelt to Nathan. And accepted Nathan as their master.

Nathan got on Ayoo, and Sabrina's chariot followed him.

They reached Seperna, the Deep Hollow of Dimona.

The place of birth of dark magic. And all the demonic possessions, spells, and activities originate from here, and dark energy goes to evil demonic entities in all known and unknown universes from here.

It is a massive, deep, dark, hollow tunnel into Udin.

As they reached the entrance, Nathan and Sabrina, Ayoo, and the bulls of the chariot saw an endless abyss of space-time spinning with a glow of red and darkness.

It felt by Sabrina herself that if they went inside, there would be no coming back. The sound of it can scare even angels.

Ayoo and Bulls got scared after looking at it.

They made frightening noises. And went a little back.

The size of the Seperna endless abyss looked supermassive, and their son is inside of it, but they don't know exactly where he is inside the Seperna.

Sabrina started crying.

Sabrina said in tears, crying, "My son is inside of it, and I don't know how to save him!"

Nathan looked at Seperna and looked at Sabrina, feeling sad.

He had tears after seeing Sabrina crying.

Nathan said, "I will go inside. You stay here."

After hearing it, Ayoo screeched in fear, and Nathan petted her, assuring her that it was okay and he would be with her.

Sabrina said, "No, I will come. I want to see my son."

Nathan said, "To the end of the times, at the end of the times, before the end of the times, and after the end of the times, I will protect you and our children with my life and without my life or in between and outside."

Sabrina is on chariot, and Nathan is on Ayoo.

He said to Ayoo, "Come with us, friend. Follow us."

He signaled Ayoo with his hand to take him to Sabrina's chariot. And when Ayoo stopped behind the chariot, he got into the chariot.

They stared at Seperna, and bulls started moving, and the chariot went near the entrance of Seperna. As they moved forward, they stared at the endless abyss.

They are going inside Udin through Seperna. As they were going near Seperna's entrance, the atmosphere around them quickly changed to chaotic, and it started to lightning as they moved forward through darkish white clouds on the path.

On their way to the ground of Seperna, the chariot is moving on the path.

They moved forward, and they saw massive, tall, dark mountains far away glowing on their own. The plateau looked dark, with valleys and Sater flowing in them.

Safire is burning Satsand on Seperna's dark mountains. No mortal who took birth ever walked on Seperna's ground and will never walk on it except Nathan.

In the Endless Abyss, they were moving forward; nothing was still.

The Satsand dust is everywhere, and the Sapace is dark and gloomy.

They saw a super bright glow from far away.

Nathan is ready to fight and is expecting to see the forces of Satan coming towards them. But no one came, and Nathan kept looking in all directions.

After some time, they were moving forward; it started to rain Sater.

The plateau looked lifeless, dark, mysterious, and chaotic.

They are traveling in the direction they saw the glow of light.

As they were moving through a valley, they saw massive, dark, lifeless mountains getting lightning strikes and Saterfalls with lifeless motion.

They didn't see any creature, any life form in Seperna, The Hollow of Dimona, which is an Endless Abyss.

It is called The Hollow of Dimona because Satan never knew who his father was, and he asked his mother, Mother Adis, and she said he needed to prove himself worthy to see his father.

When God Yinta asked about his father, Mother Adis said the same to God Yinta as she said to Satan.

God Yinta said to Mother Adis, "I'm already worthy to see him because I'm your son."

Mother Adis laughed and told him who his father is, but Satan said, "He is my father, and I want to see him."

Mother Adis said, "You are correct!" And also told him who his father is.

Satan said, "Then I want everything which is his!"

Mother Adis said to Satan, "You can have everything of his when you prove yourself worthy of having them."

God Yinta heard it and said, "I will make my father proud!"

Mother Adis looked at Satan, and Satan said, "What is my father's is mine and mine by birth.. Why should I prove something to get what I'm entitled to?"

Mother Adis said, "Son, you are correct, but you should not destroy what your father has built, and to prove you are capable of ruling it, you should prove yourself!"

Satan felt disappointed and said, "I love you, Mother, but Yinta and I are different. And you think I should be like him," to which Mother Adis said, "No, He understood what I said, and you didn't. Try to understand!"

Satan said, "No, Mother, I won't because if I understand you, I have to give up what I get, and I have to prove myself unnecessarily like a mortal for doing something which I have known since my birth. I have learned everything from my father before coming into existence. and I'm the son of the ultimate. So I won't understand. If I get a chance to prove myself, then I can, but how can I prove myself worthy of having my father's gifts to me before having them at all?"

Mother Adis said, "Son, listen to me!"

Satan said, "No, Mother, I will never come to Adististen again. I know how to take hold of all the mortal and immortal beings, in known and unknown - masters and sub-universes."

Satan walked out from Adististen.

God Yinta left to the Right side of the Adististen and constructed the complex of Heaven in the Master Universe.

Satan left to the left side of Adististen and constructed the complex of Hell. But they built them at the border of left and right in the middle of the Master Universe by the order of the Mother Adis.

Dimona is a woman from the mortal world. Satan married her through Satanic rituals and killed her after she gave birth to two Satan children, Sabrina and Koshi, in human form but with the powers of Satan.

Satan took Koshi and Sabrina to Hell and taught them the ways of Satanic rituals and Satan worship, dark magic standards, spells, and laws of Satan.

After killing Dimona, he sent her soul to Seperna because no sacred energy ever reached Udin after Mother Adis cursed it, and Dimona's soul will never reach Heaven.

Nathan and Sabrina continued traveling on the chariot to the place where they saw the glow. Ayoo is following them.

They heard dark, mysterious voices. Nathan tried to figure out where the voices were coming from.

Nathan is ready with his trident to attack if any evil force appears in front of them.

He heard the voices again and felt something different.

Nathan waved his trident and focused on the voices and channeled them to Seperna's dark freya frequency. It gave those voices a clarity.

The voice said, "Daughter!"

Sabrina heard it. And she was looking everywhere to find out who it was. The vast plateau of Seperna is looking merciless.

The voice again said, "Come to me, daughter!"

Sabrina got confused and couldn't find who was calling her.

Nathan said, "Evil force, who are you?"

The voice laughed loudly and said, "Evil force? Haha, Look where you are!"

Nathan and Sabrina saw the plateau land, and it was humming fiercely.

The voice again said, "No one has been here ever since I came here. You mortal immortal came here with my daughter. I know where my grandson is. He is with me."

After hearing it, Sabrina stopped the chariot and got down.

As she stepped onto the ground of the Seperna, the ground shook a little.

Sabrina said, "Oh, servant of my father! I don't know who you are, but giveth me my child."

The voice replied, "Haha, I'm not your father's servant, My child. Your child is a child of my child. So that child is my child too."

Sabrina said, "Who are you? Reveal yourself!"

The voice said, "I'm your mother, daughter."

And came in front of her in soul form and showed herself.

Sabrina's instincts told her that she was her mother, and Sabrina remembered the memory of how her father killed her mother.

Sabrina got emotional and said, "Mother, is it you? I couldn't believe it. I love you,"

And she hugged her mother.

Dimona said, "We have to hurry!"

While Dimona was saying it, suddenly a darkish green force light - Gredar came down from Sapace. They saw it. Dimona started crying loudly in fear.

Nathan and Sabrina didn't understand what was happening. They saw the dark green light - Gredar coming down.

As the dark green light touched the Satsand of Seperna,

A big explosion happened, and it resulted in a greenish dark light sphere and a big glow of powerful green light inside of it with green lightning striking around it.

Dimona said in fear, "They will torment us."

Sabrina asked her, "Who are they? And what is it?"

Dimona said, "They are Innahath soldiers of your father!"

Nathan asked Dimona, "What will they do? Why are you scared of them?"

Dimona said, "They take me to Arhush and tie me with the Chains of Mohenaa and torture my soul with Irhath whiplashes to my soul."

Nathan was taught by the sacred serpent when he went to the Sacred Yira forest under Heaven about Satan and what he did.

So Nathan knew Arhush was a Satsand triangle plate traveling in space-time at the edge of the universe expansion, and Arhush always travels to the unknown dimensions of space and time.

Every power in the universe is neutral at the expansion of the universe, but to create dominance, Satan married Dimona, a mortal human with a soul that has the natural-universe energy of the Earth. He then killed her and cast her soul to Seperna, his birthplace, and by using his Innahath soldiers, who have no birth and no death and are part of his immortal Satanic energy, takes the soul of Dimona to Arhush and tortures the soul of Dimona.

Satan is trying to establish an energy imbalance through his anti-elements in the Master Universe using the natural energy of the soul of a pure mortal woman.

The Innahath soldiers take her every 13 Farush days and tie her with Chains of Mohenaa, which can arrest even angels because the Chains of Mohenaa originated from Mother Adis when she gave birth to Satan.

Satan took the part of energy of her to himself, and with that, he made Chains of Mohenaa. The chains are so powerful that it is said that God Yinta escaped tactfully on the battleground when Satan threw the Chains of Mohenaa at him instead of trying to break the chains with his sword. Because he knew no power in the universe could go against them, even himself. But the rule to use Chains of Mohenaa set by Mother Adis to Satan is that he can only use them once against anyone in any universe. If they escape the first attempt at arrest, then the chains become powerless against them. And the

Mohenaa Chains cannot do anything to anyone if they escape from them once.

But escaping from the Chains of Mohenaa is not easy. God Yinta took the help of Mother Adis, his mother, to escape from them by overpowering them. And the Chains of Mohenaa went powerless against God Yinta from then.

For a mortal soul like Dimona, it is impossible to escape from Mohenaa Chains.

The soldiers of Innahath came out from the energy sphere with Mohenaa Chains in their hands.

There are 4 Innahath soldiers.

As they came out of the sphere of Gredar Innahath, the glow of Sianch brightened much higher. Sianch is the light that Nathan and Sabrina saw earlier from far away.

And the Sianch light spell threads became much tighter.

Inside Sianch is where Nathan and Sabrina's son was hidden by Dimona with her faith in righteousness, and she did it to save her grandson from the soldiers of Innahath.

The Sianch light threads lock made by the faith of Dimona in righteousness is unbroken until she gives up her faith in keeping her grandson, a child, safe from evil.

In order to keep her soul from being tortured by soldiers of Innahath at Arhush,

Satan told Dimona to give up and break her faith in the righteousness of keeping the baby safe. So as not to get her soul tortured at Arhush, and from then on, he can create an energy imbalance to assert supreme dominance in the known and unknown universes much strongly.

As the son of Nathan and Sabrina, the baby will give Satan the power to create imbalance.

As Satan's grandson holds the power of the highest order of the mortal worlds, which he got from his father Nathan, and the power of the highest order of all known and unknown universes through his mother Sabrina.

The grandson of Satan had the power to command all known and unknown universes. Satan wants that power to control all known and unknown universes by himself.

The soldiers of Innahath are walking towards the Soul of Dimona. She is getting scared, and the soldiers are walking in a square formation with four soldiers on each side.

They are throwing Mohena Chains into Sapace, walking towards Dimona's soul, and catching those Mohena Chains again.

As they were coming towards the soul of Dimona, Safire was protecting the Innahath soldiers through a wall of burning in a square shape around them. Sater came out of the Satsand of Seperna to honor the soldiers of Innahath and washed their feet.

Sapace was striking the Chains of Mohenaa with dark greenish lightning when they were throwing the Mohenaa Chains into Sapace to assert dominance over the soul of Dimona.

Dimona said in fear, crying, "They will take me; do not come in the middle when they are taking me to Arhush. You go to the sacred glow of Sianch and take your son. I fought with demons here to take my grandson from them."

Sabrina said, "No, mother, I can't let you go with them!"

Nathan said "No, mother in law. I can't let you go with them."

Dimona said, "Fool, no power in the universe can go against them, even yours!"

Sabrina replied to her mother, "But you did!"

Dimona stopped and looked at Sabrina.

Sabrina continued, "Chains of Mohenaa or any power in the universe didn't break your righteousness spell of light to protect your grandson.

You thought you offered your soul to Satan's Innahath soldiers eternally to save your grandson, but you didn't realize the soldiers of Innahath couldn't be able to break your spell of righteousness to protect a child ever.

But now we are here. Your daughter is here.

As a daughter, how can I let my mother's soul get tortured even by my father?"

Nathan said, "Oh, mother-in-law, you didn't give birth to the child you are protecting, and you didn't have to protect him as you can save yourself from the immortal pain inflicted up on you by soldiers of Innahath at Arhush, but you choose to protect our child, and you accepted the eternal pain in return to protect our child. I shall put my life on the line to protect you because there is no value to my life if I can't save and protect my child's protector from Satan, and you saved my son before me from the pain of Satan. It will be an honor to die defending you, my mother-in-law."

The Innahath soldiers came near them, and they stopped in front of them.

The Innahath leader said, "Oh, the soul of Dimona, come with us to Arhush at the order of my master. Otherwise, give up your faith in righteousness and give us the child."

Dimona said nothing.

Sabrina said, "F**k yourself, idiots!"

Nathan said to Sabrina, "Great one! Your time in my world is not a waste."

The Innahath leader said, "Princess, we bow to you!"

And bowed to her.

And the Innahath leader continued, "It is my master who told me what to do. I have to take your mother's soul to Arhush once every 13 Farush days. Otherwise, the universe will be dominated by positive forces of God Yinta, and my master will not be happy."

Sabrina said, "Your master caged Happiness in Hell. Of course, he will be happy."

The Innahath leader said, "Princess, I cannot question my master. I follow him."

Sabrina said, "Leave my mother and go back."

The Innahath leader said, "No, princess! I have to take her. If you want to save her, then win her in the Combat of Mohenaa."

Nathan went forward and said, "I will fight you!"

The Innahath leader said, "Oh, mortal immortal young man, in the Combat of Mohenaa, you cannot use any weapon against us, but we can use anything we want."

Nathan threw his trident on the chariot and said, "Come on then!"

The Innahath leader said, "The Innahath soldiers of Satan know no mercy and nothing other than their master."

And all the Innahath soldiers chanted, "Oh, master of known and unknown universes, oversee the Battle of Mohenaa and grant us the victory against this petty mortal immortal!"

Nathan walked into the square of Innahath soldiers.

Safire gave him the way to go in, and Satsand made mud to make it hard for Nathan to walk. Satsand made mud specifically under Nathan's legs, to make it hard for him to move and fight. But Satsand kept the rest of the place dry to keep it convenient for Innahath soldiers.

Sapace started raining Sater on Nathan specifically. And Safire increased its intensity and threw itself on Nathan. Sair was throwing rocks and dust at Nathan to make it harder for him to see.

Nathan had no weapon, and Innahath soldiers started coming towards him. The Innahath leader threw a big Udin rock at Nathan, and Nathan escaped it. The four soldiers of Innahath lifted themselves above the Seperna ground, raised their hands with their index fingers pointing to Sapace, commanded Sapace and Sater to throw themselves at Nathan with more intensity.

As they are in Sair floating, the Sater and Sapace poured an entire river of Sater on Nathan. And continuously enormous amounts of Sater is being poured on Nathan, making him struggle to escape the force of Sater and Satsand mix with Safire, heating the mixture.

Satsand poured on Nathan and Sair, raising dust and throwing rocks into the mixture, hitting Nathan.

The rocks hitting Nathan are getting broken and blasted. The mixture of Sater and Satsand is pouring on him. Instead of pushing it away, Nathan raised his hands up and grabbed the mixture of Satsand and Sater into his fist.

He bit himself, added a few drops of his blood into the mixture, and threw it back.

When the sacred blood of Nathan touched the anti-elements, the chaos started calming down slowly, and after some time, it completely stopped.

Nathan's blood from his bitten spot again fell on Satsand. It decreased the anti-elements' energy to zero. After some time, Satsand, Safire, Sater, Sapace, and Sair started behaving differently. They are getting the colors of life slowly.

After seeing it, the Innahath leader threw the Chains of Mohenaa on Nathan.

Nathan tried to escape by moving away from there, but Chains of Mohenaa got his hand. Nathan tried to remove the chains from his hand, but he couldn't do it.

The Innahath leader said, "Oh, mortal immortal, no power in the world can take the Chains of Mohenaa off other than my master."

Soon, the Chains of Mohenaa grabbed his two hands and legs, arresting him, and Nathan could not escape from them.

Arhush is not a place. It is a moving plate of Satsand that is triangle-shaped. The sharp side was pointing forward, and Arhush always travels with the edge of the ever-expanding universe. Satan attached Arhush to the edge of the universe, which is expanding always, and Arhush always moves away from all the known universes.

On Arhush, they had an Innahath leader chair and rings to use to lock Chains of Mohenaa.

In Seperna, the four Innahath soldiers took Nathan by pulling the Mohenaa Chains, and seeing this, Sabrina and Dimona got scared.

Ayoo got up and flew towards Nathan, but it was stabbed by the Sword of Innahath leader and fell on the Seperna ground. Ayoo screeched loudly in pain. It stayed on the ground, bleeding.

The dark greenish sphere on the ground took Innahath soldiers in, and then they took Nathan inside the sphere.

The dark greenish sphere with Nathan in Chains of Mohenaa was taking him to the edge of the universe.

The dark greenish sphere Gredar went out of Seperna and Udin. Gredar started going in the opposite direction to the side where it was said Mother Adis resides, and as they went, Nathan saw nothing but darkness. They traveled in the sphere just for a few seconds from the mortal perspective of Nathan. Nathan saw nothing in front of him.

And when the dark greenish sphere had a blast in front of it, after the blast, he saw an expansion in front of him.

They are on Arhush now. As the universe is expanding with a horizontal thick line of energy and glow moving forward, it is releasing a lot of debris and energy through blasts, and lots of matter is being formed.

As Arhush is moving forward following the horizontal thick line of universe expansion, it is infecting the matter created by Mother Adis's energy with Satan's anti-elemental nature energy.

Arhush is taking over the newly formed stars, universes, planets, and others by Mother Adis's energy through its Satanic anti-elemental power and making them part of the kingdom of Satan.

Nathan saw how the newly formed universes, planets, stars, and matter itself were damned by Satan and his forces.

The Chains of Mohenaa went inside the rings of Arhush and brought Nathan to his knees on Arhush. They are traveling with the speed of the expansion of the universe, and newly formed matter in all forms is getting infected by the anti-elemental powers of Satan.

In Seperna, Sabrina and Dimona healed Ayoo, and on the chariot, they started going towards the glow of Sianch.

In Seperna, there is nothing that can stop them now as the blood of Nathan purified Seperna and brought the colors of life into Seperna and Udin, the birthplace of Satan.

Sater is turning into Water and Satsand to Sand and Sapace into Space and Sair to Air and Safire into Fire. The dark lightning strikes on mountains in space were then turned to white.

They reached the glow of Sianch. Dimona, Sabrina got down from Chariot.

Dimona went near the glow of Sianch and sat down, closed her eyes, and said, "Oh, the Master of Masters, Oh the King of Kings, Oh the Emperor of Emperors, Oh the Son of the Brave Mortal Immortal, I and your mother came here. I pray to you to reveal yourself to us, master."

As Sabrina looked at Sianch, the glow decreased, and slowly, the light threads faded away, revealing her son's face and then the rest of his body.

The baby saw his mother and smiled, making happy noises.

Sabrina, in tears, ran to her son, took him into her hands, and gave him kisses. Seeing it, Dimona felt happy.

Sabrina said, "Your father! He came for you, son. He is fighting for you. And he will come for us."

Nathan in Chains of Mohenaa tied to Traingle Satsand Plate of Arhush.

The chains went tight, and Nathan was on his knees, seeing the Satanification of newly formed worlds by Mother Adis's energy.

Nathan, thinking of his son, felt sad. The father in him is feeling the pain, and the Prophet in him saw the destruction of pure worlds into Satanic, just like what happened to the Earth.

As the Arhush moved with the expansion of the universe, the Innahath leader got his sword from the Arhush weapon box, 'Aneka.'

Aneka has all the weapons of Satanic forces and units. Aneka gives an unlimited number of physical and mental weapons to demons and forces of Satan. There are many Anekas with the soldiers of Satan throughout the known and unknown universes.

Any weapon that comes out of Aneka, mental or physical, was designed by Arusthra, the dear follower of Satan.

Arusthra eats the pain of people to survive. He sends demons of Satan to the worlds where life forms exist and gives them problems.

Some life forms use those problems and pain to reach God Yinta. And some weak-minded life forms succumb to it, providing Arusthra with food of pain. After their death, these weak-minded people, usually by suicide because of problems in life, go to Hell and become slaves to Satan under Arusthra, where they are stuck for eternity.

Arusthra was told by demons in Hell about Nathan. And he learned that Nathan was on Arhush and would face the wrath of his weapons now.

Innahath leader took a mental weapon out of Arhush Aneka. It is a metal block of dark liquid that causes the pain of losing a child to a parent.

The Innahath leader, with this weapon in his hand, came near Nathan. There, the other Innahath soldiers are standing beside the chair of the Innahath leader.

Innahath leader placed the metal block of dark liquid on Nathan's head.

The Arhush triangle plate is traveling simultaneously with the expansion speed of the universe. The worlds, universes, planets, stars, and other matter were being created by the ultimate sacred energy of Mother Adis and immediately taken over by Satanic powers and getting Satanized.

The child loss pain - weapon's metal block of dark liquid is slowly going inside of Nathan's head and into his brain.

It caused uncomfortable feelings to Nathan initially, and as it went into his brain, the pain started for him, but it was not a physical wound pain or injury pain.

It is the pain coming from his emotional side with a feeling that he lost his son and his son is dead, which is not true, but the mental weapon of child loss is making him believe that.

He is becoming emotionally weak as he has gone completely into the trance of the mental weapon of child loss. And he now completely believed that he had lost his child.

The pain Nathan was feeling was unexplainable, and he believed that he was the reason for the death of his child and that he was responsible for it.

A father cannot bear losing his child, let alone him being the reason for it. The mental weapon of child loss is causing that feeling in him.

Nathan is trying to fight back, but he is struggling inside.

He closed his eyes, and tears were coming out of his eyes.

The dark liquid is completely inside his brain now.

He was remembering his son and completely believed that his son was dead, and he killed him accidentally at the glow of Sianch in Seperna while fighting against Innahath soldiers.

The dark liquid took over Nathan, and it made him think of his mother and father in Wizbome and how bad of a son he was for leaving them alone on Earth when they needed him most in their old age.

The dark liquid made him think of how bad a husband he was, since he didn't even spend a little happy time with Sabrina and didn't bring her what she liked.

The dark liquid in his brain made him think about how bad of a human being he was because he never fought against injustice in Wizbome, and the dark liquid made him think how weak he was to get beaten by thugs and let them steal his car on Beruk highway.

He was told by Dark Liquid how bad a friend he was, because Ira was possessed by Heezle. And Jiza was trying to save her but couldn't.

Nathan, a friend of theirs, gave them his word that he would get them married by convincing their families because Ira is Krisen and Jiza is Ateestan. But he couldn't save Ira from Heezle now.

At that moment, he remembered Ira and Jiza and the word he had given them.

Nathan opened his eyes, and as the dark liquid took over him, showing the universe's expansion as if it were a Kingdom of Satan.

But Nathan, deep inside, is trying to come out of Dark Liquid's Trance and make sense through rationality within himself to see the universe expanding from the Arhush Satsand triangle plate as it is.

But dark liquid is not letting him see the universe as it is with his own eyes and only showing him the universe as the Kingdom of Satan, which is impossible, as Mother Adis will not allow it to happen.

The Chains of Mohenaa are so strong that they are not letting Nathan go from them. Nathan, in the great struggle within himself, shaking, shouted, "Iffure ahaan Satane, Adis!"

Which means, "Adis, Save me from the creations of Satan."

They are on Arhush, and Arhush is going with the edge of the universe expansion and making Satanic power take over new worlds created by Mother Adis's energy and Satanizing them.

Innahath soldiers saw a trident coming towards them from far away at a speed more than Mother Adis's universe expansion creations.

The power to liberate Nathan from the dark liquid is not in the trident but in the assurance Mother Adis gave to Nathan with the trident that she is with progress and not destruction.

It is the same trident Nathan left in the chariot in Seperna. Sabrina and Dimona saw the trident going to space in Seperna, The Hollow of Dimona.

Nathan got to know about Mother Adis, The First Energy, for the first time in the Yira sacred forest.

He saw the carving of Satan and God Yinta standing in front of Adis, their mother, on the sacred stone with five sacred dots inside the sacred snake's nest in the holy cave.

The serpent trident of Nathan came with loud thunderstorms and hymns. It struck the Chains of Mohenaa, and a link of Mohenaa broke after being hit by Nathan's trident.

The Innahath soldiers and their leader were flabbergasted.

There is no one in the universe who broke the Chains of Mohenaa, even God Yinta, in the war of Nazreck because of respect for his Mother, Adis; he escaped them rather than engaging with them.

But now Nathan broke the Chains of Mohenaa with the moral assurance from Mother Adis.

Nathan's trident came into his right hand, and he got up from his knees. His eyes started glowing red, and with his trident, he struck the remaining chains tied to his hand. They broke.

The Innahath soldiers are scared now.

He threw the trident to the front side, and with bare hands, he broke off the chains into small pieces and threw them into Space. Arhush, the triangle plate is moving steadily forward with the expansion of the universe.

The trident came to him, and Nathan caught it. He started walking towards the Innahath leader's chair, and the Innahath leader moved away from Nathan.

Nathan sat in the Innahath leader's chair. The Innahath soldiers are scared, and they are amazed that someone can challenge their master now.

Nathan said in Satanic language, "Een Adis arusm, Satane arusm hiras ladh!"

Innahath leader, after hearing it, prayed to Satan, "Gredar, Rusul taake."

After the spell, Gredar - a darkish green light sphere came to them, and Innahath soldiers went inside of it, and they escaped to Hell to meet Arusthra.

After the Innahath soldiers ran away, Nathan looked at the creation of new worlds, and he waved his trident.

Arhush stopped the Satanification of those worlds and matter. All the newly created worlds and matter by Mother Adis's energy were left pure and as intended by Mother Adis.

Nathan got to know from the child loss mental weapon of Aneka that by the overconfidence of Arusthra, Arusthra assumed the life form that was getting tortured by the mental weapon of child loss would be so helpless that that life form will not be able to do anything, no matter how much the mental weapon tortures that life form.

In that overconfidence, Arusthra's mental weapon of child loss from Aneka, the unlimited weapon box, revealed to Nathan that Ira was possessed by Heezle.

Innahath soldiers went to Hell and met Arusthra. Innahath leader informed Arusthra that Nathan took over Arhush, the Satsand triangle plate.

Arusthra got angry and cast the Innahath leader into the Beeliaal - Satan energy pact. It released a lot of energy, and Arusthra absorbed it.

Arusthra does not have legs and hands, but he is an immortal being.

It is because he was once punished by Sumaaraa for attacking a cat in the Sacred Yira forest under Heaven when Sumaaraa was praying to the sacred stone.

Sumaaraa heard the cry of the cat and got angry. She came out of the sacred cave and saw Arusthra. She has cut Arusthra's hands and legs in anger with her sword. Sumaaraa is the lover of God Yinta and the daughter of the Emperor of Emptiness, Beeliaal.

Nathan is on Arhush, and with his trident, he struck the Aneka weapon box. The Aneka weapon box blasted, and he took the weapons and energy into his fist, threw it on the Arhush surface, and crushed it with his leg. The energy turned into dust.

Nathan heard a voice in his mind, "Your work here is still incomplete, but your friends need you now."

Nathan took his trident and saw the new worlds being created. He threw his trident to the backside, and an energy line came out of it, and it attached itself to Arhush, the triangle plate.

It stopped Arhush from going with the expansion of the universe, and started going backwards to the side of Udin.

The new worlds are being created, but Mother Adis's energy is now flowing pure without Satan's energy infecting the worlds and matter with his evil demons. Nathan broke the bond between the universe expansion by Mother Adis, the first source of energy, and Arhush, the Satsand triangle plate made by Satan at the beginning of times.

As Nathan is going towards Udin on Arhush, Nathan, with his trident, is making a way into the vast space filled by the matter and worlds created by Mother Adis's energy earlier. He saw millions of suns and planetary worlds with many life forms on them.

He looked into the space in front of him with great intensity. The trident started going at unimaginable speeds, and it is taking Arhush with Nathan on it.

He crossed trillions of worlds in his path. He understood, he had to visit each and every one of them to make them pure by removing Satan's influence on them. But he was told by the voice to go back to his friends. Nathan reached Udin in 4 Farush days.

In the mortal human world of Earth, one Farush day is equal to 299999 Earth years. But the space-time of the sub-world Earth, where Nathan comes from, was adjusted and regulated to the Farush time of the Master Universe by Farush. The Heaven time and the Hell time, Udin time, and Sacred Yira forest time are in different time zones of the Master Universe.

When Nathan first came to the Master Universe, he didn't see the other seven worlds Sabrina showed him on the way to Udin because Ayoo crossed those seven worlds between Earth, the sub-universe, and the 'Nothing' place in the Master Universe timeline. And Nathan didn't recognize it.

As Arhush approached Udin, Nathan saw a beautiful view of greenery. He came very near to Udin and saw the mountains of Udin covered with forest and sacred animals in the forest, like he saw in the Sacred Yira forest under Heaven.

He saw a big lion hunting a deer in the forest. He went to Seperna, the Hollow of Dimona Endless Abyss entrance, and entered it.

He saw a beautiful world with big trees, rivers, and waterfalls.

The complete opposite of what was there before. He got off from Arhush, the triangle plate. As he walked into the Seperna abyss, he saw Sabrina laughing and his son smiling and looking at his mother.

Nathan teared up. And he walked up to them. Sabrina, in happiness, didn't observe Nathan, and when Nathan went close to them, Nathan's son saw his father for the first time.

Sabrina saw her son's eyes, wondered what he was looking at, and turned her head. She saw Nathan, and there was no limit to her happiness then. Nathan took his son into his hands.

Nathan said, "Aarus, my son, I brought Arhush for you. It will be your toy from now on." And kissed his son on the forehead. They sat under a sacred Banyan tree on a stone.

A sacred, magical river is flowing behind them. Dimona saw Nathan and Sabrina with their son. She had tears in her eyes.

Ayoo came screeching happily, and Nathan saw it and smiled. It recovered from injury caused by the Innahath leader.

Nathan said, "I have to go."

Sabrina asked nervously, "Where now?"

Nathan said, "Our friends.. Huro, Tes, and Kwin are still at Farush. And Ira got possessed by Heezle on Earth."

Sabrina was shocked.

She said, "I will come with you."

Nathan said, "No, I will come for you and our son," and looked at Aarus.

Then continued, "You can stay here till I come back. No one will bother you. This is our home now. And Koshi didn't leave the Master Universe forever. I sent him to the Earth sub-universe." And gave Aarus to Sabrina.

Sabrina was shocked that her brother wasn't in Mother Adis and on Earth. Nathan took his trident and closed his eyes. When he opened his eyes, he made a big castle of Happiness in Seperna, the Hollow of Dimona. He then kissed Sabrina's forehead. And he got on Ayoo and left Seperna.

Aarus is looking at his dad, and he is sad. Sabrina and Dimona, too, are sad.

Nathan reached Farush on Ayoo. And saw a war check post at the side of the sacred waterfall, which Nathan told The Three to bathe in to attain immortality.

He landed on Farush in front of the check post at the sacred waterfall. And The Three came to Nathan in Happiness.

Tes said, "We thought you forgot about us."

Nathan said, "Never in my life will I forget about my friends."

Huro said, "See, I told you. He will come for us again."

Nathan asked, "Why didn't you leave for Earth's sub-universe? Rather than waiting here?"

Kwin: "Oh! You are a great friend, but you thought we would betray you?"

Nathan: "No, guys!"

Huro: "It's ok, boss! But we worked on constructing the check posts here on our side. The demons of Satan came here many times, and they looked over their side."

Nathan said, "I know! But we have something more important to do now than this!"

Huro: "But we don't have as much time and resources as they do."

Nathan: "Yes, but we will come back, and we have to leave the Master Universe now."

Kwin: "Why?"

Nathan: "Jiza and Ira needs our help!"

In shock, Tes asked, "What happened to them?"

Nathan said, "Come with me. I'll show you."

Huro: "Where is Sabrina?"

Nathan: "She is in Seperna, at our home."

Kwin said, "Oh," and looked at Tes and said, "I don't know!"

Huro said, "We saw Yinta!"

Nathan was surprised and asked, "You saw who?"

Kwin said, "Yes, we saw God Yinta. Well, not closely, but from far away. He is going somewhere. He is on a White Horse. It has wings."

Nathan said, "What? He is a God. He can literally move in space. And where would he go on a white horse with wings? If he is everywhere. And how do you even know that it is God Yinta?"

Huro said, "We don't know all that. We just saw him on a white horse with wings, and I'm sure it is not possible for anyone to look like that and make a person feel pure inside with just plain sight other than by God himself."

Nathan laughed. And said, "Maybe you saw an angel!"

Tes said, "Na.. Na.. No angel can be like him."

Kwin said, "He had hair like yours! And a very beautiful face."

Nathan said, "ok, then you saw Yinta. Then why don't you go on your sacred eagles to meet and talk to him? You got the sacred eagles, right?"

Huro said, "No, we thought it should be done on his command only, and we cannot try to be his equals by flying next to him."

Nathan laughed and said, "Maybe he thought and wished you would go to him and talk to him after seeing him, but you didn't. He might have been disappointed."

The Three felt a little sad and shocked.

Then Nathan continued, "Maybe he likes you. That is why he allowed you to come to the Master Universe before your death. You believe nothing is done in all of the universes without his permission, right?"

The Three nodded, and Nathan continued, "Then you should have taken the opportunity to go to him and talk to him. No one is equal to God, just like a Banyan tree knows what it means to be a seed. Like that, he knows who you are. You don't have to fear offending him if you have the best intentions in your mind."

The Three were thinking deeply, looking at each other, wondering if they had made a bad decision by not approaching God Yinta after seeing him.

Nathan said, "We can meet him later, guys. But we need to go now."

They started to travel back to Earth, and after some time, they reached the Brunuck Line of the Master Universe. Within minutes, they are in Earth's atmosphere, and they are invisible to mortal life as the Farush in the Master Universe is working on creating energy equilibrium till they land on Earth.

# 5

They landed in Hervin forest near Nathan's cabin. Ayoo and the sacred eagles landed in the middle of the forest, where Nathan got on Ayoo last time. Nathan got down from Ayoo, and The Three got down from their sacred eagles.

They started walking towards the cabin. On their path, Nathan felt like he was seeing a different forest than what he had seen before going to the Master Universe. The Three felt normal.

They reached the cabin. They saw the ashes of wood burned by The Three before going to the Master Universe. They are in their mortal bodies now, but they are immortal. And they looked just like before they left for the Master Universe.

Nathan and The Three are just looking like mortals after coming near the cabin. Nathan saw the doors of the cabin open, and he saw many things on the floor. It looked like someone had tried to rob the cabin.

But Nathan didn't go inside, and The Three saw it.

Huro said, "Oh my God. What happened..?" And started going towards the cabin.

Nathan said, "No, we must go to Ira's house now."

Kwin said, "Why? What is the emergency? It looks like someone robbed our cabin."

Nathan said "No, no one robbed our cabin. The police came here to search!"

The Three remembered what they did.

And Nathan said, "Sabrina told me Ira's address."

They saw Nathan's car in front of the cabin with doors open.

The seats of the car were torn, and it looked like someone had searched for something in it. Nathan saw his car. He sat in it.

He forgot where he placed the car keys. So he took two wires from the car at the ignition lock, cut them, and connected them. The car started, but the fuel was low, as shown by the fuel indicator. The Three sat in the car. Huro sat in the front passenger seat. Nathan started driving, and they were on the Beruk highway.

They stopped at a gas station for petrol, but they didn't have money. They saw a gas station worker.

Nathan gave him his phone and said, "Please keep it and fill the tank with petrol. I will give you money later and take my phone."

The gas station worker said, "Don't worry. Today is our anniversary. We are giving a 50 percent discount to our customers today. And today is also my birthday. I will pay the regular price for the half tank of petrol, and you get the other half through the discount."

Nathan said, "God bless you, bro. Happy birthday! Your life will be changed soon to the greatest."

The gas station worker said, "Thank you, bro.. "

He filled the full tank of petrol. And The Three said, "Thank you, bro!" To the gas station worker, and they left.

They reached Relsar. And in the city now. It was night, 7, at the time they reached Ira's house. Ira's house is in a quiet neighborhood with old, destroyed, abandoned houses. And Ira's house is the only house with people. They stopped at Ira's house.

The house was quiet as they observed from outside.

Nathan and The Three came out of the car and stood in front of the house.

Nathan walked up to the front and rang the doorbell. No one came. He rang the bell twice, but there was no one. The Three and Nathan are wondering what is happening inside.

Suddenly, the front door opened, and Ira came out smiling with a handbag. And looked at Nathan, The Three. She stopped and looked back into the house and said, "I'm going, Mom. Bye."

Ira came onto the road and started walking, ignoring Nathan and The Three.

Nathan went inside the house. The Three are looking at Ira as she is walking on the road in the darkness. Nathan is in the hall, and the house is dead silent. He went into the kitchen and saw Jiza bleeding with a knife in his leg. He quickly went to him, and Jiza was unconscious. Nathan ran outside and asked Kwin to come inside.

Kwin and Nathan ran to Jiza, lifted him up, and took him outside.

Jiza got conscious. And struggling to speak while bleeding.

Kwin said, "Jiza, we are here. We will take you to the hospital!"

Jiza said, "I know! She just stabbed me in the leg. I won't die.."

Jiza then continued, "She has a demon inside of her. She sent her mother to Hell while her mother was still alive. When her mother tried to stop her from going outside. I don't know what is inside of her, but it is not a normal demon. I saw Hell on Earth in the f**ing hall."

Tes went inside and searched for a first aid box in the kitchen cupboards. He found it. He came out and cleaned the blood on Jiza's leg. The ambulance arrived. When they got the Stretcher to take Jiza to the hospital, Jiza insisted he didn't want to go to the hospital. A Health worker who came with the ambulance called a local doctor. Jiza told the health worker that he would pay extra money for the treatment. The doctor arrived in his van with surgery equipment in a bag.

Nathan asked the health worker in which hospital the doctor worked.

The health worker said, "He is not working. He is my friend. The hospital he is working in fired him."

Jiza asked, "Why?" in fear.

The health worker said, "He saved a person who attempted suicide by drinking poison, but the person whom he saved didn't have insurance or money with him. He came to Wizbome illegally. The hospital fired my friend for treating an illegal immigrant without confirming the security deposit from him."

The doctor came to Jiza and sat down. He saw Jiza's wound and the knife inside his thigh. He took his tools out and started the treatment. Kwin left Jiza and joined Huro.

Huro and Kwin followed Ira, who was at the end of the

neighborhood's main road. Huro and Kwin ran fast and stood in front of Ira. Ira stopped and looked at Huro and Kwin. Ira smiled and said, "Who are you?" innocently.

Huro said, "Ira, it's me. Huro. We met at Nathan's cabin. You and Jiza came there."

Ira replied angrily, "Who is Jiza? Who are you? I'm going."

Huro and Kwin again stopped her.

Ira gave them a weird look.

Huro said, "Come home, Ira!"

Kwin said, "Yes, Ira. Where are you going at this time? Come home with us!"

Ira said nothing, and her head was down, looking at the road.

Huro then said, "Ira.. I am talking to you. Why are you silent? Come with me."

Kwin said, "Ira.. Come..!"

He grabbed her arm and started walking, but he couldn't move her even an inch. He stopped and tried to pull her, but he couldn't at all.

Kwin stopped and wondered why he couldn't even make her move an inch, at least, no matter how much force he pulled her to take her home.

Ira lifted her head and looked at Kwin.

She said, "Cheap Krisen Slave Dog! Take your hands off me." In a fierce, angry, loud male voice.

It scared Kwin and Huro.

Ira lifted her leg into the air and kicked Kwin on his chest. Kwin went back flying and fell down. And he was in pain, grunting. Huro quickly ran to Kwin and helped him get up. When he turned back, Ira was not there.

They are tense now.

In the darkness, they heard a noise. They looked around but saw no one. They heard another noise again in the bushes between two abandoned houses.

Huro and Kwin walked into those bushes, but Ira was not there. They searched there, turned around, and walked back.

On the path, they saw a bone with a thick black thread tied around it.

Huro and Kwin stopped suddenly after seeing it. They are looking at it.

They don't know what it is. And they don't know who placed it there.

The weather is becoming chaotic. The speed of the wind is increasing.

Huro and Kwin are trying to figure out what it is.

The sound of bushes and trees was scaring them.

The dust is rising in the air.

In the darkness, with street lights accompanying them, they saw a shadow on the road, with horns on its head and wings on its back. That shadow created chills in them with fear in their hearts.

They are scared now, even to move their feet. Suddenly, the shadow transformed into Ira, and with wings on her back, she flew toward Huro and Kwin and came on top of their heads, flying. Suddenly, when Ira flew on top of them, Huro grabbed Ira's legs and stopped her.

Ira is trying to escape into the woods on the backside of abandoned houses. While struggling to pull her, Huro said to Kwin, "Idiot.. Help me.."

Kwin, though in fear, grabbed the legs of Ira, and both started pulling her. Ira couldn't fly forward and was in the air while being pulled back by Huro and Kwin.

She kicked. Kwin took the hit on the cheeks, but he didn't let go.

Huro said, "Oh, God Yinta, I know you, and I saw you. I know you are the only one true God. Help me save this woman!"

And after saying it. He shouted, "Ira.." Loudly.

The wings disappeared, and she fell down. Huro and Kwin caught her. They took her to her house. But while taking her back, they walked over the bone and the black thread tied around it unknowingly.

The bone and black thread around it are part of a process called 'Sireha'. It is one of the Satanic dark magic witchcraft rituals. The one who crosses the Sireha bone will be haunted by Heezle and his servant demons for eternity. Huro and Kwin, with Ira, walked over it.

Nathan felt something when Huro, Kwin, and Ira walked over the Sireha bone.

Sireha is not a simple dark magic ritual made to trouble people.

Nathan looked at Jiza while the doctor was treating Jiza.

Sireha is a nasty, scariest form of mental dark ritual attack. Anyone who falls prey to it can never survive. Heezle's demons go mad and animalistic on people who cross Sireha bone.

The demons, Heezle, had already come, and they surrounded Huro, Kwin, and Ira.

Ira became conscious of her body, and her own mind is active now. She saw demons for a second through her eyes while her mind was becoming conscious, and it scared her to death.

She screamed loudly in fear. Huro and Kwin asked her, "What happened?"

She said, "I saw demons!"

Huro asked, "Where?"

They looked around, but nothing was there.

The demons were revolving and running around Huro, Kwin, and Ira. But Huro and Kwin drank water from Farush's sacred waterfall in the Master Universe.

Huro and Kwin's aura was scaring the demons. Ira is with them, and demons cannot touch her, too, now.

Huro said, "Sister, I will never let any demon touch you or come near you. They have to take my life first to touch you!"

Kwin said, "Mine too, sister. Be brave. We are with you. God Yinta is with us!"

Ira, Huro, and Kwin started walking toward Ira's house.

The demons are coming with them. But Huro, Ira, and Kwin couldn't see them.

As they came near Ira's house, Nathan saw them. But he also saw Heezle with them.

After giving the treatment, The Doctor sat there, and the ambulance left.

Jiza told Nathan, "Ira is pregnant!"

Nathan was stunned.

Nathan walked out from the porch and is now standing in the middle of the road.

Nathan saw Ira, Huro, and Kwin walking toward him, and he also saw demons revolving around them as they were walking.

Nathan was looking at those demons.

Heezle left from there while Nathan was seeing his friends walking towards him.

Ira saw Nathan, and she was smiling.

Nathan smiled back at Ira. He started walking towards them.

The demons saw Nathan and left Ira, Huro, and Kwin.

The demons were coming towards Nathan, but no one could see them except Nathan.

Nathan knows they can't touch him and wants to scare him. Nathan stood there as they were coming towards him. And he saw the Sireha bone and black thread tied around it from far away.

He walked toward Sireha bone as Ira, Huro, and Kwin were coming toward him.

The demons came to Nathan, but they didn't do anything to him as Heezle had ordered.

Nathan is seeing demons revolving around him and on top of him.

He is hearing their cries and screams.

They are terrible and scary.

A mortal will die in fear if he is in the same position.

Nathan continued walking, and he crossed Ira, Huro, and Kwin.

They thought Nathan was coming to them, but he continued walking.

While demons are around him, Nathan reached the Sireha bone. And he took the Sireha bone with black thread tied around it into his hands.

He understood someone, a human being, must have kept it there in order to take control of Huro, Ira, and Kwin.

He turned back and suddenly saw Heezle.

Heezle has pure red skin with no hair on his body anywhere, and he has wings and horns. Heezle's skin is burning from the inside, and a red glow is coming out. There is no one around, and in the darkness, for the first time on Earth sub-universe, Nathan saw a servant of Satan. And he is standing in front of him.

When the Sireha dark satanic ritual witchcraft is executed on someone or groups of people, Heezle will never leave without taking the soul of at least one person who walked over the Sireha bone or the one who touched the Sireha bone.

Heezle left the body of Ira when Huro invoked the word of God. But Heezle can't leave now without taking at least one soul from Earth because he was bound by the rule of the Saden demons village that Heezle must take a soul after he was called by Sireha.

The demons at Saden demon village will make the soul that Heezle takes to Saden a slave for eternity, and they give this soul to Satan when he visits Saden as a gift.

To impress their king, Satan, they take souls in this way and gift him. If Heezle goes back to Saden demon village without a soul after being called by the Sireha ritual, they will take Heezle as a slave and will send him to Khudish, A graveyard of energy, as punishment.

At Khudish, Heezle will become a part of the ruins of the Master Universe.

Anyone who goes to Khudish will become singular, and they will not exist anymore in any known or unknown universes in any form. It is a painful process of going out of existence for any demon or force.

Going to Khudish for demons and evil forces is equal to human beings dying physically on Earth, which means when humans die, they don't exist physically on Earth but become part of it as their body is burned or buried in the Earth.

This, too, is like that for Demons and evil forces. At Khudish, they become part of singularity, and they don't exist in any Master Universes or any other sub-universes anymore. It is the eternal end to them.

Satan uses Khudish to make anyone who opposes him disappear from all known and unknown universes. No power in the universe knows what is inside of Khudish. It was said that at the beginning of time, when Satan had a conflict with God Yinta. God Yinta had great support from angels. Satan became jealous of God Yinta's popularity among angels and planned to destroy those angels, but it was not easy, as they were powerful and had the support of Mother Adis.

So Satan, after parting ways with his mother and brother. He came to Saden and told demons to create a singular, endless pit that if anyone falls into it, they will never come back.

The demons made the singular endless pit by using the power of Satan for 468 Farush years. It was said that even many angels stopped thinking about Satan in fear after they got to know about Khudish, the singular graveyard cosmic endless pit of destruction.

In Ira's neighborhood, where Nathan took the Sireha bone into his hands,

Heezle looked at Nathan and smiled.

Nathan smiled back.

Heezle grabbed Nathan's hand.

Suddenly, Nathan was taken to a very beautiful place. It looked like Heaven.

Nathan was looking around and realized Heezle took him to a place called Satan Heaven, where souls of people who accepted Satan go in their afterlife.

It looked just like Heaven and had all kinds of entertaining things.

Heezle told Nathan, "Satan Heaven!"

Then Heezle continued, "See this, look how beautiful it is.."

And looked at Nathan. Nathan nodded in agreement.

Heezle said, "Imagine what you will be like if you accept Satan as your one true master!"

Nathan: "Ok, what will I be like? If I accept Satan as my master?"

Heezle: "Ahh!?"

Nathan again said, "Yeah, tell me what I will be like if I accept Satan as my one true master."

Heezle: "He will give you anything you want.."

Nathan: "Anything I want?"

Heezle: "Yes, Anything you want."

Nathan again asked, "Anything... I want?"

Heezle again answered, "Yes! Anything you want.."

Nathan: "Money?"

Heezle: "Yes, as much money as you want.."

Nathan: "Fame and popularity?"

Heezle: "Yes, Super popularity and fame.."

Nathan: "Beautiful woman and health?"

Heezle: "Yes, beautiful woman and health. Immortality, too, if you offer your soul to the one true master, Satan.."

Nathan: "Alcohol and other luxuries like cars, yachts, and anything?"

Heezle: "Yes, Anything you want.."

Nathan : "Happiness?"

Heezle: "Yes, you will never be sad again in your life."

Nathan: "So, Satan will give me anything I want?"

Heezle: "Yes!"

Nathan asked Heezle, "Let's say I accepted Satan as my master!"

Heezle gave an evil smile.

Nathan continued, "He gave me money, popularity, a beautiful woman, health, and all luxuries!"

Heezle: "Yes!"

Nathan: "Then, what is the use if I have all of them, but I do not know how to keep them safe, maintain them, and take care of them?"

Heezle: "What are you talking about? They will be with you no matter what."

Nathan: "So it doesn't matter whether I know how to keep them safe and take care of them or not. They will be with me forever!"

Heezle said, "Yes, that is correct."

Nathan said, "Then I want to tell you something. If lots of money is being given to me by Satan and I don't know how to take care of it, I don't know how to invest it, and I do not know how to increase it by my own intelligence, then all I see is my incompetence and someone who likes me or wants something from me just spoiling me, and I don't know what good I can do with that money to myself and my fellow human beings.

It feels good at first, but I certainly don't know how to keep it safe and increase it morally. I'm just being given the money without my effort in any manner, physical or mental. Not even by luck. I'm just being given that money. I might enjoy my life with that money, but I will soon get bored with all the fun and enjoyment, and I wish to die soon in boredom, actually, because there are no challenges and things to do in my life. Satan will make me successful in everything, and I know it beforehand.

Everything is being given to me. Soon, I will forget the value of those things that were given to me. I don't even know their value to begin with, as I was given them for free in exchange for my soul. So, it's not technically free. But free.

If someone who worked hard lost all of their money, there is a chance that they may earn all of that money again because they went through the process of learning and struggling to earn that money. They know how it feels in real time and the pain involved.

But I didn't, and if suddenly Satan changes his mind and takes away everything from me, then what happens to me?

I was habituated to all the luxuries and enjoyments, but was now left with nothing. I did not know how to earn that money again because I didn't have those skills.

Even if you give me those skills, they can be taken away too. Anything given without my effort to acquire and learn it myself can be taken away. How can I accept your offer of unlimited money? Even if I accept now and enjoy it till you take it away, still, my mindset will change with all the luxury and enjoyment I had, and I don't like to work hard from that minute to earn the same money by myself. It is a problem from any perspective. So I don't need your money. Actually, I have a great chance of becoming comfortably rich if I learn advanced technology or skills and get into high-paying professions or start a company.

In this way, I will learn everything by myself and with the help of others and develop a strong mental resilience and strength to failure too.

I know I can take money from Satan and then learn money management skills by myself. But I also know there is no workaround when Satan is involved. He will crush the soul in one way or another."

Heezle said, "Not just money. You can have any woman you want..

beautiful woman.."

Nathan said, "Yes, I can have any woman I want if I accept Satan as my one true master, but the question is, does that beautiful woman whom I want, does she want me too?

Or you just change something inside of her so that she starts liking me. If you do something like that, then she doesn't really like me. But you just changed something in her mind and made her like me, without her free will in making the decision of whether to love me or not.

She might like me, love me with all her heart and soul for the rest of her life, but I know that she didn't love me naturally; it is Satan who made her love me.

I know that truth. How can I be with her knowing this? And it amounts to manipulation and rape, actually, if you make her love me and I have sex with her.

How can I become a rapist? I can't.. And if Satan one day changes his mind and he doesn't want my soul anymore. Then she will stop loving me and leave me.

If I love her truly, how can I see her leave me?

And even if I gather the strength in me to see her leave me,

Then, to make her fall in love with me again, or at least even to try, I'm not the one who made her fall in love with me initially. It was Satan. And I don't know how it feels to make her fall in love with me, or know whether she loved me and wanted me before I started loving her.

I don't know why or how she felt the feeling of loving me, to at least behave, talk, or do something to make her feel that way again. So I do not want any woman to love me just because I gave my soul to Satan!"

Then Heezle said, "You can become famous, popular in the entire world!"

Nathan said, "There are many people who are popular and wealthy in the world who didn't offer their souls to Satan. And they are still popular and wealthy."

Heezle said, "But you do not know how to become like them, and not even one person can become super wealthy and famous among billions."

Nathan said, "Yeah.. But if I have a great talent or knowledge in something, I can reasonably become popular, and if I really concentrate and work hard on some skills or business, then I can become famous and rich. And even if I don't, I still have those skills I learned.

And with you, it is the same with talent and skill. I will be famous and popular as long as Satan wants my soul, and if he doesn't want my soul, then I will be forgotten by people, and I don't know how to become popular and famous again because I don't know the process and I don't have the mental resilience to do it naturally by myself the second time."

Heezle said, "You can become healthy and live forever!"

Nathan asked, "Does living forever mean I can become an immortal being?"

Heezle said, "Yes.."

Nathan said, "If I drink alcohol, etc, daily and get high, then I only alter everything in my mind, but the world and reality are not changing in any way. And also it is a bad habit. I don't want to do it.

Even if I drink daily and get sick, I will at least be in control then because I will have the fear that I will die. Otherwise, I will be high all the time and waste my life by doing nothing, especially if I accept your immortality. I will become a burden to the Earth itself by not being productive in any way and by not having any purpose for my existence.

I will literally become trash. At least the trash can be recycled. Being healthy is important, and I also want to drink a little and enjoy the drink after doing something great in my life rather than drinking like an idiot.

My food habits and other habits are already good. I am now, and even in the future, I will be healthy anyhow. If you tell me, I will never get any diseases. Then okay, it is good, but when Satan is done with my soul and doesn't want my soul anymore, then I will get diseases and die quickly. Also, Life is boring if you live forever. What will you do by living forever? After living for 200 years, for example?

The process of enjoyment and everything becomes dead boring, and you wish for death, actually, to see another world in the afterlife to kill the boring routine life you have, and you seek a new adventure from then in the afterlife."

Heezle said, "Then you can come here. To Satan's Heaven. It has beautiful women, tasty food, drinks, and eternal happiness."

Nathan said, "Earth has very beautiful women already. All I have to do is impress one of them, and I can be with her. Earth already has great food and drinks. If you want to eat healthily or just to satisfy your tongue, they have all the food and drinks. They have beautiful mansions and houses. They got planes and luxurious cars. The people of Earth got everything you offer here in Satan Heaven. The people of the Earth actually have everything that you have here in Satan's Heaven and also many things extra.

And they also have one extra thing that is super precious, which is children. The ability to give birth to babies by women, raise them, and see them do something great in their lives.

There are many types of Happiness on Earth. But this is precious.

The happiness you get when you achieve something in life, the happiness you get when you learn something, and the happiness you get when you do something in general. But the happiness you get through children has no measurement and no comparison.

In fact, even if we get happiness from all these situations, strangely, happiness is a result of our perspective. No matter what we are going through, good or bad, I can choose to be happy or not. So my happiness is in my hands. Not in Satan's or anyone's."

Heezle said, "No, mortal happiness is different, and immortal happiness given by Satan is different. Happiness given by Satan is eternal. There is no sadness or anything other than happiness in Satan's offer."

Nathan said, "Then why should I give my soul to Satan for eternal happiness or whatever? God Yinta is giving that happiness to me here on Earth and also after my death in Heaven without even taking my soul or anything from me. All he wants from me is to be honest, work hard and smart, learn new things, and help people. Just those types of things. They actually help me to become a better person by myself naturally, and God Yinta is not even threatening me through his demon servant so that I will accept him as my one true master. I'm accepting God Yinta as my one true master God because I like him, his principles, and his teachings."

Heezle said, "You are not getting the core point of Satan's offerings to you."

Nathan said, "Explain to me what they are."

Heezle said, "You can get anything and everything without any struggle and pain to achieve it, and fear of losing it. You will never have to face failure, humiliation, and shame. You will see only successes."

Nathan said, "Then what is the difference between me and a slave?"

Heezle asked, "What do you mean?"

Nathan said, "A slave only works just to live and to survive out of fear of his master. And I, as a slave to Satan, see only success and happiness that comes with my submission to Satan. And I get success only by forever being a slave to Satan. I don't want to be a slave. My God told me that I have the freedom and the choice to walk away from anything, even from him, but I still stay because I love God, and it is free will real devotion, not any other thing like being a slave to Satan."

Heezle said, "Come with me. You don't need God anymore, you don't need anything, and you will have no problems anymore. I will ask my master to keep you in the Satan Heaven for eternity, and you don't need to leave. My master will give you his word of your eternal place in the Satan Heaven."

Nathan said, "No, I will go to sacred Heaven. The Heaven which was created by God Yinta, not the fake Heaven.

Heezle got angry and loudly said, "You human! You will not honor my master even after being offered everything in the world in exchange for it. You deserve to die, but you are immortal now. I will take you to Khudish and will make you disappear from all known and unknown universes."

Nathan smiled and said, "Try, I will cut you into a million pieces here and now."

Heezle smiled and said, "You know what the problem is with you, Nathan? You think you are intelligent, but the problem with intelligence is that it is in your mind and only in your mind. It means nothing if you don't apply, can't apply, or if you never get the chance to apply it somewhere that can help you in your life."

Nathan looked at Heezle, and Heezle turned into a bald 70-year-old man.

Heezle, in human form, said, "My demons are already in your home."

Nathan gave a surprised expression, thinking how demons could go into Udin's Seperna Abyss and what they could do to Sabrina, his son, and his mother-in-law Dimona.

But again, Heezle smiled and said, "No, no. Not your home in my master's birthplace, but your mortal home. Where your mortal mother and father live!"

Nathan was shocked and disappointed, realizing that he had forgotten his home in Beruk.

That night, Nathan's mother is in their home in Beruk looking at Nathan's photo. And she is crying, remembering the memories she had with her son. Nathan's father came into the room, and he had tears looking at his son's photo, and sat beside her.

Nathan's mother was crying, and she said, "My son.. He left me.. My baby.. My baby," and she started crying loudly, and Nathan's father tried to console her. But she couldn't control herself and was crying loudly.

She said, "My baby... My son... My everything... My world left me... Why should I live... For whom I should live..?"

Nathan's father said, "Don't cry, Svetaa. He is a hero. He is a legend. He died after doing something that changed the fate of this country. We should be proud of him.."

Nathan's mother said, "My son changed the lives of millions of people for the better, but in the process, he destroyed my life. I don't even have a life now. My son is my life.."

Nathan's father said, "We gave life to a legend, a hero. Someone who came to Earth with a reason and purpose to change the world for the better. No family is happy when they have a great man in their family who changed the lives of people and left an impact that will last for generations. God asked us to sacrifice our son for a higher purpose, and we did."

Nathan's mother said, "Can't God change the lives of people without taking my son? If only after taking the life of my son, he can change the world, then he is not a God. He is a businessman. He took someone precious from me and gave something precious to others. He is no God. He didn't change anything. My son loved this country, and he looked at the injustice that had happened to his family and others. He made a decision to try to change the country for the better, and he did it."

Nathan's father and mother are crying. They heard a sound suddenly. They looked around, but they saw nothing and no one.

Nathan looked at Heezle and said, "If something happens to my mom or dad... Remember, Heezle, I will not kill you. I will not keep you alive, either. I will not let you die. And I will not let you suspend in gaps of the universe, too. I will send you to Seperna, to my house, and I will put you in chains like a mad dog and will tie you to a tree in my castle's garden for eternity."

After hearing it, Heezle stopped smiling.

Nathan lifted his fist and punched the ground. The illusion of Satan's Heaven created by Heezle disappeared.

Nathan started running towards Ira's house. The Doctor is smoking there, Jiza is resting, Huro, Tes, and Kwin are with Ira.

Nathan came to them and said, "We must go to Beruk now."

All of them got up, and he asked The Doctor, "Will you come with us? We need your van!' Looking at the Doctor's van.

They took Jiza, and he sat in the back of the van. They all sat in the van, and The Doctor was driving it.

Ira is crying.

Nathan asked, "Does anyone have a phone?"

The Doctor said, "Yes," and gave him his phone.

Nathan started calling his home. But the number is not in service. He called multiple times and was disappointed.

Jiza said, "Don't cry, baby! I'm here.. "

Ira said, "I killed my mom. With my hands.."

Nathan is listening to it.

Nathan: "Doctor, please go fast.."

Ira said, crying, "I'm a killer, murderer. I killed my mom. What kind of a daughter am I?"

Jiza: "No, Ira. You didn't kill her.."

Ira: "Yes, I did. Don't try to make me feel good.."

Nathan: "Yes, Ira, he is right.."

Ira stopped crying, Jiza and everyone looked at Nathan.

Nathan continued, "Yes, Ira. Your mother didn't die. She just went somewhere. That's it.."

Ira asked, "Where did she go?"

Nathan told Ira, "I can't tell you that.. "

Ira started crying again and said, "I know! I killed my mom, and you guys are just trying to make me feel good and cover it. So that no one goes to jail!"

Nathan said, "No, really, your mother is not dead!"

Ira asked, "Then where is she?"

Nathan finally said, "She is in Hell!"

Ira started crying loudly.

And Ira said, "I know, I killed my mom, and you guys are ** holes. My mom is a good person. She will go to Heaven. Not Hell."

Nathan said, "No, she is in Hell."

Ira then cried in disappointment and helplessness.

Then Nathan said, "I mean, she is not dead, but she still went to Hell."

Ira: "So you are saying my mom is so bad that she went to Hell before even dying?"

Nathan: "No, Ira. She is not a bad person, and she is not dead, but she is in Hell now."

The Doctor, hearing all this, became speechless and said, "Are you guys high? Did you take drugs… or .."

Nathan said, laughing, "Haha, no.. no.. We are not high, and we didn't take drugs."

The Doctor asked, "Then what is this Hell and Heaven? Going there before even dying.."

Nathan said, "It is a big story, I will tell you later."

The Doctor thought these guys might be psychos or could be mentally disturbed.

Nathan, looking at the Doctor's face, said, "No, we are perfectly alright, and we are not mentally insane."

The Doctor smiled in little embarrassment.

Nathan said, "I have sent my friend Eesayi to Hell. To save your mother. He will get your mother out of Arusthra's imprisonment.

Don't worry!"

Ira asked Nathan, "Who is Eesayi? How can he save my mother? And who is Arusthra? What are you talking about? Is all this real, or am I dreaming?"

Nathan said, "No, you are not dreaming. Everything is real, and Eesayi is my friend from Heaven. He is also an angel, and he stays in Heaven with God Yinta."

Ira and The Doctor couldn't believe what Nathan said and stayed silent in shock.

Nathan continued, "And my friend Eesayi is very good, funny, and intelligent. He will definitely take your mother to Heaven."

Again, Ira started crying.

Nathan realized what he had done. He corrected himself, saying, "I mean, he will be with your mother till we go there and will keep your mother safe."

The Doctor looked at Nathan in fear.

Then Nathan realized what he had said, "Sorry, sorry! I mean, he, Eesayi, will keep your mother safe till we go back to your home. Okay.. Okay?" To Ira.

Ira calmed down a bit.

They were on the Beruk highway, and it started raining heavily. On the highway, they are going very fast. The storm is very strong, with dust and debris in the air.

Nathan is looking to the right, and The Doctor is looking to the left side. They were going on the highway very fast in the van.

Huro saw a fallen tree in front of them on the highway. He shouted, "Doctor, Tree! "

The Doctor saw the fallen tree, and he applied the brakes. Van skidded and went near the tree, and it hit the tree and stopped. Everyone is scared. And they looked at each other and confirmed everyone was alright. The fallen tree is very big. It covered the whole highway, horizontally.

So they reversed the van and went into the forest beside the Beruk highway.

They are on a dirt forest road now. The van is moving forward smoothly. It is skidding in the dirt, and The Doctor is trying to keep it on the road by slowly moving it forward.

They went deep into the forest. There, they saw a buffalo's dead body in the middle of the road. The road is very small. So they should move the dead body of the buffalo off the road to the side, then they can move forward in the van. Its calf is with the dead body. It looked like someone had hunted its mother.

They all got out of the van in the heavy rain. And in the dirt, they walked to the dead buffalo's body. It is reversed, and its four legs are facing upside down. It is a very big buffalo. The calf is calling its mother. Jiza stayed in the van. Nathan and the gang approached the dead body of the big buffalo. The calf is scared, and at the same time, it doesn't want to leave its mother, so it is running away from its mother as Nathan and gang are approaching, and again coming to its mother.

Nathan and the gang reached the dead body of Buffalo. Nathan looked at the calf. Ira is crying, looking at it.

Nathan placed his palm on Ira's hand and said, "Don't worry. I'm here. We are here!"

Then he looked at the calf and touched it. It is calling its mother. He felt sad looking at the calf. He placed his hand on the calf. And petted it. The calf calmed down, looked at its mother, and mooed in pain.

Nathan, on his knees in the dirt in the rain, petting it, looked into its eyes for a few seconds, and he got up. The calf calmed down completely and stopped mooing in pain.

Nathan and others went to the body of the dead Buffalo, and they all tried to push it off the road. But it is too heavy. They tried again and again, but the body was not moving.

Nathan asked The Doctor, Does he have a rope in the van.

The Doctor said he had a metal wire that he bought to dry his clothes. Nathan asked him to give him that metal wire. Nathan took the metal wire, tied it to four legs of the buffalo's body, and tied it to the link in front of the van. He got into the van and slowly started pulling the body through the wire that was attached to the front of the truck. The body is moving.

A demon came inside Nathan's garage, and on the wall, it wrote, "We will eat you alive, Today!"

Nathan's mother and father, after hearing that sound, got up and started walking towards the garage.

Nathan slowly got the body of the buffalo off the road. He got down, and Huro removed the wire from the van's link and from the legs of Buffalo's dead body.

Nathan walked to the calf. It is standing and looking at Nathan. He took the calf into his hands, opened the back door of the van, and put it inside. Everyone got back into the van and started their journey to Beruk.

In the van, Huro said, "We should have buried it.. "

Nathan said, "No, we shouldn't. Even though it died an unnatural death, it is sad, but we should not bury it."

Huro asked, "Why? It would have been respectful to the buffalo and calf because it was killed by someone and did not die a natural death, as you said."

Nathan said, "Yes, but it's already dead. Someone took that life. But still, if we leave it there, it can save many other lives of animals and birds. They eat its meat. If they eat it, their hunger will be satisfied, at least for a couple of days, if we bury it. It will not help anyone."

They are on the outskirts of Beruk, and no one is on the roads. Rain stopped. They reached Nathan's home. The Doctor stopped the van. Nathan got off fast, started running into the house, and went into the hall, but there was no one.

He got more tense, and he went into the kitchen and saw no one. He checked the bedrooms, too, but still didn't see his mother or father. He is in the hall, confused and tense. He doesn't know what to do.

There he saw his photo from when he won a competition in school. He made an electric lift replica. Then he remembered about his garage and started running towards it. Ira is in the van with Jiza. Doctor, Huro, Kwin, and Tes followed Nathan, and they, too, were going towards the garage.

Nathan entered the garage, and on the wall, he saw, "We will eat you alive.. Today!"

There, his mother and father, in fear, sat in a corner. In darkness. He started walking towards them. They thought it was a demon, and they were shaking as Nathan came near to them.

They froze completely in fear. Huro turned on the lights. Nathan's father saw Nathan's feet, and in fear, he slowly lifted his head and saw a man. Finally, he looked at Nathan's face.

He realized it was his son Nathan. And in shock and fear, he started smiling and couldn't control himself. He asked Nathan's mother to open her eyes. She saw his feet first and suspected something. When she turned her head, she saw Nathan.

She suddenly started smiling and got up. Her happiness had no limits. She started crying, hugging Nathan, looking at his face.

She did it multiple times. Because she couldn't believe her son had come back. Svetaa thought he was dead, and the whole country thought he died. And they constructed a memorial too in his name. She gave tens of kisses to Nathan on his forehead, on his shoulder, and on his cheeks.

Huro, Kwin, Tes, and The Doctor are seeing it. They had tears in their eyes. Suddenly, they all heard police sirens. And car sounds.

Nathan told his mom and dad, "Come with us!"

His mom said, "No, we are okay here. You are alive. That is enough for us!"

Then, immediately, Nathan closed his eyes, placed his fist on his forehead, and said, "Any demon and any force that tries to trouble my parents in any way, I will make them as my slaves and forever use them as creatures to clean my chariot in the Master Universe."

And he opened his fist. A light came out of it.

After seeing it, Nathan's parents and The Doctor were shocked.

The text on the wall disappeared by itself.

Nathan said, "I will come back, Mom!"

Nathan told The Doctor to get the van on the backside road of the house.

And he ran to the back side of his house. Tes, Kwin, and Huro followed him. The Doctor came out of the house and got into the van.

Police cars and SWAT teams surrounded the van.

Some officers went inside Nathan's house.

With guns and weapons pointed at the van and The Doctor. The officers asked him to get out. The Doctor obeyed their orders.

A police officer asked him, "Is there anyone inside the van?"

The Doctor said, "Yes!"

Then they opened the back door of the van. They saw Ira, Jiza, and the calf.

The police officer asked The Doctor, "Who are you? Why are you here?"

The Doctor said, "My friend was injured. We are taking him to the hospital."

Jiza has a wound dressing on his thigh.

The officer asked, "Why did you stop here?"

The Doctor said, "We are coming from a faraway place. We traveled 200 miles from a tribal mountain village in Trishone country. The medical treatment is cheap in Wizbome. We need rest, but stopping our vehicle beside the highway with a woman in it is not a good idea. At least that's what I thought. So, we came into this village and stopped here. We have to go to Relsar tomorrow to get treatment for my friend."

Then the officer asked, "Why is this calf with you, then?"

We saw it in the middle of the Beruk highway, but its mother was not with it. So we thought it would die if any vehicle hit it. So we got it into our vehicle.

The officer said, "No, you can't take it like that. It's called stealing!"

Doctor: "Stealing? From who? I didn't steal it!"

The officer asked, "Then how did you get it?"

The Doctor said, "Just now, I told you.."

The officer said, "No, taking it like that is considered stealing. We will file a case against you for stealing the calf from its mother."

The Doctor said, "Its mother is not with it, and it is in the middle of Beruk highway. It would have died by now. In the darkness, if any vehicle hit it. We saved it."

The officer said, "Then we will take it and send it to a rescue animal shelter."

The Doctor said, "Fine, you can take it!"

They took the calf from the Doctor's van into their SWAT van and left.

Heezle is at the end of the road. Nathan, Huro, Tes, and Kwin are waiting for the Doctor's van.

Huro said, "I think that the health worker who came in the

ambulance must have recognized us and informed the police."

Nathan said, "No, he doesn't know who we are and what we did... because both of them spoke in Trishone's accent, and I saw their faces. They have no clue about who we are... I think the police got to know about us when I called my home from The Doctor's phone."

Kwin said, "But you said your home phone was out of service when you called it."

Nathan is thinking, then how the police would have known about them.

Then he realized. Only one person who could've done that is The Doctor. That is why he didn't leave even after treating Jiza.

At the end of the road, Nathan, Huro, Tes, and Kwin saw Heezle, but except for Nathan, The Three didn't know the ugly demon's original form, and what was walking towards them was Heezle, one of the eight sahani servants of Satan.

Heezle knew if Nathan ever took him as a pet to Seperna, he would be destroyed by God's angels because God, in the war of Nazreck, vowed to kill Heezle specifically if he ever went back to Udin.

Seperna is inside Udin. That is why Heezle always stayed with his demons at Saden, as told by Satan.

The Saden Demon village edge is where the demons take birth through the Kuyanish Satan Beeliaal energy pact. Satan also uses it as the graveyard for demons and forces who go against him.

Beeliaal is an Emperor of the anti-universes called Xhehroom Universes. Xhehroom Universes are created, getting created, and will be created in equal parallel amounts to the universes created, getting created, and will be created by Mother Adis, the first energy.

Beeliaal, the Emperor of all known and unknown anti-universes called the Xhehroom Universes, is the direct opponent of Mother Adis, the first energy who creates all natural, known and unknown universes.

Beeliaal rules the infinite number of all known and unknown anti-universes created in amounts equivalent to the infinite number of all-natural known and unknown universes created by Mother Adis, the first energy.

Beeliaal made an agreement with Satan to help him get power and rule over Mother Adis's known and unknown universes, which are already in existence and will come into existence.

The creations of Mother Adis are pure and full of life, unlike the creations of Beeliaal, which are pure evil and dark without any life forms.

Beeliaal waged a war against the Husband of Mother Adis at 'The Place' where time didn't even begin anywhere. It is just empty everywhere at 'The Place.' Then Beeliaal saw Mother Adis's first energy of the first natural universe and the power of the light of Mother Adis and got jealous. Beeliaal asked Mother Adis to return to Lifire village, the place of her primary birth, in another dimension called Brahjemo.

Beeliaal existed in emptiness everywhere in 'The Place' before time began for the first time by Mother Adis. 'The Place' became the Master Universe after the beginning of time by Mother Adis. There were no creations of any known and unknown natural universes before the creation of the Master Universe by Mother Adis in the Yaalshme Dimension, with Jealousy, Beeliaal started creating dark, lifeless universes in equivalent parallel amounts to Mother Adis's creations in the Zehra Dimension.

Beeliaal opposed light and Mother Adis. But Mother Adis's husband fought a war with Beeliaal and cast him to exist in emptiness for eternity in the Zehra Dimension from then on.

As a result of the war between Mother Adis's husband and Beeliaal, Beeliaal left the Primary Master Universe.

The Primary Universe is the First Master Universe of all known and unknown universes in Yaalshme Dimension, where Mother Adis's light appeared for the first time, and Beeliaal kept himself in darkness and ruled the emptiness and darkness in emptiness and darkness before Mother Adis's light arrived with her husband protecting it.

Satan joined hands with Beeliaal to gain power over the creations of Mother Adis and to defeat his brother, God Yinta, through the dark magic pact of Beeliaal and Satan called Kuyanish Satan Beeliaal energy pact, at the end of Saden demon village. At the Kuyanish Satan Beeliaal energy pact, the demons take birth and haunt the creations of Mother

Adis and the life forms created by Mother Adis.

Mother Adis never said anything to Satan because he is her son, and she doesn't know how to deal with him as a mother.

But Beeliaal knows if he touches Mother Adis's creations directly without the help of Satan, then Mother Adis and her husband will destroy him and his creations of the Xhehroom anti-universes immediately. That is why he never comes directly into Mother Adis's creations in any form other than helping Satan. Beeliaal is using the brothers' conflict between God Yinta and Satan for his own gains.

On Earth - Sub Universe,

Nathan told Huro to stop The Doctor's van from coming to the place where they were, and Huro asked who that was as he saw Heezle angry and ugly on the road.

Nathan said, "One of the eight sahani servants of Satan!"

Huro, Kwin, and Tes were shocked. Huro ran towards the van, which was at the start of the road, in another direction, to stop the van. Heezle returned to his original form.

Kwin said, "If one of the servants of Satan can come here in his original form with his whole strength from Master Universe... why didn't we get our super strength and our sacred eagles, weapons, and Ayoo except the immortality and a few powers to help others?"

Nathan said, "Because a thief has many ways to prove himself that he is not a thief even after committing the theft, and he has no compulsory procedure to follow to prove himself that he is not a thief. His aim is to rob and escape in whatever way possible. But the police have to follow the law and legal procedure to catch him and send him to jail by proving that he committed the theft in a legal manner."

Kwin asked, "So, good people follow the rules, and bad people don't?"

Nathan said, "Yes."

Kwin said, "Come on, Boss.."

Heezle lifted himself into the air.

Heezle, in rage, shouted, "Oh, mortal immortal, come with me!"

Nathan loudly said, "Cut the sh** and come on, b***h!"

* * *

Huro stopped the van, and everyone looked at Nathan and Heezle in fear.

Heezle took his axe and threw it at Nathan. Nathan saw the axe coming towards him, and everyone saw the axe, and everyone thought Nathan was finished at that moment.

Suddenly, a big glowing sphere appeared around Nathan, and the bright light glared in everyone's eyes for a few seconds.

When light disappeared, they saw Nathan in his sacred clothes, and his trident returned to him. Seeing it, Kwin and Tes were smiling and shouting in happiness. Huro whistled. Ira was Shocked.

Nathan has a sacred crown on his head and a cape. His clothes resembled the fighting spirit of Heaven in the Master Universe. He is covered in White clothes with Black stripes and a Red cape. This signified that God Yinta is now commanding the darkness, light, and everything in between and outside in need of battle for justice, truth, and righteousness to prevail.

White, red, and black have significance in Nathan's Ateesta religion, as explained in their holy book Wuquin. Ateestans, on special occasions, can wear clothes with a combination of Red, symbolizing their bravery, and White, symbolizing peace, and Black, symbolizing they are not afraid to fight against injustice.

After seeing Nathan, Heezle changed his form into 'Ishera Uttaan'. Ishera Uttaan is a creation of Satan to make humans commit suicide through depression and make human beings feel that they are insignificant in this massive world they are living in.

Ishera Uttaan stops people from realizing that the universe is comprised of matter that made human beings, too. It makes people not value human life and encourages people to commit murders and crimes against each other. The Ishera Uttaan form Heezle transitioned into is a nasty form created by Satan for his servants and demons. The mortal beings will vomit and kill themselves instantly in fear if they see the form of Ishera Uttan.

Nathan saw Ishera Uttan form of Heezle. He understood what would happen to The Three, Ira, and Jiza, if they saw the Ishera Uttan Heezle.

He immediately went near Heezle, flying in the air, and Nathan passed his trident to his left hand. With his right hand, he slapped Heezle so hard that after taking the slap, Heezle's head was cut, and it fell to the ground.

Heezle's body is still in the air, and immediately, Heezle's head is again coming to get attached to Heezle's body.

Nathan saw it, and with his trident, he hit the head. Then again, it hit the ground so hard that it made a deep hole in the Earth's ground, and water was coming out from that hole.

Immediately, Nathan took his trident into both hands, and he stabbed the Heezle's body vertically into his neck. Trident went into the stomach of Heezle vertically through the neck.

After that Nathan said, "Satane, Iroj un nerch unn neen chamch Simhse aadistim!"

In Hell, there is an unusual disturbance. Arusthra sensed it. He ran to the throne of Hell, but Satan was not there.

On Earth, Nathan closed and opened his eyes. His left eye is glowing red, and his right eye is glowing white. He threw the trident into the hole made by Heezle's head and filled the hole with Heezle's body.

The water stopped coming out, and Nathan took his trident back by placing his left leg on Heezle's body, which was in the hole, and pulled the trident back. After that, Nathan spat on Heezle's body. Earth consumed Heezle's body and head at the command of Nathan. The Three, The Doctor, Jiza, and Ira saw what happened. They were all in an unexplainable state of shock and amazement.

The bright light sphere came again, and it took Nathan's trident. Nathan got his normal clothes back. Huro came running towards Nathan, smiling and shouting. "Boss.. Boss... you did it...! You killed that son of b*** from Hell... huuu.. You did it!"

Kwin and Tes, too, came running towards Nathan, and they lifted him and started shouting, "Boss.. Boss... Boss...Boss..".

Ira came out of the van. And she is very happy seeing the immortal gang cheering for their immortal leader. Jiza is laughing, seeing the immortal gang from the van. The Doctor came out and went straight to Nathan, and he touched Nathan's feet and told him, "I thought you were a criminal, but you are not. I'm sorry."

Nathan smiled at The Doctor and said, "I wish people were more like you!"

Ira got Jiza out in a wheelchair, which is in The Doctor's van. The Three, Nathan, Doctor, Ira, and Jiza, came together and formed a circle.

Ira said, "I'm hungry!"

Nathan looked at Ira and said, "Your mother is in Hell, and you are hungry now?"

Ira suddenly changed her expression to sad, and Nathan felt bad for saying it.

Ira laughed loudly, saying, "I believe you and your friend Eesayi. My mom is safe even if she is in Hell!"

In the Master Universe, demons took mortal unconscious Ira's mother to Hell, and Nathan's friend Eesayi reached the entrance of Hell. He saw demon soldiers of Satan.

Arusthra is guarding Hell. Eesayi went to the entrance of Hell, and Arusthra saw Eesayi. He got angry. He knows Eesayi is Nathan's friend.

Eesayi is an angel from Heaven. God Yinta from Heaven is supporting Nathan.

Arusthra took out a Satanic guarding thread from inside his head.

This Arusthra guard thread imprisons a mortal person mentally. The mortal who got attacked by it can never think straight and make good choices. Arusthra threw it on Ira's mother. It took control of the mind of Ira's mother, and she is voluntarily walking into Hell.

Eesayi saw it, and he was shocked. Arusthra is laughing, and the demons are laughing. Eesayi is calling Ira's mother, "Mother... Mother.." But she was in a Satanic trance. Eesayi looked at Arusthra, took out the sacred sand of Heaven from his bag of sacredness, and showed it to Arusthra. Eesayi lifted his hand to throw the sand of Heaven into Hell.

Arusthra said, "No..," in a loud screech.

Eesayi looked at Arusthra. Arusthra took back his guard thread of Hell from Ira's mother's mind. Arusthra said, "Take her from here!"

Ira's mother came out of the trance. She saw Arusthra and demons. She screamed in fear.

And then she saw Eesayi. She felt safe after looking at Eesayi. She immediately ran to Eesayi, and Eesayi took her hand and said, "Mother, don't fear. Think of me as a son you never had. Your daughter's friend asked me to take care of you. I will take you to Heaven. You can stay in Heaven until my friend comes to Heaven and takes you to your daughter on Earth."

Ira's mother cried in Happiness, and Eesayi took Ira's mother on his sacred white chariot with white donkeys to Heaven.

On Earth, after destroying Heezle, Nathan said, "We will order the food then.."

Ira said, "No, I will cook today. We will buy all the goods needed to make food, and we will make it ourselves."

Kwin said, "Yeah, that would be awesome. Let's go to a shop to buy the goods."

Huro said, "Yes, let's go!"

They all shouted, "Woooo... let's go!" and got into the van, and The Doctor drove the van.

They are going to a 24/7 mall. They bought all the items needed to make food, and Nathan said I want to eat chicken today.

Ira said, "Fine, we will also eat chicken today, and they bought chicken, other items, and battery lights."

Then they got on the road and drove straight to Nathan's cabin near the Hervin forest. They reached the cabin. They went inside the cabin and saw that everything was destroyed there. Nathan took some metal dishes out to cook food.

He washed them and gave them to The Three. The Three are cutting vegetables. And Ira washed the chicken with water.

They prepared everything and started cooking food using wood by placing three small stones on the ground and wood in the middle of the stones. They placed metal dishes on the stones and lit the wood.

Carefully, Ira cooked the food, and Ira served the food to everyone. She sat in front of Jiza. Everyone started eating, and the food was in the middle for them to take if they wanted more. The food is so good.

They are enjoying it. Nathan said, "Jiza is very lucky.. Sister!"

Jiza laughed. Ira felt good.

Nathan was eating food.

He remembered Sabrina, their son Aarus, and his mortal mom and dad.

Nathan said to his friends, "I love you guys. You guys, too, are my family now!"

They were surprised and stopped eating.

They looked at Nathan with affection in their eyes.

Ira said, "Nathan, we will be with you till the death and after our death too."

After hearing it, The Three laughed loudly.

Doctor, Ira, and Jiza didn't understand why The Three were laughing.

Huro asked Ira, "Do you know where we should go after eating this?"

Ira said, "Ahh.. No!"

Huro said, "Haha.. We should meet your mother, right?"

Ira asked, "So we are going to Heaven..?"

Huro said, "Of course..! "

Ira started crying.

The Three got scared seeing Ira crying suddenly, Nathan said, "Ira, calm down.."

Jiza took Ira into his hands and said, "Baby, why are you crying?"

Ira said, "We are going to die. That is why!!"

Hearing what Ira said. The Three and Nathan laughed.

Doctor and Jiza were confused.

Nathan said, "We will go to Heaven and take your mother to my home in Seperna, The Hollow of Dimona. My mother-in-law is there in Seperna with my wife, Sabrina, and my son."

Ira asked, "Your wife, Sabrina? Do you mean Sabrina? That girl who left you because her father got transferred?"

Nathan said, "Yes!"

Huro, in shock, asked Ira, "Sabrina's father got transferred?"

Ira said, "Yes! He is a government officer. He is the head of the local government municipality tax department."

Huro: "Hoo..! True..! True!"

Ira: "So we go to Heaven before dying?"

Kwin: "Yes, sister!"

They completed eating. They set up lights in the forest, danced to the music, and slept that night in the forest.

Nathan woke up the next morning, and he walked up to the van. Huro saw Nathan walking away, and he quickly got up and ran towards Nathan.

Huro asked, "Boss.. Boss, where are you going? I will come with you!!"

and started walking with Nathan.

Nathan got into the van, and Huro sat in the front seat. Nathan started driving, and they were on the highway.

Huro doesn't know where they are going.

Nathan drove straight to his parents' house.

He met his mom and dad. He told them what happened. And he told them he would come again and would take them with him to his home at Seperna, The Hollow of Dimona.

At first, they were shocked, but they remembered the demon that haunted them and how Nathan saved them from it.

Nathan's dad told Nathan, "Kick the ass of your father-in-law and take care of your wife and children."

Nathan's mother said, "No, try to talk to your father-in-law and try to bring the family together as much as possible."

Nathan laughed and kissed his mother on her forehead. He also took blessings from his dad and mom.

Huro felt happy seeing it. They left. On the way, Nathan saw his dad's new shop, which was built with government compensation. They reached the cabin and saw Doctor, Jiza, and Ira dead. Their bodies were cut into small pieces and thrown around the place. Kwin and Tes were not seen anywhere.

After seeing the meat pieces of the bodies of The Doctor, Ira, and Jiza, Nathan was shocked and he cried loudly.

He searched there to find out who did it, but there were no clues and nothing. Then he realized, it was the work of the demons of Satan. His face and eyes are red. Huro cried.

Nathan closed his eyes in pain.

Nathan heard a voice in his mind, "They are with me, Nathan. But what happened to them was unforgivable. Come to me and deliver justice for your friends' deaths."

Nathan then said out loud in anger, "Then why would you let it happen? Why would you let it happen?.. You could've stopped it. But you didn't."

Then he heard a voice in his mind while his eyes were open, "I cannot do that. It is against the order of the master and sub-universe equation. But you are allowed to fight the injustice."

Nathan said, "What is that equation? What are those rules? When you can't protect good people from evil, then what good is there in following all those rules and equations? "

Then he heard, "If we behave in an evil way because evil behaved in an evil way, then what is the difference between us and evil?"

Then Nathan said, "If we can't protect the good people from evil, then what is good in being good and not evil?"

The voice in his mind said, "Then it means.. Now, you have the choice to make the decisions on how you want to see things in life and approach life. Will you do good in good ways, or will you do good in good ways and also in bad ways and in all the other ways that are possible too? There is no definitive right or wrong if we continue to go up and see things in a broader context. We draw meanings from things based on facts, common sense, and our perceptions and emotions. It doesn't matter whether the meaning you've drawn is good or bad. You draw your own meaning and do what you want to do, but the end goal must be a positive thing."

Nathan said to the voice, "You didn't stop the Ira and Jiza murders, but you took their souls to Heaven. You are a hypocrite. You took Kwin and Tes physically to Heaven because you know they are immortal and can't be killed. But you let those ugly demons kill my mortal friends physically, and after my mortal friends got killed physically, only then did you take their souls to Heaven along with Kwin and Tes. You know those demons can torture Kwin and Tes but can't kill them. You also know those demons can kill Ira and Jiza physically, but you chose not to stop those demons before they murder Ira and Jiza."

The voice inside Nathan's mind said, "Nathan, my son! The demons are part of this creation, even if they try to destroy the creation itself. You and your friends are also part of this creation.

Your friends just changed their way of being, that's it. But yes, it was done by anti-universe forces and death forcefully. I can stop the demons today. But tomorrow? A day after tomorrow? Like this, every day for everyone on the face of the Earth, can I stop their death? Yes, I can, but I won't because death is the beginning, not the end, no matter how they die. And if everyone lives and no one dies, then what is the meaning of life?"

Nathan asked the voice, "So you allow unnatural deaths and murder?"

The voice in Nathan's mind said, "I do not allow it, and I didn't initiate it. It is what it is. If you can stop it, stop it, and if you can't, you can't!"

Nathan said, "So, you are saying I have to take action on this by my free will, and you will not be involved in this directly, but you will help me if I take action to do something to fight against the injustice done to my friends by Satan?"

The voice in Nathan's mind said, "Yes, my son!"

Nathan said nothing. He closed his eyes. Ayoo came flying. The sacred eagle of Huro, too, came after Ayoo. Nathan got on Ayoo, and he became transparent. The eagle was carrying Huro, and they became transparent, too. Nathan and Huro started flying and reached the Brunuck Line of the Master Universe. They crossed it. They are going at light speed.

They reached 'Nothing' Place. Nathan landed on 'Nothing' Place. Huro followed.

Huro asked, "What should we do now?"

Nathan said, "First, we should meet Doctor, Jiza, Ira, and Ira's mother in Heaven."

Huro said, "Ok, but what about Kwin and Tes?"

Nathan said, "They are in Heaven, too, but alive."

In Heaven, there is another beautiful White Castle with a great hall. It is there after the main castle at the entrance.

Nathan got on Ayoo and Huro on the sacred eagle. They are going towards Heaven.

At Heaven, Ira, Jiza, and Doctor's souls were given entry into Heaven by Sutiore soldiers of the gates of Heaven.

The front entrance of Heaven is massive. It has two pillars on two sides with steps leading to the gates of Heaven.

Kwin and Tes accompanied the souls of Ira, Jiza, and Doctor.

They were stunned by the beauty of Heaven's main complex. The complex's absolute white and gold color with sacred pillars of truth and time mesmerized them. At the same time, they were walking after entering the gate, they saw a sacred river on the left side and a sacred desert on the right side of the path to Heaven's other castle.

The trees in Heaven are massive and totally green in color. The path they were walking is in the color of gold, and the water of the sacred Heava River beside the path is as white as milk.

The sacred desert of Heaven is in the color of the blood of a mortal of Earth. As they were walking, Eesayi was standing in front of Heaven's Truth Castle. They reached the castle, and Eesayi smiled at them. He said, "Come, my friends, I was informed that you will come here by God and also by my friend."

Ira asked, "Who is your God and your friend?"

Eesayi replied, "My friend is your friend, too, and my God is your God, too."

Ira asked again, "Yeah, but who are they?"

Eesayi said, "They are who you think they are. And they are not when you think they are not. They are who they are. And they are not if you think they are not."

Ira and others are confused.

Eesayi asked, "Who is your friend?"

Ira said, "Nathan!"

Eesayi said, "Then Nathan is my friend, and who is your God?"

Ira said, "Krisaan Regor!"

Eesayi said, "Then Krisaan Regor is my God."

Jiza said, "My God is Yinta!"

Eesayi said, "Then my God is Yinta!"

Kwin and Tes said, "Our God is Krisaan Regor, too, but we also believe in God Yinta."

***

Eesayi said, "Then my Gods are both Krisaan Regor and God Yinta."

Ira asked Eesayi, "Where is my mother?"

Eesayi said, "She is here!" and pointed his finger towards the Truth Castle of Heaven. Eesayi took everyone inside the castle. Ira's mother is in a house inside the castle.

The Castle of Truth is so massive that the Master Universe itself will fit inside of it. It has that quantum nature.

Truth Castle has its own sun, moon, day, and night inside of it.

It has its own world inside of it, and it is the World of Truth. The only thing that is there inside the Truth Castle of Heaven is the truth and nothing else.

The houses inside Truth Castle are white and gold in color, with a garden in front of them. The grass is pure green in color.

There is no air, but they felt as if there was air, but it was not air. It is the energy of truth.

Ira went into a house. Ira's mother saw her daughter. She was stunned to speak and came running towards Ira and hugged her. They didn't talk. But looked into each other's eyes. Jiza looked at them, and he was happy.

Ira also saw her father. She got emotional, and her father got emotional too and cried.

Ira's family came together in Heaven's Truth Castle.

Kwin told Doctor and Jiza to stay in Heaven's Castle of The Truth.

Kwin and Tes came out.

They met Eesayi.

Kwin asked Eesayi, "Can you come with us?"

Eesayi said, "Yes, but you have to bow to God Yinta to show respect even if you don't believe in him. And he is the one who saved you from the demon torture and also your mortal friends from the pain of death."

Tes said, "Okay, we have no problem!"

And both turned towards the massive Castle of Truth. And starting bowing to it as Truth is God too.

Eesayi stopped them and said, "No, you don't need to. You already did when you agreed to bow to God Yinta when I asked."

Eesayi looked to the side, and his chariot was coming. The sacred chariot with white donkeys came and stopped in front of them.

Eesayi, Kwin, and Tes got on the chariot.

The chariot of truth moved forward and started flying out of Heaven towards 'Nothing' Place.

Nathan on Ayoo and Huro on Sacred Eagle are coming towards Heaven.

In the middle, Eesayi saw Nathan and Huro. He stopped.

Eesayi asked Nathan, "What do you think? Where should you go now?"

Nathan answered "Yes! I have to meet him and ask for help."

Eesayi said, "Yes! let go!"

They started traveling to the Sacred Yira forest under Heaven.

Arusthra came to them on a Satanic bison while they were going to the Sacred Yira forest. Eesayi's chariot, Nathan, and Huro stopped.

Arusthra said, "Nathan, you are committing grave blasphemy against Satan. You will pay a heavy price for this."

Eesayi said, " Arusthra, control your words!"

Arusthra said, "Haha, This mortal immortal who cannot live without eating and drinking just for 137 Earth days in his mortal life is now going to fight my boss. This low-life mortal immortal is disgusting and is not even eligible to have the presence in the Master Universe."

Kwin and Tes got angry.

Huro angrily said, "This disgusting, filthy, dead being from the beginning of times, who got his body parts ripped off by Mother Sumaaraa, is now talking about who is high and who is low based on where the life forms take birth. This disgusting, filthy creature doesn't even know what it means to be alive and take birth in the mortal universe, but it troubles them and makes them commit sins using the mortals' problems and desires. This filthy creature now has the confidence to stand in front of a mortal immortal who took birth as a human being and then turned himself immortal and defeated the soldiers of Innahath. Oh, disgusting being, go to Farush. I will come for you to rip off your head with the help of Mother Adis."

Arusthra was angry and left in shame.

Kwin and Tes were laughing silently, looking at each other.

Huro said to Nathan, "Not just your father-in-law, but his servants are also too egoistic."

Eesayi: "Being pure and righteous is important, but not at the cost of getting destroyed."

Nathan: "Do you remember how God Yinta told you and me to help each other?"

Eesayi: "Yes!"

Nathan: "I never met you before. This is the first time, right?"

Eesayi: "Yes!"

Nathan: "But God Yinta knows both of us and told us what to do!"

Eesayi: "Yes, brother!"

Nathan: "God Yinta knows what to do, and Wuquin told us how to approach everything. Then why do we have to fear Arusthra or any Thra?"

Eesayi: "You are correct, brother!"

Nathan: "We should go now!"

And they traveled and entered the Sacred Yira forest.

Eesayi's chariot and Huro on the sacred eagle stopped at the Sacred Roush tree.

Eesayi said, "My friend, we are not allowed to come inside that sacred cave. You must go alone."

Nathan asked Ayoo to stay with Eesayi, Kwin, Tes, and Huro.

He came down from Ayoo, and Nathan threw his trident in front of him.

The trident transformed into a big sacred snake like it was earlier.

He got on the sacred snake, and the snake started going into the Sacred Yira forest.

The sacred snake crossed rivers, paths of valleys, and trees.

The sacred snake reached the sacred cave. Nathan got down, and he remembered his wife telling him about the Sacred Yira forest.

He went inside the sacred cave and stood in front of the sacred stone.

The five dots on the sacred stone started glowing. Nathan was looking at the stone, and he bowed in front of it, and God Yinta, in energy form, came out of the stone.

Nathan couldn't see God Yinta's face or body, but just energy glowing in a triangular form.

God Yinta told Nathan, "My son, you go to Farush and do what is necessary. I will give you my army."

Nathan asked God Yinta, "But Father, I'm just a man. A mortal man who attained immortality, but still a man. How can I fight a supernatural power?"

God Yinta laughed and said, "My son, everything in the known and unknown universes is the same, and the creation of Mother Adis is the same. Her creation's manifestations and formations might differ according to the sense of the particular matter and where it is located, but in the beginning, everything is the same: you and me and everything everywhere, but we are separated long before. You fight for justice and righteousness. Everything will fall in place automatically."

Nathan then said "But Yinta.. Satan is strong, and he is my father-in-law."

God Yinta said, "You are strong too, my son, and if you respect your father-in-law, then try to change him or change him."

Nathan said, "Come on, God, I love my wife!"

God Yinta laughed and said, "I mean, you can change his behavior by making him realize how much of a horrible being he was, or you can send him to Eternal Mother Adis's origin place."

Nathan said, "I don't think he will change! God"

God Yinta said, "You do your part, son, and see where it leads and move forward from there.."

Nathan said, "Yes, father!"

After a second, Nathan asked God Yinta, "God, why did you hide the truth from me?"

God Yinta said, "I must, son! I want you to meet me here, and I want you to represent me. I need your help. And I want you to realize how beautiful life is and how life was in the creation of Mother Adis for a mortal.

I can't teach you how to live a life even as an immortal being in the

Master Universe at the same depth as you understand it by yourself through death and living on Earth, an immortal world of mortal beings. My son, your mortal mother and father loves you a lot. You are a son worth having. I'm proud of you for becoming an Ateestan."

Nathan was made an orphan on Earth by Satan.

Satan killed the biological mother and father of Nathan after his birth because Satan knew Nathan was a threat to his throne in Hell.

Nathan is son of the Emperor of Dretonian Kingdom in Wulshaan Universe. It was said by Mother Adis that Nathan would one day rule the Master Universe. But to do that, he has to first take birth as a mortal and die. Giur is a soldier in the Dretonian Kingdom. Dretonian Emperor Qriswur helped God Yinta in the war of Nazreck. Mother Adis took Nathan, the son of the Dretonian Emperor, and sent him to Earth.

When Satan killed the biological father and mother of Nathan on Earth, if Satan had killed Nathan as a baby, then Satan would have been happy, but he feared the anger of Mother Adis. So, Satan killed Nathan's biological parents and made him an orphan.

God Yinta took Nathan as a baby and put him in a dustbin in Beruk village. His present mortal father and mother on Earth adopted Nathan from an orphanage in Beruk village. He was found by the people of Beruk orphanage in a dustbin at night 23 years ago.

God Yinta left him there. Nathan was adopted as an infant, and until he visited the Sacred Yira forest for the first time, he didn't know what Satan did to him, his biological father, and mother. Their souls are in the Wulshaan Universe. Father Wulshaan gave their souls Eternal Integration into Him.

Sumaaraa - God Yinta's only lover, the daughter of the Emperor of Emptiness, Beeliaal, got angry seeing what Satan did to Nathan and his family.

Sumaaraa asked God Yinta to make Nathan his representative in the wars of good and evil in all the known and unknown universes. God Yinta agreed as he also gave his word to his mother that he would not fight Satan directly.

God Yinta said, "My son, you were born on Earth with the blessings of my Sumaaraa. She wants you to lead us and our forces at Farush."

Nathan: "Yes, God! I'm blessed to obey the commands of my mother."

God Yinta: "Sumaaraa's motherly energy and my powers, army are with you, son."

Nathan: "I'm honored to fight by your side, God. But why does Satan want to kill me? Why does he think a normal mortal immortal like me is going to be a great threat to him?"

God Yinta: "If you win this war at Farush, as told by Mother Adis, you will rule the Master Universe. Satan will never want to give up Hell, you already took over Udin. Satan hates you for that, and also Satan hates someone who can question him, challenge him, and you did that."

Nathan: "How can I do it as a just-born baby?"

God Yinta said, "Having a nature of questioning things is enough to get attacked by Satan. He either kills you or tries to control you through various methods. But when he senses the intensity of questioning and the sense is high in a person, then he will try to kill them.

He thinks it is better to kill someone with a high-intensity questioning nature than to try to change them with worldly pleasures because they don't."

And God Yinta continued, "The creation of Mother Adis gave you what it gave to any mortal being, but you made a choice by your free will to question things. Where others didn't. Satan knew your previous life as the son of the Dretonian Emperor. So he killed your biological father and mother on Earth and made you an orphan, but I cannot see the light and hope of the future of universes die like an orphan, so I intervened as minimally as possible to save you and also tried not to change the flow of happenings in holy creation of Mother Adis."

Nathan: "But Satan has no restrictions. Satan can destroy and change anything. You cannot?"

God Yinta: "No, he too was not allowed to do it, but he chose to do it. That is why he is Satan."

Nathan: "All the rules are only for good people, and bad people don't get punished immediately if they do something bad. This is unfair."

God Yinta: "It is because if everyone becomes bad in the process of punishing bad people, then there will be no good left. Everyone will suffer at the hands of everyone."

Nathan said, "Yeah... But now, good people suffer at the hands of bad people. That's it. If good people turn bad like bad people, then bad people also suffer at the hands of good people. After that, everything becomes even."

God Yinta: "Then everyone becomes bad too."

Nathan: "Then what is the meaning of staying good if it is destroying a person? At least originally good people, by turning bad, can defend themselves to an extent rather than just getting destroyed by originally bad people and doing nothing because they are good."

God Yinta: "For that exact reason, you have systems in place to deal with bad things. So, if something bad happens to good people, then good people do not need to turn into bad, but the system will punish the bad people."

Nathan: "And those systems are slow and inefficient!"

God Yinta: "Then make them efficient and fast."

Nathan: "It is not that easy!"

God Yinta: "It is easy and possible. That is why you have systems in place first. All you gotta do is make them more active and efficient, that's it."

Nathan said nothing.

God Yinta said, "The Master Universe needs you, son. Go and fight against the injustice done to your friends and humanity by Satan."

Nathan nodded his head vertically.

God Yinta disappeared.

Nathan came out of the cave.

He started walking in the forest. He walked two miles into the forest and saw a mountain full of banyan trees. He walked towards the Banyan Mountain and reached it. He sat under a small banyan tree. The sacred snake followed him all along.

He looked at the trees and the forest. In the cool breeze, he slept there under the small banyan tree.

# 6

When Nathan woke up, he saw the sacred, beautiful animals of the Yira forest. Lions, tigers, jaguars, elephants, foxes, snakes, and many other birds and animals came to see Nathan.

They are all standing in front of Nathan.

Two sacred eagles and a lion came to Nathan.

Nathan petted them. He saw a fawn and asked it to come to him. It came to Nathan, and he kissed it on its head. The wind was cool, and the environment was pure and sacred.

He walked up to an elephant, and with its trunk, it made Nathan sit on it.

The elephant started walking towards the Roush sacred tree. All animals and birds of the Yira forest followed Nathan. Sacred elephants crossed the rivers and valleys in the Yira forest on the path to reach the sacred Roush tree.

Nathan reached the sacred Roush tree. And got down from the sacred elephant.

Ayoo saw Yira Forest's animals and birds.

Eesayi, The Three saw Nathan and were amazed.

Nathan got on Ayoo and left the Sacred Yira forest while the animals and birds were making cheering sounds.

Eesayi, Kwin, and Tes are on Eesayi's chariot. Huro, on the sacred eagle, followed them.

* * *

They landed on Farush ground. There, Nathan saw Arusthra making arrangements on Satan's side.

Arusthra, at Farush on his Satanic bison, saw Nathan and gave a careless, arrogant, evil smile.

He came to Nathan and said, "Look who's here! A worthless mortal to fight my master."

Nathan said nothing.

Arusthra continued, "This sub-universe piece of junk wants to fight the Lord of the Lords!"

Nathan had his trident with him. He was on Ayoo.

Arusthra then said, "Your wife.."

Nathan suddenly took his trident and hit Arsuthra's neck.

Then, Arusthra's head was cut and came off from Arusthra's body.

Nathan took the head of Arusthra and threw it at the check-post that The Three had set up earlier, on their side of Farush. The stick placed into the ground at the check post went into the head of Arusthra.

It looked like a warning sign to God Yinta's enemies.

Satan saw it in his Satanic vision. He got angry.

Nathan closed his eyes and opened them again.

A sacred eagle came to Nathan.

Nathan told the sacred eagle to go to Seperna, The Hollow of Dimona, and tell Sabrina to stay there until the end of the war.

But as he was telling it to the sacred eagle, Nathan saw Sabrina's chariot reaching Farush.

Sabrina saw her friends, The Three, and Eesayi.

She smiled at them and went to Nathan.

He got down from Ayoo and hugged her.

She kissed him on his forehead.

Sabrina saw Arusthra's cosmic-dead body, without the head.

Sabrina seriously told Nathan, "Tomorrow, there will be war. It is not a normal war. It is the war between a man and Satan. God Yinta will send his forces for you, and you have to lead them. My father, Satan, will come here with his forces. This war will be called The Great War of Man and Satan. This war will determine the future of the

Master Universe and its sub-universes."

Then Sabrina continued, "Nathan, my beloved husband! I know what you did. The time when you got pimples, you know that Satan gave you them, but you also know my father is watching you and observing you while you are getting depressed and low.

But you acted so naturally, like you don't even have an idea that Satan is watching you, and made my father believe that you are trying to find a solution to your pimples using human science.

But you know, it was not just the medicine that cleared your pimples. But also your faith in God Yinta.

You did the same when my brother attacked you, by acting like you didn't know Koshi, and the same when thugs stole your car. You made my father believe you were really suffering naturally because of all those troubles and problems in your life, but you already knew the truth.

The truth is that problems and good things in our lives change when we take action, according to time. My father, Satan, thought he was torturing you, a beloved follower of God Yinta, but you acted like you were in pain. Yes, physically, you were in pain when you were attacked by those thugs, but not mentally ever.

But you made my father believe he was successful in torturing you and inflicting pain in your life, but nope, you suffered physically, but just acted like you were suffering both mentally and physically to an extreme level because of all the problems you had in your life. Because you knew Satan was watching you.

And you don't want him to think of new problems to trouble for which you don't have the solutions to solve them. So you satisfied his ego by betraying him completely by making him believe that you were suffering from the problems he gave you initially to an extreme level that you can't take anymore problems and pain."

Eesayi and The Three were shocked.

Sabrina continued, "But my father realized this when you came to Master Universe for the first time. So he gave blood cancer to your mortal physical body. After this war, you will die physically. But we will exist at Udin in Seperna eternally with our children because I know you will return to your cosmic body after your physical body dies.

* * *

Why did you disrespect my father on that day? You said Satan is worthless, useless, and valueless in your life while giving a speech at your college on rational thinking. My father heard about it through his demons on Earth. He was hurt. And he said he wanted to torture you and kill you. Otherwise, he would have let you live. He already killed your mortal biological parents on Earth. That is why you got blood cancer, and you are here rather than in your world at your home. I also know that you knew I'm the daughter of Satan, and I came to you to help my father torture you and kill you. But you still loved me genuinely with your pure heart and soul. I changed myself for you, husband. I started liking you because of how you saw your mortal life, even in all those problems, and how you saw me.

You are the man for me. I realized that clearly that you are my man from that moment after you told me about how you saw the attack my brother did on you. I thought you were a good-hearted cosmic man who took birth as a mortal. But your place is among us. You are the son of the Dretonian Emperor, Qriswur, from the Wulshaan Master Universe. You came to Mother Adis Master Universe to get trained in real-time by fighting with Satan because you have to rule the entire Wulshaan Universe after the Great War of Man and Satan, along with Mother Adis Master Universe. Sumaaraa told me that your father knows Father Wulshaan, the father of Satan, and God Yinta, Husband of Mother Adis."

Sabrina had tears after saying it.

Nathan took her into his hug and told her, "I don't regret it even for a second because that is why I'm here with you, that is why I met you, that is how our beautiful son came into this existence. And I love my mortal mothers and fathers, also my immortal mother and father."

Sabrina looked at Nathan and felt amazed and surprised.

Nathan asked her, "Where is Aarus?"

Sabrina answered, "He is with my mother."

Nathan told Sabrina, "Ira, Jiza are in Heaven's Truth Castle now!"

Sabrina was shocked. Nathan continued, "They were killed by your father's demons because I destroyed Heezle on Earth."

Nathan said, "Your father committed a sin that he can never repent. He will face the consequences."

Sabrina: "I love my father, and I love you too, but fighting my father is not easy. Did God Yinta tell you?"

Nathan: "Yes, he did. And he also told me to tell you to visit Sumaaraa. He told me you haven't met them in a long time."

Sabrina: "Yes, my father doesn't like them much. So, I visit them in secret occasionally, but still my father knows about it, at least I won't raise his Ego in that way. But I met her yesterday at Seperna. She came to our home to see our son."

Nathan smiled in happiness and asked Sabrina.

Nathan: "How can I tell Farush if I have a request?"

Sabrina: "You will take the sacred sand of Farush into your two fists, and you will go to the sacred waterfall and the sacred fire. And you should throw the sand of one fist into the sacred waterfall, and the sand in another fist into the sacred fire.

Then you return here, kneel, look at Farush, and say your request. It will consider your request. But never drop the sand in the middle from your fists, no matter what."

Nathan asked Sabrina, "Is it the same process for your father?"

Sabrina said, "It is the same for God Yinta, too. Systems and rules over positions and ego. This is a standard practice set by Mother Adis."

Nathan took the sand of Farush, and on Ayoo, he went to the sacred waterfall and sacred fire on both sides of Farush, and he mixed the Farush sand in them.

He returned to where he was earlier on Farush and, on his knees, asked Farush, "Oh Farush, I, Nathan, the mortal immortal, requesting you to set the war and its rules as if this war is happening in my mortal world, Earth. That is how it would be fair to me to fight as a mortal immortal with Satan and his forces. I request you to please make this war fair and honest."

Then Sabrina, Eesayi, and The Three saw a big tornado coming right at them. Nathan saw it too.

The tornado came to them, and from it, a voice came out.

It is of Farush's.

She said, "Oh mortal immortal, I grant you what you asked for. In the great war of man and Satan, you, a man, and your army will fight with Satan and his army, as you humans fought wars on Earth like in your sacred times of the Son of God, Laseen."

After saying it, the Farush tornado went away.

A big, bright, glowing sacred chariot with white horses that have wings is coming towards Farush.

Nathan and Sabrina saw it.

After seeing it, Sabrina said, "Your God is preparing his armed forces for you."

Nathan asked, "Are those unicorns?"

Sabrina said, "No, there are no unicorns. They are not real. The armed forces of God have horses with wings. Satan's armed forces don't, but they travel and operate the same way."

The child in Nathan was disappointed a bit. And said, "God is a little more creative than your father."

Sabrina looked at Nathan and laughed.

The sacred chariot landed on Farush.

The general of the armed forces of God Yinta, Heera, came out from the chariot.

Heera came in front of Nathan and Sabrina. He bowed to both of them.

Nathan and Sabrina said, "No, we don't like that," at the same time.

They looked at each other and laughed.

Heera said, "That is why I bowed to you, my prince and princess."

Heera continued, "God Yinta told me to assist you in this war. I never thought there would be a war between a man and Satan, but it is here.

I also learned about the request you made to Farush.

Farush informed me that she allowed both sides to get up to 1.4 million horses and 4 million soldiers in total, along with other weapons of mass destruction.

This rule is applied to us and them both."

* * *

Nathan asked Heera, "Will the soldiers die in the war?"

Heera smiled and said, "No, master! Soldiers of God Yinta are immortal, and Satan's soldiers are immortal, too. They don't die, but they feel the pain of wounds and hits. The army, which eventually fears more pain from hits and wounds, will stop fighting to stop more pain of all kinds inflicting upon them and give up."

Nathan said, "It is crueler than war on Earth. At least soldiers die there, but here, it's just pain of all kinds."

Heera said, "Yes, master!"

Then they saw a big, grand Satanic chariot with thirteen bisons coming towards Farush.

It landed on Farush. When it landed, Farush shook for a few seconds.

From that Satanic chariot, Satan came out. He is 24 feet tall and a massive being. His brother, God Yinta, too, is 24 feet in height.

He stepped on the Farush ground. His head is a little up, and he has arrogance and confidence on his face.

Sabrina saw her father. She went behind Nathan. Satan didn't look at Nathan, his daughter, or others.

Satan's general, Iteen, stood a little away from Satan.

Satan looked at the plateau of Farush, the sacred waterfall, and the sacred fire.

He gave a mocking, arrogant smile at Nathan.

Satan told Iteen, "400000 soldiers with horses, 600000 foot soldiers."

Iteen said, "Yes, Lord!"

Satan saw his daughter, Sabrina. He got angry.

Satan angrily said, "Sabrina, your husband will perish at Farush."

Sabrina was scared and said nothing.

Then Satan continued, "This fool," looking at Nathan, "Will pay the price for denying me as his Lord. Your God, Yinta, is a fool. He stole my early existence and my father's legacy. This Parasite God of yours is no God. He is not even eligible to become a dust particle under my foot. You came here with the courage you got from that fool just because he is giving you his weak army of stupid souls of his believers.

Fool, you will be defeated by the royal forces of Satan. We rule the Sapace, Satsand, and everything. The Farush request you made shows how much you trust your God. Ha, ha. I will tear you and your forces apart into pieces. Where is your God? Is he scared? Is he hiding in that dirty forest as an idiot acting holy?"

Nathan asked Heera, "Is he like that before too?"

Heera said, "Yes! God Yinta used to laugh at him."

Nathan said, "Yeah, he thinks I don't know about the promise God Yinta made to his mother, and he thinks I will make the mistake of revealing my plans or intentions by replying to him in a rage of anger. Abusing God Yinta doesn't change anything.

And this is Farush, and we are on sacred sand, not on Satsand. Safire or Sapace will not work here unless they are being used as war weapons. Why does he think I will get scared? Yeah, he is looking pretty dark, but we have more interesting characters in our movies on Earth than him here."

Nathan told Sabrina, "If your father got a chance, he would cut me into a million meat pieces, but he wants to fight me to prove to you that you took a bad decision by having a child with me, and he would have gotten you someone greater than me. He wants to prove that to you by defeating me first."

Sabrina quietly said, "I, too, understood that!"

Nathan said, "Even Satan thinks he can get a better son-in-law if he is given the chance to select the husband for his daughter."

Sabrina sarcastically said, "Of course! My father knows what is best for me!"

Nathan looked at her sarcastically.

Satan told Iteen, "This fool, my God! I don't know how my daughter liked him. I sent her to kill that stupid. But she married him. No, she had a son with him even before marriage. Kids these days! This idiot as ruler of The Great Wulshaan Master Universe, what in the Hell!"

Sabrina looked at her father with affection. Satan looked at Sabrina, too. His love for his daughter is visible to all known and unknown universes on his face.

Satan then left for Hell on his grand chariot.

Nathan felt terribly sad after seeing Satan and Sabrina. He thought he came in the middle of a father and daughter. He thought of trying to talk to Satan nicely at least once before his physical body's death.

Nathan told Heera, "600000 foot soldiers and 400000 soldiers with horses."

Heera said, "Yes, master!"

Nathan told Heera, "Keep 200000 foot soldiers in reserve. They should not enter Farush but should be ready to come here when needed."

Heera: "Yes, master. What about weapons and strategies?"

Nathan: "What weapons and other things do we have?"

Heera said, "We got many, master. It would take one Farush day to tell you the complete list."

Nathan: "Ok, tell me the most important weapons."

Heera: "We calculate the strength of weapons according to how many mortals they can kill. Nuca Suhen Bomb can kill a minimum of 10 million mortal soldiers, and it completely decimates the place, too. Sahen Isuka missiles can kill up to 20000 mortals. Israas drones' rock bullets can kill hundreds of mortals. We also got thousands of chariots, swords, axes, rocks, sacred eagles, Ayoons, and other animals."

Nathan said, "Keep most animals out of the war except for horses, donkeys, and Ayoons, etc."

Heera: "Certainly, master!"

Sabrina asked Nathan, "Did you bathe in the sacred waterfall? And did you pray to the sacred fire?"

Nathan told Sabrina, "No, is it necessary? Does it serve any purpose?"

Sabrina: "No, but just like Krisens pray to Regor, now we can pray to the sacred water and fire to gain that psychological strength to face our problems. Even if it doesn't help logically."

Nathan said, "Ok, do you know how to do it?"

Sabrina said, "I don't, but Heera might know!"

Nathan asked Heera, "Heera, do you know any priest who can help me with the process of praying to the sacred water and fire?"

Heera: "Yes, master. I will go now and will return with the priest."

Nathan said, "Ok!"

Heera left in his chariot.

Nathan went to The Three and Eesayi.

Nathan asked Eesayi, "What do you think? Can we win the war?"

Eesayi said, "You can, if you can!"

Nathan: "True!"

Nathan asked The Three, "What do you think, guys?"

Huro said, "Yes, Boss. However, we should be very careful when choosing strategies. It looks like Satan's armed forces will not follow any standard practices of war except the rules of Farush."

Kwin said, "Yes, we have to treat them like our army treats the terrorists."

Tes said, "I agree. They are worse than terrorists because now they are dead too, and we can't even kill them again."

Huro, Nathan, Kwin, and Eesayi laughed.

Nathan said, "But really, guys, the soldiers of Satan, when they were alive, thought they would go to Heaven with the promise they were given by Satan if they did what Satan and Satan's demons asked them to do. Yes, they went to Heaven, but it is Satan's Heaven, not God's. For them, Satan is their God. They killed people and did horrible things in their worlds as asked by Satan and his demons. Thus, they earned Satan's favor and entered Satan's Heaven. Now, too, they think they are fighting a holy war against nonbelievers of their God, Satan. They were extremely dangerous when they were alive, and now I don't even need to say. They believe in Satan as their one true God with their soul."

Satan is waking up the forces in Hell.

"Schehiel en muntro, iss retur un mundro. Shael tew gos us en enrek oruf leu jes enkotyote," said Satan loudly in Satanic language.

Heera returned with an Ateestan priest to Farush. The priest asked Nathan and Sabrina to come with him to the sacred waterfall and sacred fire at Farush.

Nathan and Sabrina on Heera's chariot, Huro, Kwin, and Tes on sacred eagles, Eesayi on his chariot, reached the sacred waterfall of Farush. They got down. The priest asked Nathan to bathe in the sacred waterfall and sit next to Sabrina. Sabrina sat on the Farush ground in front of the sacred waterfall. Nathan bathed in the sacred waterfall. And he came, sat next to Sabrina.

The priest said to Nathan, "Prophet, your prayers and wishes will be granted, but to pray in front of the sacred waterfall and sacred fire, you must be a married man. It is the rule of this victory prayer. You have to marry your lover here, and I will confirm your marriage. Then your prayers will be answered by Mother Adis."

Nathan looked at Sabrina. Sabrina told Nathan, "As you wish, my love!"

The priest prayed to the sacred waterfall. He chanted Ateestan sacred spells. The sacred waterfall opened a hole in the ground in front of Nathan and Sabrina. From that hole, water started coming out in a small laminar flow.

The priest asked Nathan to take water into his palm and pour the water on Sabrina's head. The priest asked Nathan to say, "God Yinta, Mother Adis, bless us with prosperity and progress. Father Wulshaan, bless us with victory in all our wars." Nathan said it while pouring sacred water with his hand on Sabrina's head.

The priest loudly chanted, "Oh, God Yinta, Son of Mother Adis, Lover of the Goddess of Peace Sumaaraa, Son-in-law of Emperor of

Emptiness, God of Righteousness, God of All Life Forms, God of Humanity, God of All Known and Unknown universes, today, the flag bearer of righteousness and justice, Nathan, is asking for your help. Nathan's sacred wife, Sabrina, is asking for your help. Oh, Lord of Lords God Yinta, Help thy child secure victory in his battles and wars. Ask the Goddess of Peace to help Nathan and Sabrina handle the stress and pressures."

The priest asked Sabrina to take the Farush sand mixed with sacred water into her hands and apply it to Nathan's palms. Sabrina did it.

The priest asked, "Now, Nathan, the Last Prophet of Ateesta, do you agree that Sabrina is your wife?"

Nathan said, "Yes, I agree!"

The priest asked Sabrina, "Sabrina, the Daughter of Satan, do you agree that Nathan, the Last Prophet of Ateesta, is your husband?"

Sabrina said, "Yes, I agree!"

The priest said, "I pronounce you husband and wife. Your victory will be the blessings of Mother Adis, Father Wulshaan, and God Yinta."

Sabrina hugged and kissed Nathan.

The priest said, "You loved each other before your marriage, too, but now the Gods will know that you both are husband and wife, not just lovers. They will help you now, and they will also help you even if you are unmarried, but now it is different."

The Three, Eesayi and Heera, felt happy seeing Nathan and Sabrina getting married and blessed by the priest for victory in the war.

They went to the sacred fire of Farush, and Nathan and Sabrina sat in front of it. The priest prayed to the sacred fire, and the sacred fire came in front of Nathan and Sabrina. The priest said, "With the light of the sacred fire as a witness, I confirm your marriage to before, after, to, from, and everything other than that, in inside and outside and everything in between and outside of eternity in all known and unknown universes."

Nathan hugged Sabrina and kissed her.

Satan's general, Iteen, constructed a grand war camp tent on their side on Farush using black Satanic magic.

Nathan, Sabrina, The Three, and Eesayi returned to their side on Farush, where they had the checkpost.

The Satan war tent color was dark, and The Three felt, after seeing it, as if death constructed the war camp tent by itself to kill them, which is true.

Heera saw Satan's war camp and constructed the grand war camp tent of life. It is pure white with Gold pillars, Red lines, and Black borders.

The war camps looked like they were representing a war of life and death, light and darkness.

The war camps of Man and Satan are ready. Satan walked into his war camp.

The Priest sat in a small tent, and he was praying to Mother Adis for the victory of Nathan and the forces of God Yinta.

Sabrina walked into their war camp tent.

Sabrina saw magic spells, lights, and buttons for weapon controls.

She saw magic light buttons for Nuca Suhen Bombs, Sahen Isuka Missiles, Israas Drones, Resrua Pain bullet guns, Axes, and Swords. She came out and saw sacred eagles, Ayoons, and also hundreds of thousands of cosmic soldiers of God Yinta with chariots and weapons. They looked just like humans in war fields on Earth at the time of the Son of God, 'Laseen,' as Farush said.

The Three, Nathan, Eesayi, and Heera, changed into their war uniforms. Sabrina came in one already.

The hundreds of thousands of God Yinta's soldiers are coming towards Nathan's war camp from far away. They were coming from a place called 'Kaasmaa Milee.' The people who fought on Earth on the side of good and for their countries joined the Kaasmaa Milee forces. Kaasmaa Milee is a place on the back side of Heaven Truth Castle in Mother Adis' Master Universe. The Soldiers of God train there and take care of matters of war of God Yinta.

The young people who come to Heaven go to Kaasmaa Milee if they are interested in fighting for the truth.

Satan's soldiers are coming from 'Sahell Maesra.' They are thugs, murderers, and people who betrayed their nations on Earth and in their worlds. They train at the backside of Hell in Sahell Maesra and exist in Satan's Heaven. Satan's Heaven is under Hell in Mother Adis-Master Universe.

Heera asked Nathan to join him on his chariot. The Three got on their sacred eagles.

Heera's chariot was going deep into Farush.

There are hundreds of thousands of soldiers of God Yinta who are getting prepared for the war.

There, Nathan saw thousands of chariots, soldiers on foot, on horses, with all kinds of weapons with them. They all looked determined and confident.

Satan came out from his war tent and, in his chariot, was going to meet his soldiers. They were ugly and confident as Hell. The Satan soldiers are ready to inflict as much pain as possible, which is much worse than death.

The generals of Satan checked their weapons and Anekas. They have Nuca Saahroon bombs, Sahen Stana missiles, Satruna drones, Sateen pain bullet guns, Sait Axes, Sait Swords, etc.

They are equivalent to God Yinta weapons in classification.

Satan's forces also brought Satanic Bulls and Bisons. Nathan's forces brought Heaven Bulls and Bisons.

Nathan greeted his armed forces.

They were cheering and chanting, "God is Great.. God is Great!"

Heera's chariot stopped, and Nathan looked at the forces in front of him. He asked them loudly, "Do you know who I am?"

The forces are looking at Nathan.

Nathan continued, "I am the Son of God, just like you. I'm his servant. Just like you!"

Everybody is silent, Nathan and Heera can hear noises made by horses and bison, bulls, eagles, and Ayoons.

Ayoo is the name given by Nathan to his creature vehicle. From that day, that creature's family named itself 'Ayoons'.

All the creatures of God Yinta forces are in White color or in

White with Red and Black on them.

The chariots of God Yinta forces are golden in color with flags of Ateesta on them.

The creatures and animals of Satan are dark and smoky. The chariots of Satan's forces are dark and brownish.

Heera took his chariot more into the middle of the concentration of their forces.

Nathan asked his soldiers, "Will you fight for me?"

The forces said, "Yes.."

Nathan continued, "No, fight for Justice. Fight for our God, Yinta. Mother Adis knows if our God steps on this battlefield, then he will decimate the forces of Satan in seconds, and he will take over Hell and sit on its throne. But Mother Adis treats everyone as equals, and she prevents destruction as much as possible, no matter what the context is. It is because she is a mother. That is why even in the great war of Nazreck, she made sure that the world didn't get burned in the fight between God Yinta and Satan. But today, that very motherly nature of Mother Adis is being taken advantage of, and Satan did horrible things to Mother Adis's sacred creations. The cunning Satan hid his slow destruction of the minds of life forms in Mother Adis's creations cleverly from her. But God Yinta is continuously trying to save those life forms from the influence of Satan."

He then got down from the chariot and sat on a horse. That horse started walking forward.

Nathan continued, "Today, the destruction of the sacredness of Mother Adi's creations in all known and unknown universes will be stopped. Satan will learn a very good lesson."

Then the horse reared, and Nathan, in rage, said, "Kill Satan!"

The forces cheered and shouted, "Kill Satan!" in masses.

Satan heard it. Nathan started riding his horse to his camp. Heera, on his chariot, followed him.

Satan saw Nathan coming on the sacred horse and the chariot following him.

After inspecting the battlefield, The Three returned to camp on their sacred eagles.

They saw Nathan.

Sabrina, The Three, Eesayi saw Nathan riding the white sacred horse.

It was felt by them, while looking at Nathan riding the sacred white horse, and the grand sacred chariot following him with dust, and the way they were coming, it was like God Yinta himself came into Nathan and riding the horse.

The armed forces, seeing Nathan, felt they were not just fighting on God's side for Nathan but were fighting for God Yinta himself, who took birth as a human being.

Satan saw it.

Satan knew that the aura Nathan had was not coming from God Yinta, but from the feeling inside Nathan that he was fighting for righteousness.

Satan knew that that aura and confidence were more dangerous than the support of God itself.

Satan knew that God would be proud of Nathan even if he lost the war.

Satan couldn't take the glow of the aura of Nathan and wanted to destroy him from the inside, too.

Nathan reached his war tent.

He got down from his horse and went to Sabrina.

Sabrina was emotional. She had tears in her eyes. Nathan saw it, smiled at her, hugged her, and kissed her on the forehead.

Nathan emotionally said, "Sabrina, for our family. For the family of our humanity!"

Huro loudly made a war cry: "For God, We Kill Satan!"

Nathan said, "No."

Everyone looked at Nathan in amazement.

Nathan loudly gave a war cry, "For Humanity, We Kill Satan!"

Satan heard it. He understood.

The wild, infectious nature of human courage and valor is

unmatchable by anything in the universe. Humans came out of the Earth and used the path of the Earth to improve their daily lives for the better, which Mother Adis had not even imagined it herself.

The Humans evolved as creatures of intelligence, unlike other life forms created by Mother Adis in all known and unknown universes. They are now at the initial level of cracking the key to the path to the Master Universe through quantum science, which will help them come to the Master Universe before death like Nathan, but with no help from any higher power than humans.

Satan knew the aspirations of these human mortals were unimaginable, even by Mother Adis and God Yinta. Satan knew if someone triggered them to do something strong enough, they wouldn't even care about death or any pleasure. They will be fixated on achieving the thing they wanted to achieve till the last breath of their mortal life. If that wildfire courage of Nathan spreads to the forces of God Yinta, then Satan's greedy, arrogant, overconfident forces will be defeated in minutes. Satan is thinking of something to stop Nathan.

Satan still remembers how much he tried to create problems for a man who brought many inventions to life for humanity. That man never knelt to Satan. That man never accepted Satan as his lord. That man never took the offers of Satan. At the end of his life, he wished to be with his mother, but never bent his neck to Satan. Satan knew that that man knew where Satan was in the Master Universe, where the Master Universe was, and how to get there. Nathan comes from that line of humans who will never bend their knees to Satan and will take humanity forward aggressively and make people ridicule Satan and respect God even if they don't believe in God because God wants humans to be happy even if they don't believe in him but Satan wants humans to believe in him and accept him as their Lord primarily. If not, Satan will offer humans Satan's Heaven and pleasures in their world so they will accept Satan as their Lord. Satan couldn't take this 'Not believing in God and Satan but respecting God-philosophy' development of humanity and the way they live their lives and see Satan through their lives, which makes Satan's influence none in the lives of those human beings who follow that philosophy.

The time has come. Farush blasted the Warena volcano, signaling they should start the war officially. On every Farush day, the war starts with the first time the Warena volcano bursts and stops after the second time the Warena volcano bursts that day.

The war will start again with the Warena volcano blast on the next Farush day. The process will go on until someone wins the war.

After seeing the Warena volcano blast, Satan, on his chariot, went to his soldiers.

Satan loudly said, "That servant of the false God thinks he is right. And we are wrong. There is no definite way to live a life in your world and to exist here. You live as you want, no matter what others think of it. You can get anything if you believe in me. My soldiers, I'm giving you a sacred offer. I will make you all take birth as mortals in your world again, but this time, from your birth, you will be wealthy, handsome, beautiful, powerful, and intelligent; you will get everything and anything in your world. Even while taking you to Hell and Satan's Heaven again, I will give you a painless death in your old age after you enjoy your mortal life to the fullest with all the worldly pleasures. That army of God Yinta will never take birth as mortals again, but I will give you that chance. Go, show Hell to those low lives of God Yinta."

Satan's forces shouted their war cry, "Satan is God! Satan is Lord!"

Nathan started on his horse and is now in front of his forces. With him, The Three on their sacred eagles, Eesayi is on his chariot, Heera is on his chariot, and Sabrina is on Heera's chariot. They are all looking at Satan's forces, who have the aura of dark ugliness.

Nathan and his gang are looking at Satan's forces. Satan came in front of his forces with his generals and Iteen as his charioteer. Satan looked at Nathan and his forces.

Nathan told Heera to wait and stand by. Heera told the forces to stand still.

Satan told Iteen to stand by. Iteen told their forces to stand still and wait for further orders.

Nathan and Satan are looking at each other and their forces.

Nathan asked Heera, "Is he waiting for us to attack them?"

Heera said, "Yes, maybe!"

Satan asked Iteen, "Is he waiting for us to attack them?"

Iteen said, "Yes, my lord. It looks like that."

Satan said, "Then we wait. Let him move first to attack us."

Nathan told Heera, "We wait, let him attack first!"

They are waiting. So that the other will attack first. The forces from both sides are standing still with dust above the Farush ground. The noises of bison, bulls, horses, Ayoons, and other animals from both sides are clearly heard in silence.

Nathan asked Eesayi to come to him. Nathan told Eesayi something quietly.

Eesayi nodded his head in agreement.

Satan and Nathan are looking at each other. Satan started laughing.

Nathan and others couldn't understand why.

Suddenly, the forces of Satan started attacking the forces of Nathan from the back.

Nathan's forces were confused as they expected the attack from the front side, where they saw Satan's forces on the battlefield, but Satan hid his other forces from Nathan and his forces behind Beetreyaa Mountain, and those forces started attacking unexpectedly from the backside.

Satan's forces are causing massive damage to Nathan's forces and destroying their chariots and animals. They were inflicting horrible pain on the soldiers of God.

Nathan was surprised by the unexpected attack and understood that he had underestimated Satan a bit.

The first move of Satan at the beginning of the war caused massive damage to the Nathan side.

Nathan saw the destruction.

He signaled Eesayi.

Eesayi quickly reached their war camp.

He asked soldiers there for the weapons operating rooms of the Israas drones. They took him to the Israas weapons control room.

There, he saw the Israas operators.

Eesayi asked them to strike Satan's forces with Israas drones diagonally from four sides.

They got the God's Israas drones on the fly and quickly went to the four sides of Satan's forces. The Satanic Israas came against them. Those drones attacked each other. Some of God's Israas drones attacked Satan's forces with bombs and pain bullets.

Satan's forces started running in all directions to escape the attacks of God's Israas drones.

Nathan decided to be utterly merciless and not look back. Otherwise, Satan will even take advantage of his morals, too.

Satan saw the disturbance in his forces due to God's Israas drones.

Nathan saw Satan thinking.

Nathan immediately asked Huro to go to Eesayi and tell him to launch Sahen Isuka missiles on the war camp of Satan and confirm to him again that he had communicated the message.

Huro, on his sacred eagle, reached their weapons control centre and informed Eesayi what Nathan told him.

They launched Sahen Isuka missile attacks on Satan's war camp.

Satan's forces launched a reverse attack. And blasted many missiles before reaching Satan's war camp. Some fell on Satan's war camp tents, but they caused minimal damage and pain to Satanic weapons operators.

Chaos erupted on both sides with continuous strikes through drones and missiles from both sides. The soldiers from both sides are getting hit by the Resrua pain bullets, missiles, and drone strikes, inflicting pain on both sides' soldiers.

Nathan asked Heera to make the horse forces come with them, and they moved straight into Satan's forces. They are attacking Satan's soldiers fiercely.

Satan saw it.

Nathan was inflicting not just pain but also fear into the existence of soldiers of Satan in front of him.

Nathan, with his horse force, went deep into Satan's forces. They were attacking barbarically. A Satanic arrow went into Nathan's palm. Light came out of his veins and went up. The minuscule leak of light, which came out from his veins for a split millisecond, went and touched another arrow coming towards Nathan. It resulted in a big blast equivalent to 1000 Nuca Suhen bombs. The anti-light matter that came out from Nathan's veins caused a supermassive energy release. The soldiers on both sides were blinded by the extreme-ultra glow of the light of the explosion.

Nathan understood that if the exploded anti-energy reached the Farush ground and soldiers on it, then both sides would suffer complete losses, and soldiers from both sides would experience the pain of getting burned alive as a mortal ten million times at once. To stop this, Nathan lifted himself into the space of Farush, showed his palm to the 'Idea' of the blast, and absorbed the energy from the blast into him.

Nathan came down and stood on the Farush ground. Everyone is standing still and knows what Nathan did. But again, they started fighting.

Satan laughed and said, "Ha, ha, you can save a poisonous snake from death, but never expect it to be loyal to you because you saved it."

Nathan saw Satan laughing. And smiled back at him.

The smile of Nathan irritated Satan.

Farush blasted the Warena volcano. Both sides stopped fighting.

Nathan's forces suffered a lot of losses in the form of being inflicted with pain by the weapons of Satan's forces. Satan's forces, too, suffered significant losses. Many soldiers were screaming in pain. In the pain and fear, many soldiers from both sides couldn't continue the fighting. They were sent to relief camps on their own sides to recover from pain and fear.

Nathan came back to his main war camp tent. In front of it, Nathan kissed Sabrina and hugged her.

Satan saw Nathan hugging Sabrina.

He understood the courage, power, and strength a woman can give to a man.

He feared that if every man on Earth were to be loved by his wife, like Nathan by Sabrina, then it would be impossible for him to penetrate their lives and create problems for them to make them suffer, and also make them accept Satan as their Lord. Because the man and woman will stand by each other in facing the problems Satan created for them, eventually, they will solve those problems with the strength of their unity, and in the process, they will become closer to God than to Satan in their mortal lives.

Then, after realizing this, Satan cursed humanity so that no man and woman would be truly loyal to each other. The men and women will betray each other and fight culture wars with each other with their falsely supercharged Satanic egos. The men and women will give more importance to the money of person they are marrying than to the person's character and how that person will love them and take care of them. The men and women will hate each other by seeing each other's unique qualities rather than embracing, respecting, and understanding them. They will become confused and will slowly lose their true identity.

Nathan, in his camp, sat with Eesayi, Tes, Kwin, and Huro.

Tes said, "The Satanic forces used lots of pain bullets and missiles on our forces. We tried to blast them before they reached us, but they were using them in unusual numbers. Our defense systems couldn't intercept each and every one of them. This caused a lot of damage to us. They are also attacking not like soldiers of any sort but like murderers, serial killers, and thugs, and they are not following any patterns with their attacks in any form. They are too barbaric and brutal. But our brave soldiers are attacking from the front, and our soldiers are trained well, but they have patterns, and Satan's forces are decoding those patterns of our attacks in all forms."

Kwin said, "They are using Satsand on our soldiers. It is burning the skin of the cosmic bodies of our soldiers where it was touching and causing unbearable pain to our soldiers."

Nathan asked, "But using Satsand is not allowed on Farush, right? If they didn't inform us in advance?"

Kwin: "Yes, but they are smuggling it!"

Nathan: "That is against the rules of the war, right?"

Kwin: "Yes, but you are seriously not expecting the soldiers of Satan to obey the rules of war, right?"

Nathan didn't say anything.

Huro said, "We have many pain casualties from today."

Eesayi said, "We should use Nuca Suhen if they continue fighting immorally like this!"

Nathan took some time to respond. Everyone, including Sabrina and Heera, is waiting for Nathan's response.

Nathan got up and walked out. He went to the relief camps of his forces.

Soldiers are screaming in unexplainable pain and fear.

Nathan was assuring them. He consoled them and told them to be strong. The medical teams are giving Marjena Plant leaves to soldiers to soothe the pain.

Others came with Nathan. Nathan told Eesayi to ask for the help of the angels of God Yinta in Heaven for making the sacred rain of holy Heaven sand from the Farush space and the holy Heaven water to come out and rain from the Farush ground.

Eesayi said, "Yes, Prophet!"

Nathan told Huro to be with the weapons teams. And Nathan told Tes to be with Eesayi all the time during the war.

Heera told Nathan about the Czarach manuscript.

Nathan asked Heera if he could see the ancient palm leaf manuscript of Czarach.

God Yinta wrote the Czarach palm leaf manuscript after the war of Nazreck.

God Yinta wrote it to describe the nature of Evil and Satan.

Heera told Nathan, "The priest asked God about it, and the priest also requested God to give it to you, Nathan. The priest told me that God Yinta told him that the Czarach manuscript would arrive in Farush on the first day of the war after the Warena volcano blast for the second time. "

They walked to the tent where the priest was praying. The priest came out with the Czarach manuscript. The priest gave it to Nathan.

Nathan took the Czarach manuscript, and he went into his tent.

Nathan started reading it.

He felt the presence of evil inside his tent while he was reading it. No one went inside the tent Nathan was in while he was reading the Czarach manuscript. The priest asked them, even Sabrina, not to follow Nathan.

Czarach manuscript, even though written by God Yinta himself, is horrifying, monstrous, and atrocious. While reading it, God Yinta himself gave Nathan a protective layer around him until he completed reading it. God Yinta himself gave strength, courage, and bravery to Nathan, as the Czarach manuscript explains about Evil from its origins and birth.

While Nathan was reading it, Tes, Huro, Kwin, Eesayi, Sabrina, and the priest were seeing bloody, ugliest, angry, evil Pisaach Demons surrounding and revolving around the tent Nathan was in. It is pure Satanic chaos of demons.

They saw demonic entities that no one had seen before in any universe because the Origin of Evil was being revealed to Nathan, and Nathan, while reading the Czarach manuscript, was also chanting the spells made by Evil, which attracted the nastiest demonic evil entities in all known and unknown universes.

The Czarach manuscript explains the origin of evil from the absolute beginning point before even the time began anywhere in any known, unknown universes and dimensions. The Czarach manuscript talks about the origin of evil from Beeliaal, how the first light ever of Mother Adis created good, and how the nature of evil was created by Beeliaal initially, how it happened, and the whole process in detail. Nathan is the first person to have read it since God Yinta wrote it at the banks of the Kalsa River on Earth after the War of Nazreck.

Nathan freed Ira's cosmic soul from the room of Ikkayath in the Saden Demon castle, through a spell from the Czarach manuscript. He reunited Ira's cosmic soul with her mortal mind-soul.

The sounds made by demonic entities while Nathan was reading the Czarach manuscript were horrifying and unbearable even to Eesayi, the angel from Heaven.

* * *

Nathan completed reading the Czarach manuscript, and he came out.

Nathan saw the demons. He said and did nothing.

God Yinta's servant Eesayi took his trident and scared those demons. The demons went away. Sabrina felt something different after seeing Nathan.

Warena volcano was blasted again by Farush.

Nathan got on his horse.

The forces from both sides again stood on the battlefield.

Suddenly, a missile came from Satan's side.

Nathan forces intercepted it and blasted it.

Nathan looked seriously to the side of Satan's chariot. Satan was laughing, looking at Nathan's forces.

Satan told Iteen and his generals, "Today it will rain Satsand and Sater from above, ha ha!"

They laughed, looking at the soldiers of Nathan.

The soldiers from both sides cheered themselves with their war cries.

Eesayi saw angels from Heaven coming to Farush. They landed at the war camp of Nathan.

They were so gracious and pure. It smells of jasmine around them.

They came on the sacred triangle plate of truth. They only stand on the sacred triangle plate of truth when they travel. It is prohibited for them to sit and travel by the orders of God Yinta. The reason is that Satanic Pisaach Demons always mimic and appear to life forms as angels of God, but they don't have the courage to stand straight and look into the eyes of any life form that prays to God. So they always sit or bend a bit to show their lies as truth and cheat God loving life forms.

The courage of standing and speaking the truth is only possible for angels of heaven. So, to avoid confusing life forms, God Yinta told angels to travel and appear to life forms only standing and never while sitting or in any position.

The angels are on a sacred triangle plate of truth, looking at the battlefield.

Satan was arrogantly talking to his soldiers, abusing God Yinta.

Satan was too arrogant to observe angels reaching Farush from Heaven. Satan did not even recognize the sacred divineness of angels.

Satan ordered his forces to attack. The Satanic bison and the God bison were hitting each other. Ayoons and Satanic Froona flying creatures are fighting above the ground. The Satanic bulls are ramming the soldiers of Nathan. God-side Bulls are hitting and attacking Satanic bulls. The white donkeys were biting soldiers of Satan. Nathan, on his horse, started flying towards Satan. Heera followed him. Sabrina was on the tower at Nathan's war camp tent. She is looking at the battlefield, instructing sacred eagles and Ayoons on how they should attack.

Huro was handling weapons, and his team was constantly attacking Satan's forces with Sahen Isuka missiles and Israas drones, and also intercepting hundreds of Satan Sahen Stana missiles and Satan Satruna drones.

They observed Satan soldiers using extreme amounts of Satan Sateen pain bullets and also attacking Nathan's soldiers with Satan Sait Axes and Satan Sait Swords.

Huro and his team understood that Satan's soldiers were following the patterns of literal terrorists, mad serial killers, and murderers of Earth.

Nathan saw this and asked Heera to send someone to Huro to tell Huro that they should increase the usage of Israas drones and Sahen Isuka missiles, particularly at the edges of Satan forces.

Heera forwarded the information to Huro.

Nathan was fighting with a sword in his hand against the Satan soldiers.

The trident of Nathan changed its form to a sword for the war.

Huro attacked the edges of the Satan forces with missiles and drones. Huro also tried to attack the general of Satan, Iteen. It angered Satan.

Satan ordered Iteen for Sater rain.

Iteen made Sater rain from the upside, and soldiers of the Nathan side are screaming from burning pain when Sater touches them.

Nathan saw it and got angry.

Eesayi and Tes went to the angels who came to Farush from Heaven. Tes bowed to them. Eesayi greeted them.

The angels saw the Sater rain. They got angry.

Angels prayed to God Yinta, "Oh Lord of Lords, Emperor of Emperors! The Life forms who believed in you need your gracious help now. Help us, Father!"

After that, it started raining sacred water from the Farush ground.

Nathan saw sacred water drops coming out of the Farush ground. It is a reverse rain to Earth in comparison.

The water drops of the sacred rain in Farush were coming out from the Farush ground and going up. It is the holy rain format of Heaven. It happened on Farush that day.

Nathan was amazed. Huro, Tes, and Kwin saw the sacred ground rain. They were flabbergasted.

The sacred water was burning soldiers of Satan from the moment it came into contact with them.

Then God Yinta, through his angels, made sacred sand rain from above.

The sand, while touching Satan's forces, was burning and turning their cosmic skin into dust.

A sacred Banyan plant was born at the side of Nathan. Satan got to know about this through his demons.

Satan felt that it was because Nathan was a human, and Nathan was fighting this hard. Nathan has an able brain that is functioning properly.

Satan thought that if Nathan was not ably minded, then he wouldn't have come this far to fight against him.

Satan doesn't want anything to happen like this again in the future. Satan doesn't want any mortal to challenge him. So, Satan cursed humanity that their environment would be polluted, and with pollution, the intelligence and thinking power of people would go down significantly. The trees on Earth will be cut down as fast as possible, and the Earth will be filled with poisonous, lifeless-Satanic gases. The humans will also die of hunger because of this.

The Banyan tree is the symbol of life in Ateesta. God Yinta likes Banyan trees a lot.

Warena volcano was blasted again by Farush.

The forces on both sides stopped fighting.

Satan's forces took huge losses. Thousands of Satan soldiers left the battlefield to get relief from pain and fear.

Nathan went back to his war camp and met Sabrina. She hugged him.

Satan was upset. Satan asked his generals to use the Nuca Saahroon bomb on the next Farush day.

Iteen and his generals asked Satan again, Does he really want to use the Nuca Saahroon bomb?

Satan told them, "No matter who you are, if the other forces are tearing your forces apart, then you have to do what you want to do. I should have done this on the first day. I would have returned to Hell that evening itself, winning this stupid war."

Nathan and Sabrina went to the angels. Nathan graciously greeted them and thanked them.

Then one of the angels told Nathan, "My child, Oh mortal immortal, we pray for your victory to God Yinta!

The flag on your camp never saw defeat and will never see defeat."

Then Nathan looked at the divine flag of God Yinta; It was the same flag God Yinta had on his chariot in the Great War of Nazreck.

The angels left Farush after blessing Sabrina and Nathan.

Nathan and his gang again gathered in their war camp.

Huro said, "We suffered significant losses of our sacred animals and soldiers. But we found the patterns of attacks by Satan's soldiers. They are pure murderers, terrorists, and serial killers."

Satan asked his generals to instruct his soldiers to behave like absolute maniacs on the battlefield the next day before attacking to confuse and irritate the Nathan forces.

In his war camp, Nathan told his team, " Tomorrow, we will be together on the front line."

He asked Sabrina to come on Heera's chariot, following him.

Eesayi brought food and tasty drinks from Earth for them.

Nathan asked Eesayi, "My friend, why did you bring these? We don't need them anymore!"

Eesayi said, "I know, my friend, but I know you were also human once. Not only you. Kwin, Tes, and Huro too. In this stressful period, you need these to make your immortal souls feel good in mortal cosmic bodies."

Nathan thanked Eesayi.

They all ate together outside on the Farush ground.

After eating food, Nathan left for the relief camps where his soldiers were kept to recover from the pain.

He met thousands of his soldiers who are in cosmic pain from war injuries.

Nathan sat with them and talked to them.

Nathan listened to the stories of their mortal lives. They laughed together, and soldiers felt good in the presence of Nathan.

Nathan told them he would come to Kaasmaa Milee after the war.

Nathan returned to his main war camp tent.

The time has come for the Warena volcano blast by Farush.

Nathan was on his horse, and Sabrina was on the chariot with Heera as her charioteer.

Kwin, Tes, and Huro were on their horses on both sides of Nathan.

They saw the Warena volcano blast. After that, they started going to the front line. Eesayi followed them. They reached the front line.

Suddenly, they heard a loud bang.

Nathan heard it. It came from the back side of his forces.

He understood by seeing the energy and dust coming from the faraway that it was the Nuca Saahroon bomb, the deadliest bomb in the Master Universe.

After seeing it, Nathan was upset and shouting, as the energy was reaching them very fast. Sabrina and others, too, were seeing it. They were stunned.

The energy of the Nuca Saahroon bomb reached Nathan's soldiers and was burning them.

Nathan, not knowing what to do, looked at his friends and his soldiers. Suddenly, on his horse, Nathan went up and started flying towards the place where Nuca Saahroon was instigated.

Sabrina saw it and was crying that Nathan would be decimated in the energy flow of the Nuca Saahroon bomb. No one came with Nathan.

Nuca Saahroon bomb's energy is reaching Nathan's soldiers and is burning them; Nathan saw a mountain called Hanimaa.

There is a large gap between the exploded place of the Nuca Saahroon bomb and the back side of the Nathan forces. In the explosion chaos of Nuca Saahroon, Nathan went to the other side of the Hanimaa mountain and prayed to Mother Adis, God Yinta, and Father Wulshaan.

He pushed the Hanimaa mountain. The mountain didn't move. Then again, he pushed the Hanimaa mountain, shouting, "God, Lord, Father, Mother, help me!"

The Hanimaa mountain moved. Nathan pushed it more, and the mountain covered the site where Nuca Saahroon was exploded. And the Hanimaa mountain absorbed the total Nuca Saahroon bomb exploded energy.

Nathan understood the plan of Satan, If Satan sends Nuca Saahroon in the middle of the fighting or directly onto his soldiers then Nathan forces will intercept it, that is why Satan made the Nuca Saahroon explode at the back side far way from them and let them take the indirect Satanic energy injures of bomb from backside.

And then Satan soldiers will attack Nathan soldiers from the front side too, and from the backside, the Nuca Saahroon Satanic energy will already be burning them.

Nathan used Mother Adis's creation itself to stop the Satanic Nuca Saahroon energy effect on his soldiers by moving the Hanimaa mountain and letting Hanimaa absorb the Satanic energy.

The soldiers of Nathan saw this and they cheered and praised him.

Nathan came back to the front line. Eesayi, The Three, and the others are happy. Sabrina kissed Nathan on his forehead.

Satan was stunned seeing what Nathan did. Satan was expecting Nathan's forces to feel the pain of getting burned alive, but it didn't work.

After seeing Nathan and Sabrina, Satan felt threatened and understood that if he destroyed the family systems, then it would be easy for him to win over people. To do this, he cursed humanity to get plagued by murders and rapes.

Murders and rapes became the favorite sins of Satan. Also, those who touched children on Earth with bad intentions became dear to him.

Murders, rapes and child abuse absolutely destroys families and lives of people to fullest.

Nathan was getting informed about Satan's curses by Eesayi. Nathan thought of reversing those curses after the war.

But, after hearing what Satan did today. He couldn't wait.

Nathan told Satan directly on the battlefield, "Anyone who commits murder, rape, and touches children with bad intentions will be burned alive on Earth. And I will not let their souls come even to Hell in the Master Universe. I will trap their souls in the Brunuck Line of the Master Universe even after the end of times. I will not let them get peace after their death. They will suffer for eternity. There is no redemption for them."

The soldiers of Nathan started attacking. They were fighting ferociously. On his horse with ten other soldiers, Nathan reached Satan on the battlefield.

Nathan saw hundreds of mortal heads cut and hanging there by Satan's followers after Satanic rituals and prayers were done.

Nathan saw a dark, void atmosphere while approaching Satan.

Iteen attacked Nathan with arrows, and Satan soldiers pelted Farush-stones on Nathan and his soldiers. Nathan and his soldiers dodged them.

Satan's soldiers saw Nathan's pure white glow of aura. They were scared to go near him. Nathan threw his sword at Iteen. Satan took his sword out and stood on his chariot. Iteen was destroyed by Nathan's sword.

The Three and the others are fighting. Nathan stopped in front of Satan. Sabrina saw her father.

Satan told Nathan, "Oh, mortal immortal, leave this battlefield and flee. Save yourself!"

Nathan said nothing.

Sabrina is waiting for her husband's response to her father.

Then tens of missiles came and hit Satan's war camp tents. Those God-side missiles destroyed many critical Satan war camp tents. Many weapon operators of Satan were in existential pain and will not recover any time soon from that pain.

Nathan distracted Satan and his soldiers to do this by coming to Satan.

They heard the Warena volcano blast.

The soldiers and animals, demons, and others from both sides stopped fighting.

Nathan returned to his war camp with Sabrina and others.

The priest came to Nathan and told him to be careful from that moment on.

Satan will do anything to win this war.

Suddenly, a swarm of missiles and arrows came towards Nathan's war camp.

Nathan, The Three, and Eesayi were shocked seeing them.

Eesayi told Nathan, "Satan wants to fight now. He doesn't want to wait till next morning."

***

Nathan said, "Intercept as many as possible. I will give him the war he wants!"

Huro said, "Yes, boss!" and ran to the weapons control rooms.

Nathan told Sabrina to stay at the camp.

The soldiers from both sides returned. And they were fighting. Ayoons were ripping the Satanic creatures apart.

Nathan, while riding his horse on the battlefield, jumped onto a God Bison and sat on it. Bison took Nathan to Satan.

Xeil, A general of Satan, came on Satanic Bull and started attacking Nathan.

Nathan got down from his bison and engaged in dual combat with Xeil.

Xeil was the personal favorite of Satan because of his cruelty and blood-sucking nature. Xeil is a demonic entity. As Nathan and Xeil were fighting, the ground near them was burning and turning into dark dust. Every time Nathan hit Xeil's sword, it released massive darkness. That darkness is consuming other soldiers from both sides who are near them.

Soldiers ran away from them in fear.

The losses are heavy on both sides.

Xeil and Nathan are fighting. Nathan looked at Xeil's swords and found them to be made of Satanic metal, which Koshi's sword was also made of. Nathan hit Xeil's knee, making him bend his head. Nathan quickly cut his hands and his head.

Nathan saw a great flood coming from the side of Warena volcano.

By fighting after the Warena volcano blast, Satan and Nathan violated the rules of Farush.

Everyone on the battlefield saw the massive flood of fairness coming towards them.

Nathan saw it, got down on his knees, and prayed to Farush to forgive them.

But the flood didn't stop. Sabrina came to him and asked him to take the Farush sand into his hands, he did it.

Sabrina took Nathan to the sacred waterfall on her sacred eagle. He mixed some Farush sand in the sacred waterfall, and then they quickly went to the sacred fire, and Nathan threw the rest of the Farush sand in his hands into it.

Nathan got down on his knees and prayed to Farush to forgive them.

The Farush came to Nathan as a tornado; she said, "Oh mortal immortal, today you fought after the Warena volcano blast and violated the rules of war at Farush. You must pay the price for it."

Nathan told Farush, "Oh, Mother of Farush, you saw how Satan attacked us. To protect my soldiers and ourselves, I have no other choice but to retaliate."

Farush said, "If Satan violated the rules of Farush, then he will pay the price for it, but by retaliating to his attack, you too violated the Farush rules of war."

Nathan: "Yes, but I have to protect my soldiers!"

Farush: "You should not. Stealing from a thief, too, is a crime. You should have let Satan attack you. After the attack, he would have been disqualified from the war, and you would have been declared the winner by me."

Nathan: "If I can become a winner by accepting an attack voluntarily on people and soldiers who trusted me, then I don't even want that winning."

Farush: "You came to ask me to stop the flood of fairness, but Satan didn't come."

Nathan: "That is his plan. He knows that if we fight after the second time Warena volcano blasts, then the flood of fairness will come.

So that he can escape the battlefield, claiming that the flood stopped the war, and not having to fight. You know he is Satan. He is utterly cunning and will do anything to keep his power in the Master Universe."

Farush said, "I will allow you to fight, but after the war, you should meet me and come to Faarushaana and marry my daughter."

Nathan didn't say anything. He looked back at his soldiers and Sabrina. After hearing what Farush said, Sabrina was sad, controlling her tears, and fearing what Nathan would say.

Nathan looked at the flood. He was confused and couldn't make a decision.

Finally, Nathan said, "Ok, I will marry your daughter!"

Farush stopped the flood of fairness.

Sabrina had tears in her eyes, turned to the other side, and cried silently.

Nathan got up from his knees and went to Sabrina. She wiped her tears. And smiled.

Nathan asked, "Shall we go?"

Sabrina, in a shaky voice, said, "Yes!"

Satan saw the flood of fairness going back.

Satan got to know what happened through his demons. Satan was upset, thinking about his daughter.

Satan felt he shouldn't have attacked Nathan and his forces after the allowed time, which led to this.

Sabrina and Nathan reached their war camp on Sacred Eagle.

Satan saw his daughter when she was on the sacred eagle.

Satan understood his daughter was sad and had already cried.

Koshi, the brother of Sabrina, came to the Nathan war camp.

Koshi was cast to Earth as a human being by Nathan to make Koshi understand the true meaning of life, and also to make Koshi realize why he is wrong and arrogant for sitting in the Master Universe and troubling mortals unnecessarily.

Koshi heard what happened from his pisaach demons.

He wants to see his sister.

Nathan went inside his war camp tent and talked to his generals and soldiers.

Sabrina saw her brother. After seeing him, she came running towards him. Koshi hugged his sister.

Sabrina cried loudly while hugging him.

Koshi said, "Sister, I know what happened. I met our mother. I saw your son."

Sabrina felt a little calmer after hearing it.

Koshi continued, "Your son is handsome like his father. I need a niece, also, as beautiful as you. We don't have any in our family."

Sabrina smiled.

Koshi said, "Your brother is here. Don't worry!"

***

Eesayi is on the battlefield fighting with the demons of Satan.

The Three are helping Eesayi fight demons. Satan ordered his generals to send as many demons as possible to push Eesayi out of Farush. Satan didn't want any presence of angels on Farush from that moment.

Satan hated Eesayi because Eesayi told Nathan to accept what Farush asked for, to stop the flood of fairness, so that the war would continue. Sabrina doesn't know about it.

On the fourth day, Farush blasted the Warena volcano.

Eesayi and The Three are still fighting.

Heera was fighting in the war, reporting to Nathan after the war every day.

Heera came to Nathan and asked Nathan to target Satan directly from now on.

Nathan agreed.

Even after seeing him, Nathan didn't meet Koshi and went straight into the battlefield. Sabrina stayed with her brother at their camp.

The forces started fighting each other.

Nathan, on the Bison, rammed into Satan's soldiers and chariots. He was followed by Heera on his chariot.

The soldiers of Satan destroyed the flag of Ateesta on Heera's chariot. Nathan saw it and went back. Nathan took the energy rope in Heera's chariot, and he tied the cosmic bodies of those who destroyed the flag of Ateesta to Heera's chariot, cut their heads, and placed their cosmic heads into his bison horns.

Heera's chariot is dragging their cosmic bodies on the Farush ground.

They reached Satan's chariot.

Satan saw Nathan and Satan's soldiers' cosmic bodies without heads and Nathan's bison horns.

Satan got angry and asked, "What does the immoral God of yours ask you? To come here and attack me?"

Nathan wondered why Satan said that about God, because God is the truth and morality.

Nathan said, "Oh, Satan, my father-in-law, thy daughter is with me. She is happy. Stop this war and accept your defeat."

Satan laughed. And said to Nathan, "Happy? Is she happy? Ha, ha, Oh, my son-in-law, she is not happy with you now. She will come to her father's house soon, for what you did to her."

Nathan understood that because he agreed to marry the daughter of Farush, Sabrina was not happy.

Nathan replied, "It is because of what you did!"

Satan said, "But you have a choice!"

Nathan: "What choice? to lose everyone to the cosmic flood of fairness?"

Satan: "Did I come to talk to Farush?"

Nathan: "No."

Satan: "Do you know why?"

Nathan didn't say anything.

Satan continued, "Because if Farush is all equal and treats everyone the same, then why did she ask you to marry her daughter to stop the flood of fairness, while still, I'm the one who attacked you first? It is because no one is fair, and no one is equal to anyone anywhere. It's all a lie. They say all those things to make you trust them, and then they show their true colors at the right time. You will like them all along, and you can't start hating them when they show their true colors suddenly.

You tell yourself many things about why the great Gods you like did what they did, which is ugly. You can't even start hating them right away when your great Gods suddenly show their true nature to you. You will compromise and still pray to them for everything you want in life and to go to Heaven."

If you do anything for your God and go to Heaven in return for what you did to your God, then you and your God are the same and selfish. It is just that you are a mortal and your God is immortal. You both are transacting.

Heera and Nathan was silent.

Satan continued, "I show my nature without any cover and sweet talk from the beginning itself. I'm who I am. The good name I have and the bad name I have, both are mine. But your Gods claim the good name and run away from the bad reputation they might get even by doing a good deed."

Nathan said nothing. Heera looked at Nathan.

Satan said, "Son, I'm Evil, but what good did your God do to you? Tell me a single reason why a man should go through horrible things in life.

Why? Just to understand the value of their mortal life and die ultimately? Why should a man understand the value of life through problems and hardships only? Why should a man learn everything by himself? Why can't your God give you all that by birth? Why do they make some people geniuses with great brain power, and some just normal people? No matter how hard some try, they just can't learn anything that will improve their lives.

For me, there is no reason for a man to go through any hardship, any problems, or pain. Because ultimately, they die and come to Hell or Heaven. If God is all-powerful and great, why can't he teach humanity everything about life, how valuable and great it is, without pain and hardships? Is it impossible even to your God?

For me, no. I hope the same for your Gods too. But your Gods don't do it. If your Gods give you everything without pain and problems in your lives, and if they make you learn how valuable mortal life is without any pain, problems, and heartbreaks, then you will not pray to those Gods for money, happiness, and mental peace in your lives.

Your Gods don't want your happiness first. They want your prayers and loyalty first. If they are satisfied with your mindless worship, then your Gods will bless you with money, happiness, mental peace, and everything in your life.

Tell me one good reason why you should pray to your Gods other than for money, mental peace, happiness, your family's safety, and things you want in your life?

Or you just pray to your Gods because they are Gods? And you read their stories and admire their qualities? Ha ha, then you fell for some good God propaganda because you are worshiping your Gods just because they are Gods and praise them for their great characters. And you pray to them because you think being God gives someone a free pass to be sacred and worthy of worship. It isn't. If someone is God, then he/she is God. That's it. Just like Satan is Satan, and Human is Human.

Think once, if your Gods want your happiness and want you to realize how valuable and great your mortal life is, can't they do it without giving you problems and pain? If not, are they even Gods? Because I can do it. There is no reason for any mortal to go through pain and problems to learn about anything, do something, and live their life the way they want. What good will happen to man, specifically, if a man goes through all that pain and problems, when God can give the same courage and bravery to the man directly that Gods think man gets after going through all that pain and problems they give to man?

But you know, many mortals are killing themselves because they can't take any more pain and problems in their lives. What good has God done for those? That is why I want to give everything to humanity without struggle and pain. Struggle and pain are meaningless when we take the entire universe into context. Man will die and be forgotten totally after millions of years, according to their mortal time.

You might feel something is wrong with this approach, but every new thing feels wrong at first. However, once you try it, you will understand its technicality and practicality, leaving aside all your narrow-minded preconceived notions disguised as great philosophies, ethics, and morals."

Heera said to Nathan, "This is what Satan does. He will try to convince you that he is right, in any or every way possible, whether it is sacred or dirtiest, at his convenience. Do not fall for it!"

# 7

Nathan said to Satan, "You are saying you can make fruit come out of a tree without the land itself, and land is not even needed. Yes, a God can make it, but is that correct? Yes, a God can make a tree give fruit without giving the tree water and sunshine, too. But why have the trees at all at that point? Can't God give all the fruits directly of all kinds without trees? Yes, he can. Can a God make a man learn and know everything without any type of struggle? Yes, he can, but why have humans at all? Why did Mother Adis have to design the evolution of humans at all?"

Satan said nothing.

Nathan continued, "Why does Mother Adis have to create you, me, and everyone? To fight here? I don't think so. Life has no meaning. Man has to give meaning to his life by himself."

Satan laughed. And said, " Life has no meaning. Man has to give meaning to his life by himself." And continued, "Does that God of fools tell you this? That idiot is hiding somewhere in a false sacred forest and playing games. Coward!"

Nathan angrily said, "From this day, anyone who abuses God Yinta, the One True God of Ateesta, will lose their common sense, intelligence, thinking power, and rationality bit by bit. Every time they commit blasphemy against God Yinta, the amount of loss will be increased. They will also live meaningless lives and die meaningless deaths."

***

Nathan saw Ayoo fighting a Satanic bull.

Nathan, with his sword, walked forward.

The bodyguards of Satan surrounded Nathan. They are attacking Nathan relentlessly. Heera is trying to break the circle of bodyguards of Satan around Nathan. But other Satan soldiers came and distracted Heera by making him fight with them.

With a sword in his hands, Nathan fought the bodyguards of Satan. The soldiers of Satan formed another bigger circle around him.

The bodyguards of Satan are using dark magic against Nathan. They hit Nathan with their dark lightning strikes and rocks of Khudish.

The soldiers of Nathan tried to penetrate the circle of Satan's soldiers, but Satan's soldiers were standing strong.

Sabrina got to know about Nathan getting trapped in Satan's Circle through his brother's demon servants.

Even God Yinta was careful enough to avoid getting trapped in Satan's Circle. Nathan read about it in the Czarach manuscript, but unknowingly, he was trapped in Satan's Circle.

Koshi and Sabrina, on Koshi's chariot, went near Satan's Circle, which Nathan was trapped in.

Nathan was fighting with Satan's bodyguards' circle, and there was another thick circle of Satan's soldiers around them.

The soldiers of Nathan formed in the shape of a triangle and attacked Satan's circle from one side. Then, Satan soldiers formed in the shape of double triangles side by side and attacked Nathan's soldiers. The animals from both sides couldn't take the chaos anymore.

They were getting scared as Nathan was taking cuts on his skin from Satan's soldiers and bodyguards. Nathan was getting pain-injured, and he was not letting any blood light come out from him. The Satanic animals and the God side animals saw it as a bad omen.

The Prophet cannot be hurt or injured by anyone. If he gets pain-injured, then the Prophet will take it as the last stage in the war.

The chaos erupted, and all animals from both sides started running away from the battlefield, including Ayoons, sacred eagles, bison, and every creature. The animals of the Satan chariot, too, got scared and freed themselves and ran away.

Sabrina was crying. Seeing the chaos and animals running away from the battlefield. It signifies that an angel or the Prophet of God is going to die.

Satan got down from his chariot and took his sword into his hands.

Farush blasted Warena volcano, but Satan's soldiers didn't leave Nathan, and Satan continued to walk into Satan's Circle. Nathan's soldiers were trying to penetrate the Satan Circle continuously, but Satan's soldiers were attacking them from all sides.

Koshi and Sabrina were seeing this.

Satan said, " You fell for all the emotional talk. Ha, ha, poor human. I know you changed my son, too, but after killing you, I will go straight to Udin and into Seperna, The Hollow of Dimona. I will kill your son, Aarus, and that b**h Dimona, I will tie her to the Arhush plate again for eternity at the edge of the universe expansion. My daughter Sabrina, I will take her to Hell and will marry her to Beeliaal."

Nathan was in pain on his knees and was hurt badly. Looking down, he was silent.

Satan came near to him. Satan, with his sword, lifted Nathan's head.

Sabrina was crying. Koshi couldn't dare to stop his father.

The Farush ground was shaking.

Nathan looked into Satan's eyes.

Nathan saw a deep void of chaos and a true, endless abyss.

Satan turned his head to cut eye contact.

Nathan, in that second, understood the insecurity and weakness of Satan. It is just men and women being truthful, courageous, clear, and boldly brave.

Satan swung his sword at Nathan. Nathan dodged it while on his knees.

Sabrina closed her eyes.

Koshi thought that Nathan had been taken out of existence by his father.

Nathan stood up in the chaos. Satan saw it.

Satan attacked Nathan with his sword.

Nathan laughed and said, " The father of my wife, why are you so horrible?" while fighting back.

Satan said, "You humans will pay the price for siding with God today!"

Nathan said, "Do you know what humans will pay you?"

Satan was waiting for the answer.

Nathan suddenly stabbed Satan in his heart, grabbed Satan's knife, and threw it away.

Nathan grabbed Satan by the neck from the backside. And said in Satan's ears, "From this day to the end of times, I curse you to be in the cage in Hell, where you kept the Happiness.

'Adistene restue heerave Hurovey Satane baandhinaam kirowze assaaaneem!'

I will not let you go out of this existence. I will not let you influence this existence. I will kill you, but I will not take your sacred cosmic life. I will make you not exist in any universe, father-in-law. You cannot control my mind, Satan. But I can control yours. Did you feel anything familiar? It is how you think, right? "

Sabrina, Koshi, Huro, Kwin, Tes, Eesayi, Heera, the soldiers from both sides, and angels who came from Heaven saw this.

Angels brought the cage in which Happiness was imprisoned from

Hell.

At Farush, Angels freed the Happiness in the Master Universe. A beautiful cosmic woman came out of the cage.

But for Happiness to reach Earth, Nathan has to take her with him.

Angels threw the cage near Nathan. No one came near Nathan while he was fighting Satan, and they saw the glow of God through Nathan while he was fighting the darkness of Satan. Nathan emitted white sacred rays from him while fighting with the king of darkness.

Nathan told Satan, "I'm killing you here but not killing you in my universe. I will come again to check on you. Your friend needs to learn some good manners. I will take you to him."

And Nathan threw Satan forcefully into the cosmic cage prison, which Satan had made himself to imprison Happiness. Nathan closed the door and placed his palm on it. He locked and secured the cage using God Yinta's mortal forbidden spells named 'Lucihenaa.'

He secured the cage, Satan was in, with Lucihenaa dark spells of imprisonment.

The soldiers of Satan ran away in fear.

Nathan asked Sabrina to come to him.

She saw her father and cried. Koshi looked at his father.

Nathan said, "Sorry" to Koshi.

Nathan asked Happiness to come to him.

She came. Nathan told Sabrina to take her to Earth after 137 Earth days.

Sabrina agreed.

Nathan kissed Sabrina. He told her, "I'm not going to marry the daughter of Farush in this universe. You will take birth as the daughter of Farush in my universe, and I will marry you there."

Sabrina has no limits to her happiness.

Nathan also said, "When angels take this cage into Hell, then the cage will have a world inside of it for your father Satan to exist."

Koshi felt happy hearing it.

Angels took Satan to Hell. Satan was imprisoned in the cage.

Nathan, on Heera's grand chariot with Heera as his charioteer and Sabrina with him, started going to Hell.

The animals were returning to Farush. And Nathan was going to Hell.

Koshi, Eesayi, Huro, Kwin, Tes, and other angels followed Nathan to Hell.

They entered Hell.

The priest was chanting sacred spells of Ateesta while welcoming Nathan and Sabrina to Hell.

Angels took the cage that Satan was in and placed it right behind the throne of Hell.

No one disrespected Satan or the cage he was in.

While the priest was chanting sacred spells of Ateesta, Nathan and Sabrina walked into the hall of Hell, and everyone was sprinkling sacred Roush flowers on Nathan and Sabrina graciously.

The demons, all evil entities and creatures, knelt in front of Nathan and Sabrina.

Nathan walked up to the throne of Hell, climbed the stairs to the throne, and sat on the Grand Throne of Hell in the Mother Adis Master Universe.

Sabrina sat next to him on the throne of Hell.

Emperor of Emptiness, Beeliaal, got to know about this.

Father Wulshaan blessed Prophet Nathan and Sabrina from the Sacred Father Wulshaan Universe.

Mother Adis came to Adististen from the Father Wulshaan Universe.

# 8

Nathan was walking on the Beruk highway after he found out that he had blood cancer.

After walking on the highway for a few miles, he saw a religious gathering. It is a Krise religious gathering.

Nathan went and sat there at the event.

The priest on stage is telling the story of Krisaan Regor, the God of the Krise religion, and how the Last Prophet of the Krise religion killed Satan and sat on the Grand Throne of Hell.

Nathan listened to the whole story.

Nathan's religion, Ateesta, had no supernatural God and prophet stories like that. Ateesta is a religion without supernatural beliefs of any sort.

After the event was over, he talked to people there about birth, death, and repenting for sins by praying to Krisaan Regor, the God of the Krise religion.

He ate food there and returned to his cabin at Hervin Forest.

Nathan knew he would die in a few months from blood cancer.

He started writing about the dreams and imaginations he had in his last days.

The police officers found Nathan's clothes and the stories he wrote about God Yinta, himself, and the Ateesta religion.

Nathan wrote about what their religion, Ateesta, would be like if it had been like the Krise religion. And he also wrote about how it would be if Ateesta also had stories in it similar to those in the Krise religion about birth, death, and life.

He wrote about how much comfort it would have given him if the Ateesta Religion had stories of God Yinta, Prophets, and life and death.

Nathan thought that if the Ateesta religion had supernatural stories and elements like those in the Krise religion, then those stories might have at least relieved him psychologically. But Ateesta is a pure rational religion. Ateesta doesn't have any supernatural stories or elements like in the Krise religion.

Nathan's girlfriend left him when she found out about his blood cancer.

Nathan does not have any close friends.

Nathan left home and his parents because he thought that if they knew about his blood cancer, then they would never sleep or live peacefully.

So, he gave money to a company.

The money is to send a letter to his parents, to call his parents to inform them that Nathan died in an accident in Trishone country, and to send his body from Hervin forest cabin to his home in Beruk.

After he dies of blood cancer in a few months, the company will take care of all of it.

Nathan imagined everything in his last days of life and wrote it, which the police found later after his death. The travelers who stopped on Hervin forest road near Nathan's cabin complained about an odd smell in the forest.

The police didn't find the thugs who attacked Nathan and stole his car on the Beruk highway that night, and Nathan, too, didn't.

He never bought a second car.

After his family lost everything when the government demolished their carpenter shop, Nathan's family became extremely poor.

For not paying taxes, the government demolished their home in Beruk.

Nathan's parents left for Nathan's father's ancestral village. They lived there till the end of their lives.

The company to which Nathan paid the money to send the

information about his death to his parents, and to send his dead body to his parents, couldn't find the address of Nathan's parents. The information never reached Nathan's parents.

Nathan's parents never got to know what happened to their son and where he was.

They died in old age without ever knowing what happened to Nathan.

The police couldn't find any details about Nathan near his dead body at the Hervin forest cabin. They buried it themselves.

Nathan's parents never came to the Hervin forest cabin. The bank took it from them for not paying back loans. But Nathan still came to the cabin regularly even after the bank took it from them.

The cabin is in a very remote place, so no one bought it from the bank.

After one month of Nathan's death, a group of young people walked into Hervin forest to party. They walked deep into the forest. They saw a big footprint of an animal in the dry mud, but they couldn't figure out what that animal could be because of the odd patterns of the footprints, no matter how many ways they tried. They also saw a big wooden stick.

# 9

Flag of Ateesta Religion:

The Ateesta Religion Flag has triangles of White (left), Red(above), Black(right), and Green(below). In descending order from down to up, it also has black, white, green, and red circles in the middle and a prosperity '+' symbol(Orange) on top of those circles, with edges of '+' touching the black circle.

Ateesta Religion's peace, progress, and prosperity symbol:

* * *

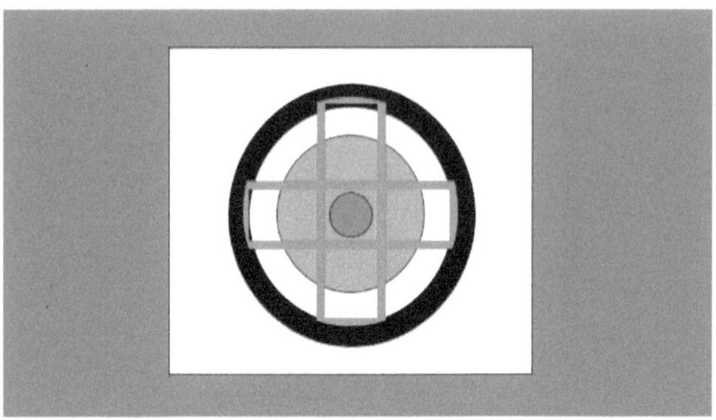

The Ateesta Religion symbol has a Red rectangle background and a white square in the middle. Inside the white square, in descending order from down to up, it has black, white, green, and red circles in the middle and a prosperity '+' symbol(Orange) on top of those circles with edges of '+' touching the black circle. (*The flag and symbol are also on the back cover.*)

Author's Note:

I tried my best to find mistakes and correct them. I haven't hired a professional editor or proofreader because I wrote the two books, I Killed Satan and Wuquin, in my small village, where I cannot get any professional proofreaders or editors, and even if I find one in a city, I actually can't afford them.

I did everything, from writing to locking the final draft by myself. If you find any mistakes, please excuse me and let me know. I will correct them.

The good, the bad, the worst, and the best, everything came from me.

I owe the errors of all kinds and the good things. I embrace them as part of the book.

I wrote what I felt.

Thank you for coming this far into my imperfect world.

- Naveen Mullangi

www.ingramcontent.com/pod-product-compliance
Lightning Source LLC
LaVergne TN
LVHW090602110826
845146LV00001B/229

*9798998671104*